VIGILANTE

VIGILANTE

A SARA VALLÉN THRILLER

CECILIA SAHLSTRÖM

Translated from Swedish by Emma Ericson

Published in 2023 by Podium Publishing, ULC
www.podiumaudio.com

Podium

VIGILANTE

1

"Finally," he whispered.

"Finally." He kissed her and held her close. She felt the heat of his body and started to breathe more calmly. His scent, his warm lips against hers, and his calm heartbeats relaxed her and made her feel safe. His big hands stroking her hair.

Their clothes in piles on the floor.

Their naked bodies met and moved together in perfect synchronisation. She reached climax long before he did, and when he finally came, it was time for them to say goodbye. It hurt more and more each time.

On her way home, she walked in silence along the streets. She took Slagtoftavägen and turned right on Storgatan. The air was cool and clear and the stars glistened in the black sky. She passed the deserted car repair shop. As always, she was worried about someone seeing her or following her. Worried about someone knowing what she had done. She had met up with him–the man she loved more than anything–once a week for months now, and just like after all the other times, she was overcome by a feeling of unease. She clenched her fists, focused her eyes on the street ahead, and frowned. She was almost too scared to breathe. She scanned her surroundings for danger. Not sure what was dangerous. And what wasn't.

Suddenly, she heard a noise behind her. It sounded like gravel underneath heavy feet. Her heart raced. She turned around and her long braid danced across her back. But she didn't see anything. There was nobody there. She told herself she was only imagining things and stood still for a while to allow her pounding heart to calm down and the noise in her head to disappear. Then she kept moving, silently. She walked past Sandahl's fashion boutique, crossed Hörby's old square, and finally made it home.

She slipped into her bed. Her heart was filled with love for him but she couldn't shake the fear she had felt on the street. Her parents were asleep and she could hear her father snoring through the wall.

2

Tobias walked briskly towards the car, opened the door, and was just about to sit down behind the wheel when he heard something behind him. Before he had the chance to see what or who it was, he felt a powerful arm wrap around his throat. It suddenly became hard to breathe, and his head started spinning. Spots began to flicker in his vision. A thought started to form in the back of his mind but refused to reveal itself.

He had a feeling he should know who was attacking him. But he couldn't figure it out. He tried twisting out of the attacker's grip but the more he moved, the harder it became for the air to find its way into his lungs. He tried to breathe through his nose and did his best to stay calm. He was a pretty big guy and realised that the person attacking him must be even bigger. He tried to relax as he knew it would make it easier to breathe, think, and act.

The man was panting heavily, and Tobias could feel the heat from his breath against his neck. He smelled the sharp scent of sweat mixed with perfume under the attacker's armpit.

"You'll never see her again," the man whispered into Tobias's right ear.

The man's breath smelled metallic.

Her. Of course it was about her. He tried to answer, but couldn't speak.

"This is your first and final warning."

Tobias's head was pounding. His heart raced.

"Don't look," the man whispered as he released his grip around Tobias's neck. He heard footsteps move away from him, but didn't move until they were completely gone.

The car door was still open. His mobile phone was on the seat. He started to dial 112, but changed his mind. He stepped into the car, drove out of the car park, and turned left on Slagtoftavägen. He continued until he reached highway E22 and turned left towards Lund. As he was driving, his legs started trembling so violently that he had to stop the car by the side of the road. Suddenly, he received a text message.

3

Chief Inspector Sara Vallén woke up and reached for her phone. When she saw it was only 8 a.m., she let out a relieved sigh. The sun shone in through the blinds and the light bounced off the mirror on the wall. It gave her hope. *I love autumn*, Sara thought as she stretched out in bed.

Today it was her turn to testify in the trial against Peter Matsson. The trial had been going on for days and this was the last day before the closing arguments tomorrow. Then it would all be over and Sara would be able to move on. Up until now, the trial had focused on the years of abuse Peter had subjected his wife to. Sara really felt for Linda Matsson, even though she couldn't help feeling annoyed with her for letting it go on for so long. After years on the force, Sara knew how hard it could be for women to get out of destructive and abusive relationships. The process of normalisation was powerful. *Just look at how you reacted*, she thought, and brushed her hair away from her face.

She sat up on the edge of the bed and shook her body to get rid of the weight on her shoulders. She was filled with anxiety.

It hadn't been long since summer, but what had happened felt like a distant memory from another life. It had been a summer she would never forget. Probably the worst summer of her life. The boy who had been so full of sadness and who had shot himself after committing multiple murders. Her dear Johannes, who had been arrested for a crime he didn't commit. And Peter Matsson, of course. The colleague who she had fallen in love with and who had turned out to be a devil in disguise. Today, she would expose him for what he really was.

The events of the past summer had also made her realise how fragile life can be and how important it is to stick together with those close to her.

Sara stepped into the shower and allowed the hot water to relax her stiff muscles. She cupped her hands over her breasts and made sure they were soft and even–a habit she had picked up since she had started going to mammography screenings. *No breast cancer today either*, she thought to herself, and stepped out of the shower.

She tried on the clothes she had laid out the night before. Then she pulled another outfit out of the wardrobe and tried it on too. No, it didn't feel right either. Finally, she decided to go with black jeans, a white shirt, and a black blazer. She put on the boots she had bought in Simrishamn. "Look out, here I come," Jonny Svensson had said when she wore them to work once. She smiled at the memory. She loved the boots for a reason. They were black and covered with colourful embroidery.

4

Sara hurried down Kalendegatan and in through the doors to Malmö District Court. She waved to the receptionist and ran up the stairs. Her lawyer, Marit Ståhl, was waiting for her.

"Bloody city. Nowhere to park and parking attendants everywhere."

"That's the city for you. That's why I bike. Did you go over your testimony?"

"Yes," Sara said, "I still can't believe that I was once in love with this guy. I really should have known better after working major crimes for all these years."

"Well," Marit said with a friendly smile, "it happens more often than you might think."

"I know," Sara said with a stiff laugh, "but I still can't believe I accepted his behaviour. I noticed the red flags right from the beginning. But still—"

Sara interrupted herself. The prosecutor specially assigned for cases involving officers of the law, Stig Malmsten, stepped out into the waiting room at the same time that Peter Matsson and his defence lawyer made their entrance. They all entered the courtroom and sat down at their assigned seats. The prosecutor, Sara Vallén, and Marit Ståhl sat on one side of the courtroom and Peter Matsson and his lawyer on the other. Sara didn't want to look at Peter, but forced herself to do so. She locked eyes with him until he looked away.

Although the room was chilly, Sara's face felt hot. She reminded herself of Rita Anker's comforting words. "You're not the embarrassing one here. He is," she had said.

The prosecutor presented his case and the defence lawyer presented his. Both Rita Anker and Peter Matsson's partner, Sergeant Malva Gran, testified. Then it was the medical examiner's turn. Time moved slowly. When Sara was questioned by the defence lawyer, she had to bite her lip to contain her temper.

"Didn't you provoke Peter Matsson?" he said, and pointed at the defendant.

"How do you mean?"

"I'm the one with the questions here," he snapped.

"I can't answer your question as I'm not sure what you mean," Sara snapped back. Her eyes were full of rage.

"Let me rephrase," the defence lawyer said, and leaned back. "Do you sometimes have issues controlling your temper?"

Sara stared at him.

"Issues? No!"

"You practice judo, right?"

"Yes."

"And you've used your judo skills to subdue a man, right?"

"Yes, a man who attacked me."

"So, I ask you again, do you have issues controlling your temper? Because you assaulted Peter Matsson once, didn't you?"

"What?"

The chief judge frowned. The prosecutor stood up, but the judge signalled to him to sit down again.

"Would you please tell me where you're going with this?" he said.

"Sure. Peter Matsson has documentation of injuries that prove he was assaulted as well. Injuries caused by Sara Vallén. So, does Sara Vallén have anger management issues? I mean, this is not the first time she's assaulted a man."

Sara couldn't believe what she was hearing. The prosecutor stood up again.

"What kind of injuries are these and why is this the first time we're hearing about them?" he asked, and shrugged his shoulders dramatically.

"Yes, what injuries?" Marit Ståhl and the chief judge asked at the same time.

"I want to present a couple of photos."

The chief judge nodded at the defence lawyer, who walked over to him with a folder. Then he handed a copy of the photos to the prosecutor and Sara's lawyer. The photos had been taken on the same day as Sara had gone to the doctor and had her injuries documented. They showed a scratch next to Peter's right eye, another one above his right collarbone, and a tiny bruise on his chin.

The chief judge didn't look impressed.

"What is this? I would appreciate it if we all showed some respect for the court's time. The witness does not have to answer the question," the chief judge said, and looked at Sara.

"The principle of unfettered evaluation of evidence," the defence lawyer said, and looked slightly nauseous.

"It seems to me that you're suggesting that these injuries are proportionate to the violence Sara Vallén was subjected to. As I said, let's show this court some respect."

The defence lawyer protested, but when the chief judge didn't budge, he gave up.

The hearing continued all day. Sara's lawyer demanded damages. When Sara came out of the courtroom, she heaved a sigh of relief. She felt that the worst part was over. Her lawyer patted her on the shoulder.

"It went great," she said.

"Yes, but it was bloody hard."

"I know. Let's talk after the closing arguments."

The prosecutor had filed a prosecution for gross violation of a woman's integrity. And considering how Peter Matsson had treated both his wife and Sara, they were all convinced he would be convicted.

Before Sara drove home, she called Rita.

"I don't exactly feel relieved. Just empty. Empty and sad. But thanks for being there for me," she said when Rita asked her how she was feeling.

"I understand. It's a very normal reaction," Rita said. "What happened, happened. Our system is flawed when it comes to crimes like these. We all know that."

"I know. But what's most important here is that he'll never work for the police again. He doesn't belong on the force."

5

Sara was on her way out to have lunch in town. Her phone had been ringing all morning. She needed to move. Just as she closed the door behind her, her phone rang again.

"Hello, this is Marit Ståhl."

"Hi."

"Could I talk to you for a minute?"

"Sure, is the verdict in?"

"Yes, he will lose his job and serve a year and four months in prison. And he'll have to pay you twenty-five thousand SEK."

Sara scoffed.

"One year and four months. Is that all he gets for assaulting me and beating up his wife for years? Not much to celebrate if you ask me."

"No, that's one way to look at it. But as it was impossible to prove all occasions of abuse as separate offences, I think we should be pretty happy with the outcome. At least he'll be fired and never work with people again."

Sara scoffed again.

"Sure. But still . . . Does he even have any money? What is he paying Linda Matsson?"

"Seventy thousand."

Sara could hear that Marit Ståhl had hoped not to have to share that particular information with her.

"Seventy thousand. That's ridiculous. For all those years of suffering."

"I know."

Sara knew that she sounded like a squeaky old door.

"Oh well, at least it's over now. As long as he doesn't appeal."

"Yes, I guess we'll see."

"It wouldn't surprise me."

"Me neither. But even if he does, I'm convinced the verdict won't change."

"You're probably right. Well, take care and I'll talk to you later."

"You too, Sara. Goodbye for now," Marit Ståhl said, and hung up.

Sara arrived at La Cucina on Hantverksgatan and sat down at a table next to the window.

The waiter came over with a menu.

"Hi there. Welcome. What can I get for you? Pasta Arrabiata?" he asked with a smile.

"Yes, the usual," Sara said, and laughed. "And some sparkling water. Thank you."

When Sara got back to the office, she continued working on one of the cold cases they had been investigating for what seemed like forever. It was moving forwards, slowly. But at least it was moving forwards and not backwards.

At 4:30 p.m., she decided to go home. She had just put one arm in her jacket when her phone rang again.

"This thing won't stop ringing," she mumbled to herself before picking up. "Sara Vallén. I'm just on my way out."

"Hi, this is the duty officer. I'm sorry to bother you, but an old couple has found a dead man in the cottage on their allotment. I want you to check it out. A patrol car is on its way. I've already called forensics. Let me know when you're on the scene."

"I'm on it," Sara sighed, and ended the call as she walked out into the corridor to call her colleagues over. Rita peeked out of her office.

"Dead guy found on an allotment," Sara summed up.

Multiple patrol cars were parked on Maskinvägen and the little street leading into Palettskolan. The gates to the allotment gardens were open and there was an ambulance and a patrol car in front of one of the little cottages. The lights on the vehicles danced on the dark sky and curious bystanders had gathered outside the police tape. Sara and Rita ducked under the blue-and-white tape and walked into the garden, where the flowers were in full bloom and the apple trees' branches were heavy with fruit. An older couple with blankets thrown over their shoulders stood on the gravelled path next to a little cottage.

"Hi there," Sara said, and walked over to the couple. She reached her hand out. "My name is Chief Inspector Sara Vallén and I'm the lead investigator. This is Inspector Rita Anker," Sara said, and nodded towards her tall blonde colleague, who was standing right behind her.

"Roland Bruhn," the man said.

"Anja Bruhn," the woman filled in. Her voice broke when she said her surname. "We don't understand what is going on. Who would do something like this?"

"We don't know yet," Sara said, and put a hand on the woman's thin arm. "I think you should come with me to the ambulance. It'll be warmer there and we'll find someone for you to talk to. We can speak more later. It's okay." She nodded towards the ambulance.

"But we don't want to ride in the same ambulance as the dead man," Anja Bruhn said as her chin began to tremble.

"Oh, no, of course not," Sara said. "But he won't need an ambulance, unfortunately. As he's dead there is another type of vehicle that will pick him up. Don't worry."

The man pulled a face and brought his hands to his chest. For a second, Sara thought he was about to suffer a heart attack.

"I need a nurse over here," she shouted in the direction of the ambulance. A nurse hurried over to them and Sara nodded towards Roland Bruhn. The nurse walked him over to the ambulance while Anja Bruhn was left standing alone.

"Don't worry, I'm sure he's fine," Rita said. "But let's walk over to the ambulance so both of you can go to the hospital. Just in case. Come on."

Rita's voice was friendly but stern and the woman finally gave in. Sara walked up to the little cottage and bumped into the medical examiner, who was on his way out.

"This isn't pretty," he said with a grimace. "Multiple stab wounds all over his body. The perpetrator must have been furious. And his nails have been pulled out, meaning the victim was subjected to torture. Forensics is in there as we speak."

He grimaced again, nodded, and kept walking. Sara saw him talking to Rita and smiled to herself when she saw how he straightened his back as he spoke to her.

Rita wiped her shoes on the doormat and put a hand on Sara's back before they went inside.

The man was still on the floor. Sara took a step back. *Shit*, she thought. The medical examiner was right. Torture.

"Bloody hell. What is this?" Rita exclaimed.

The head of the forensics team, Ove Ovesson, was leaning over the body, examining something that looked like fingernails. He turned around and looked at them.

"Yes, his throat has been slit. And he was tortured before that. He has burn marks on his face and his nails have been pulled out. We'll have to wait and see what the medical examiner says about the genitalia, but there are bloodstains all over the victim's crotch area."

6

Commissioner Beatrice Larsson sat on the edge of her desk and looked at Sara and the other four officers she had called into her office to form a major investigation team. She rubbed her left temple with two fingers. A bead of sweat glistened on her hairline.

"The victim hasn't been identified yet, but we looked into the record of missing persons and found a likely match. A Tobias Klingström was reported missing yesterday. He disappeared a couple of days ago. Our victim matches his description, and unfortunately we'll have to ask the parents to identify him. It won't be fun. Sara?"

"Yes, we'll launch an investigation right away. I'm not sure what to think about this murder. In a way, it looks like a crime motivated by immense fury, but at the same time the torture seems calculated and shows little to no signs of lack of impulse control."

Sara turned to her colleagues. Jonny Svensson had been called in from Malmö together with Torsten Venngren. Jörgen Berg leaned against the doorframe and Rita Anker stood next to the window.

"Hate," Rita said, and threw her hands out in front of her.

"Yes, very likely," Jörgen agreed.

"Very likely," Sara repeated. "But let's start from the beginning. With identifying the body, that is."

"Do you want me to call the Klingströms and meet them at the hospital?" Torsten Venngren asked.

Sara nodded. Torsten was the right man for the job. He was good with all sorts of people. And all sorts of emotions.

"I need you to start looking into Tobias Klingström. Find out if he appears in our records; look into who he hangs out with and stuff like that," Sara said, and pointed at Jörgen, who didn't look too happy about the assignment.

"We're not even sure if it's him."

"It doesn't matter right now. We have to get going right away. Most likely, it's him."

Jörgen shook his head before he left Beatrice Larsson's office.

"And what about me?" Jonny said, and threw his hands out.

"Call the medical examiner and check on their progress." Sara's voice sounded mechanical. Her brain was already working hard, coming up with different possible scenarios.

Torsten and Jonny walked out of the office and left the three women alone.

"You, come with me," Sara said quickly to Rita before heading for the door.

"Remember to identify the victim before you do anything drastic," the commissioner shouted after them.

Sara waved dismissively at her boss. Although Sara knew Beatrice was only trying to help, she was experienced enough not to have to deal with unnecessary advice like that.

7

Torsten walked towards the entrance of the police station. He was shaken by his visit to the hospital and full of regret. He should have used dental records to identify the victim. The parents shouldn't have been allowed to see their son in the state he was in. He should have been cleaned up and the moment should have been more respectful. Not clinical and ruthless. *It could all have been handled a lot better*, he thought, and wiped the sweat off his forehead.

The summer had ended abruptly and the air was cool and crisp. The leaves were starting to turn orange and red and the rowanberries made it look like the trees were on fire. It was beautiful. Within a month, the leaves would have fallen off the trees and left everything naked and dull. The fields surrounding Lund would be nothing but dark mud.

Torsten stepped into the building and felt the heat of the police station warm up his cold muscles. He hurried up the stairs and walked right into Sara Vallén's office. She was sitting next to Rita in front of the computer, lost in the online labyrinth that made up a person's life.

"It's him," Torsten said. "Tobias Klingström. His mother identified him."

Sara and Rita both looked up and nodded solemnly.

"Great. He's identified. Did they have any idea of what might have happened?" Sara asked while her eyelid started to droop. She blinked to regain control over it as she looked at Torsten.

"What's up with the superior look on your face?" he asked.

"You know I can't help it," Sara said.

Torsten nodded.

"To answer your question . . . no, they had no idea. Probably because they were so shocked. I had to take them to the grief counsellor, who in turn had to call the hospital chaplain. Okay?"

"Sorry, I didn't mean to be insensitive. But we have to talk to the parents."

"Tomorrow," Torsten said. "I'm sure Jörgen will find enough information for us to get a good idea of who he was."

8

When Samira woke up, she was still tired and had a strange feeling in her stomach. As if something had happened. She heard a noise behind her and sat up.

"Why are you staring at me?" she asked her father, who looked at her with his arms crossed and his thick eyebrows in a furrow.

She pulled the duvet up to her chin.

"Say something. I have to go to Lund for a lecture in an hour," she continued, trying her best to sound confident and ignore the shiver that ran down her spine.

"Leave," she said when he didn't answer her. "Get out of my room."

Her father turned around and walked away. She could see by his posture that he was upset. Very upset. He mumbled something in their language. All she could make out was the word *away*.

Samira jumped out of bed and got dressed. Then she made her way to the kitchen, where her mother sat by the table with her hands resting in her lap.

"What did you do?" her mother complained.

What does she mean? Do they know? Samira thought. She had been so careful. Fear took hold of her at the same time as she felt a wave of loathing wash over her.

"Nothing. I have done nothing," she answered stubbornly, and felt her voice tremble slightly. "Nothing," she repeated.

She left the kitchen and walked into the bathroom. She applied her makeup. Brushed her teeth. Walked into the hallway, wrapped a head-scarf around her hair, and opened the front door. She heard her father's heavy footsteps behind her and started running down the stairs. She tripped and fell down the last set of stairs, hitting her head against the stone floor. She quickly got up and stumbled out through the front door. She made it to the bus stop just as the bus driver closed the doors, but he opened them again when she slammed her fists against the glass. The bus driver stared at her without asking for a ticket and she hurried past him. She took a seat at the back of the bus and looked out the window as the bus drove off.

9

ost of the students had already taken their seats. The only person who reacted when she rushed into the classroom was Martin. Judging by the expression on his face, something wasn't right. He got up, grabbed her by the arm, and dragged her out into the corridor again.

"You're covered in blood," he whispered to her.

Samira brought her hands to her face. Her skin felt sticky.

They hurried into the bathroom, and when Samira saw her bloody face in the mirror, she couldn't believe that she hadn't realised how bad it was. She turned on the water and washed her face. Martin inspected the wound to see where all the blood was coming from.

"It doesn't look very deep. I think I can fix it with some surgical tape."

Martin ran off while Samira stayed in the bathroom. She took off her white wool sweater, which was now red with bloodstains. She turned it inside out and tied it around her hips.

She blushed and tears burned behind her eyelids. She should have understood that her fall on the stairs had left a mark. What would her friends think?

Martin patched up her wound and when he was done, they walked back to the classroom. Samira carefully opened the door and the professor glared at them as they returned to their seats.

"You know how I feel about students being late," was all he said.

They both nodded. They didn't speak more until the lecture was over.

"Are you seeing my sister today?" Martin asked.

Samira shook her head. "I don't think so. Do you know if she's at uni?"

"No idea, but I can check."

"No need. I'll call her later," she said, and hurried out of the classroom at the same time as it filled with new students, ready for their next lecture. Samira threw a glance over her shoulder and saw that the steady stream of people had stopped Martin from following her. She kept going without him, heading for her next class.

On her lunch break, she called Elin, who was the only one she could fully trust. But still, she didn't feel comfortable telling her the real reason why she had been in such a rush down the stairs, or what she had feared would happen if her father had caught up with her.

"I fell down the stairs as I was running for the bus," Samira said. It wasn't a total lie. They had known each other for years, but there were still things Elin didn't know about. Elin loved Samira's family. When she was around, her family behaved well and didn't seem more controlling than most caring families. Maybe Elin suspected something, but she had never mentioned it.

"Oh no, you could've been really hurt. Are you okay? You could've broken your neck, Samira."

"Don't be so dramatic. I'm fine. Martin took care of me. My favourite sweater is covered in blood, though."

"Don't worry about that. You can always buy a new one. You're so spoiled." Elin giggled.

"I'm not spoiled."

"It was a joke," Elin said. "Anyway, I'm glad you're okay."

"I just wanted you to hear it from me. Martin will probably tell you all about it. But now you know."

They hung up and Samira went about her day without anyone asking her what had happened to her face. Martin kept looking at her, but for some reason, he didn't make any further efforts to talk to her.

10

This is what we know," Sara said, and pointed to the whiteboard where she had written a bunch of names and drawn arrows between them. "Tobias Klingström works for the Social Services Administration in Hörby. More specifically, he works with families and children in need. Or, well, he used to work there."

"Hörby, what a dump," Jonny Svensson scoffed.

Sara shot him a sour look.

"He never showed up to work on Monday and has been missing since then. His parents reported him missing Tuesday night. He doesn't have a record. I've talked to the social services director. I'm going to Hörby after this meeting to pay a visit to Tobias Klingström's office. Torsten and Rita will question his parents. They'll be here at 10 a.m."

Sara turned to Jörgen.

"I need you to contact the medical examiner again and find out what has really happened here. And then we need to talk to forensics, of course. I'm sure Ove Ovesson has something to tell us."

Jörgen Berg nodded. He sat in front of his computer and his fingers moved quickly across the keyboard as Sara spoke.

"Jonny, I need you to talk to the couple who own the allotment."

"Why do you always want me to talk to the old ones?"

"Someone has to."

Jonny shrugged his shoulders and sighed. But for once, he kept quiet about his feelings. Sara nodded to her colleagues and went to her office to make a phone call.

"You've reached the Social Services Administration. This is Karin Thorsson."

"Hi, I'm Chief Inspector Sara Vallén from the Lund Police Department. I would like to come to Hörby and talk to you about Tobias Klingström. I assume you've heard that he has been found dead."

"Yes, we heard. The whole thing feels very scary. Tobias was a very appreciated colleague around here."

Sara chewed over what the woman had just said. *Wouldn't it have been just as scary if he weren't so appreciated?* she thought to herself, but decided not to say anything about it.

"I would like to come right away if that's okay. I've talked to Social Services Director Gertrud Hagberg."

"Yes, of course. It's important that we sort this out as soon as possible. You're welcome at any time. Most people are at the office today. We've just had a staff meeting."

"I'll get in the car immediately. I'll be there in about forty minutes."

The autumn landscape was beautiful, but Sara was so focused on her own thoughts and the road ahead of her that she barely noticed it.

Guilty. Why did I feel guilty when Peter abused me? And why didn't I leave him the first time he hit me? She knew the answer. *Because you have a destructive relationship with men.* It felt as if she had two tiny people sitting on her shoulders. One of them tried to be nice to her and the other one was convinced she only had herself to blame for what had happened. She tried to ignore both of them, but couldn't.

She couldn't even answer the questions she usually asked other women who had been beaten by their partners. Sara thought about the defence lawyer's attempt to make her look as guilty as Peter Matsson. She had found herself thinking along the same lines more than once. But the trial had been a wake-up call. *Funny how you can convince yourself of the strangest things,* she thought, and as she turned off highway E22 and drove towards the city centre, she realised she had been driving far too fast. She immediately stopped thinking about Peter Matsson.

She parked the car outside the social services office at Slagtoftavägen 1. The office was located in a rundown and rough-looking neighbourhood and Sara threw a glance at a man who stood on one of the balconies, smoking.

"You wanna come up and keep me company for a while?" he slurred.

It was obvious that he was drunk. *This seems like an appropriate location for a social services office,* Sara thought. Or perhaps not appropriate at all.

11

She rang the doorbell, but nobody came to the door. She rang it again and finally heard footsteps in the hallway. A woman opened the door.

"Welcome," she said, and took Sara's hand. "Karin Thorsson."

"Sara Vallén, Lund Police Department."

Karin Thorsson let Sara inside and Sara was baffled when she saw that the inside of the office looked as rundown as its exterior. She had driven past the quite modern municipal office and assumed the Social Services Administration would operate in a similar building. Karin Thorsson aimed a tired smile Sara's way and showed her into a conference room. They sat down by the large table.

"Do you want me to bring the rest of the staff?" she asked Sara, who shook her head.

"It's probably better if I speak to you alone first. Then I'm happy to speak to anyone who wants to share information that might be of interest to the investigation. It would be helpful if I could talk to someone close to Tobias."

Karin Thorsson thought about it for a while. "Then you'll probably want to talk to Staffan."

"Why do you think that?"

"He knows Tobias very well. They're also friends privately."

Sara nodded.

"Tell me about Tobias," she encouraged Karin Thorsson.

"Well, he was an honest man who was positive and kind to his colleagues. He was kind to people in general."

"What did his colleagues think of him?" Sara asked.

"They all liked him. He was someone who made others feel important. He was thoughtful and attentive, if you know what I mean."

"How was he lately? Did you notice any mood swings or other signs that something wasn't right?"

"To be honest, he has seemed weighed down by something for the past couple of months. At least at times. If I had to guess, I would say it had to do with his love life, but I'm definitely not sure. I heard him tell someone that he loved them over the phone once."

"But he hasn't shared anything about this with you?"

"No, not at all."

"Could you describe him some more?"

Sara studied the woman, trying to determine if she seemed insecure or nervous in any way. Karin Thorsson didn't seem completely comfortable being interrogated, but she showed no signs of lying or hiding something.

"He is . . . I mean, he was a big guy. Athletic. He got along with everyone. He was social and mature. Thirty years old. Smart, but maybe more practically skilled than analytical. At times he was chatty, but sometimes he could be quiet. I guess that's about all I can tell you about him."

Sara reassured the woman by nodding as she spoke. When she leaned back in her chair, Sara did the same.

"At what times was he chatty?"

"At staff meetings or in the lunchroom, for example. When we were all gathered, he often spoke for the whole group."

"And when could he be quiet?"

Karin Thorsson thought about it.

"When he was handling a case, for example. Then he was always incredibly focused. Even if a couple of us were working on a case together, he kept his head down and didn't say much."

Sara nodded.

"Did he have any enemies?"

"I'm not sure, but I find it hard to believe. He was a truly charming man who was liked by both his clients and his colleagues."

Sara wondered what it was with the woman's description of Tobias that made her curious. Then it hit her.

"Could you describe in what way Tobias seemed weighed down by something lately?"

"It's hard to explain. He didn't seem depressed or anything, but he disappeared into his office more and more often. He clearly showed that he wanted to be left alone. I guess that's not all that strange, but I got the feeling he was sad about something. Or weighed down, as I said."

Karin Thorsson let her pen wander back and forth between her right and left hands. It was the only sign of emotion that she showed.

12

Chief Inspector Sara Vallén," Sara said as she stood up and reached her hand out towards the man who had just stepped into the conference room. She noticed that he was red under his nose and around his eyes. He had been crying.

"Staffan Davidsson," he said, and shook Sara's hand. When she tried to look him in the eye, he lowered his gaze. It surprised her.

"Please, have a seat," Sara said.

Sara waved at his boss, who backed out of the room and carefully closed the door behind her.

He sat down in the chair with his back straight, still not looking at Sara. She started recording the interview on her phone and read out the date and time of the interrogation, as well as both of their names, before turning the microphone towards Staffan.

"I understand that you've just found out about Tobias Klingström's death."

Staffan nodded and it looked as if he was about to cry again. He took a deep breath.

"Yes," he said. "It's bloody horrendous."

"Yes, it is." Sara nodded to verify his feelings.

"And hard to believe," he continued. "He's probably the nicest guy I know. Or . . . he was. Have you talked to his parents?"

"Yes. They were the first ones we talked to. How well did you know Tobias?"

"I would say we were best buddies," Staffan said. "We met at uni, and we've been friends since."

"It sounds nice. Would you mind telling me about Tobias? Who was he, and how did he live his life?"

The young man nodded and started sobbing. Sara gave him a minute.

"He was a person who everyone liked. He was a great listener, friendly, loving, and thoughtful. He had skills that everyone wants but few possess. He was intelligent, but never looked down on people who weren't as bright as he was. He was respectful and smart at the same time. He had a great childhood. You know, almost too good."

"Didn't he have any bad habits or personality traits that were less charming?" Sara asked, and felt her eyelid slip down. She noticed how the man looked at her and blinked hard.

"I'm sure he had, but none that I could see. Or, well, yes, actually. He always thought the best of people. It's a good quality, I guess, but only as long as people are actually as good as you think. If they're not, it can come back to bite you."

It sounded rehearsed, but Sara didn't say anything.

"Who did he hang out with?"

"A few of us normally hung out together. I'll give you everyone's name if you want?"

"We'll get to that," Sara said. "Please continue."

"He had another group of friends as well. They used to play golf and tennis together. I think he had known them since childhood."

Sara smiled to hide her suspicion.

"Girlfriend?" she asked.

"He hasn't said anything, but I think there was a girl. I have no idea who she is. For some reason, he never told me about her. But I've suspected it for a while."

"So, why didn't he tell you about her if you were such good friends?"

"How would I know? Maybe he didn't think it was going to work out between them."

Staffan Davidsson ran both his hands over his beard. *Beautiful hands,*

Sara thought. *Graceful, slender, with long fingers.* She thought about her stepfather–the painter. His hands had looked just like them.

"And you don't know who this girl could be?"

Staffan sighed. "No, I have no idea. But something felt strange about it as he kept her a secret. It wasn't like him. We all thought so, but he refused to tell us about her. We tried many times, but he kept quiet about it. He denied seeing anyone, but he did it in a way that left us convinced he was lying. We assumed he wanted to keep it a secret. Very strange, really."

His answer was full of things that made Sara suspicious. Why wouldn't Tobias want to tell his friends about his girlfriend? The way she saw it, there were two possible reasons. Either he wasn't sure if he wanted to be seen in public together with her, or their relationship could lead to negative consequences for one or both of them if it was exposed. What was Tobias Klingström hiding?

13

Torsten and Rita sat in two separate interrogation rooms. Torsten was interviewing Anna Klingström, and Rita was interviewing Karl Klingström. Tobias Klingström's parents both showed signs of shock. As always, Torsten felt like a villain when he forced a parent to reveal their child's deepest secrets. It was always sickening. Although, for some reason, it was always easier when the parents were still in shock. It was as if the questions he asked didn't feel completely real before reality sank in. And he was great at what he did. His never-failing attention to detail, his ability to ask questions respectfully, and the fact that he never stepped on anyone's toes made his job easier. Maybe he even helped the victim's family to work through their grief in a way. At least that's what he wanted to believe.

"Could you tell me about who Tobias is?" Torsten said carefully, deliberately talking about him as if he were still alive.

Anna Klingström's eyes were empty. She was as pale as a white sheet and her mouth was slightly open. Her shoulders slumped in a way that looked unnatural somehow. *Deflated and lethargic,* Torsten thought to himself.

The woman tried to pull herself together, blinked hard, and shook her head.

"He's everything a parent could wish for. He has a huge heart and he's thoughtful, loving, and beautiful. More beautiful than all the others, but I guess all parents say that?"

"They probably do, but it doesn't matter," Torsten said with a friendly smile.

"He has a lot of friends and he's good at what he does. He's intelligent, sensitive . . ."

"Does he have a girlfriend?"

"Yes, an amazing young woman. Her name is Samira. We only met her once. It's a bit complicated," Anna Klingström said, then hesitated.

Torsten was immediately interested. "In what way?"

"Well, her family is from Pakistan. You should see her. She is beautiful. Almost surreally so."

It was obvious to Torsten that the woman wanted to avoid getting into why it was complicated. He ran his hand though his hair, and when one of his fingers got stuck in a knot, he freed it with an irritated jerk.

"Do you think you could be a bit more specific?" he asked as casually as he could.

"I'm not sure if her parents were happy about her dating a Swedish man, or men in general. I think they're a bit conservative. At least that's the idea I got from what Tobias told me."

"Do you know Samira's surname?"

"No, actually. We only got to see her once. And she didn't stay for very long. I'm sorry."

"Is Tobias in love with her?"

The woman seemed comfortable talking about her son as if he were still alive, which made it easier for Torsten to speak to her. But grief shone through in her sad smile and eyes.

"Yes, I'm convinced he is. I think he loves her. But it's all very hush-hush. I assume it has to do with her family. Do you think it's important somehow?" Anna Klingström asked, and looked at Torsten.

"Well, it could be . . ."

He thought about his next question for a while, worried about spooking the woman.

"Do you think you and your husband could help us find the girl?"

"Sure, if we can. It's important that we find whoever murdered Tobias."

The word *murdered* cut like a knife. The air filled with grief in a heartbeat. Anna Klingström collapsed on the floor and started shaking. Torsten jumped out of his chair and rushed over to her side. He squatted next to her and held her hand.

"Come on," he said, and helped her up. "Let's get out of here."

The woman didn't answer but followed Torsten out of the room.

14

Sara came back to the office. She walked past the interrogation rooms and saw Torsten and a woman in one of them and Rita and a man in the other. The parents. She continued to Jörgen's office. He was leaning back in his office chair with his arms behind his neck, deep in thought.

Sara knocked on his door. Jörgen flinched and jumped so high that his chair rolled away behind him.

Sara grinned.

"Oh, did I scare you?"

"Yes, you did! Jesus, I almost had a heart attack."

"I'm sorry. Do you want to come to the allotment where the body was found?"

"Sure thing," Jörgen said. and smiled.

They walked briskly along Trollebergsvägen and passed Polhemsskolan. The school looked empty. Although Sara knew that classes were being held inside the building, it looked deserted. She thought about the hundreds of young people who would take to the streets, bus stops, and pedestrian crossings in the summer, walking or cycling.

She broke the silence.

"Did you find out anything useful?"

"No, not much. How did you do?"

"Well, I got some names of Klingström's friends. According to every-one I talk to, he's almost saint-like. They all have nothing but good things to say about him. It makes me suspicious. We'll do a briefing as soon as the interrogations of the parents are over. Where is Jonny?"

"He's back from questioning the old couple. They were shaken up by the whole thing but had nothing more to add."

"That's what I thought. But we obviously have a gap of two days between when Tobias disappeared and when he was found. What did the medical examiner say?"

"They're not done, unfortunately."

Jörgen pulled up his shoulders and let them down again as if he was practising a mindfulness exercise.

They walked straight ahead at the roundabout and turned left by the flower shop. After hesitating for a moment, Sara decided to go down Van Dürens Väg before turning left on Murarevägen. They reached Målarevä-gen and walked up to Palettskolan. They hurried along the front of the building until they reached the entrance gate to the allotment gardens. The air smelled like dirt and autumn. They walked past beautiful gardens full of autumn flowers. Sara leaned over and ran her hand over a row of asters and marigolds. She was overcome by the same loving sensation she had felt when she woke up earlier that morning. Anders Magnusson had tickled the palm of her hand until she opened her eyes and looked right into his warm, tender gaze. Anders, a friend from her past whom she had met again after many years. He had been her lawyer. But she had switched counsel to Marit Ståhl as soon as she and Anders realised they belonged together.

In the beginning, she had questioned their relationship and wondered if she had settled for Anders as a substitute for what never happened with Peter Matsson. But that wasn't the case. They had fallen in love with each other and one thing led to another. Anders was her polar opposite. He was quiet and reflective and much more physical than she was when it came to showing affection. He was good for her. And both her girls and Johannes liked him. Anders had a son. Things were moving slower with him. And Sara knew she was being compared. Compared and judged in more ways than one. *It'll get better*, she thought to herself.

A long sigh full of longing left her lips.

The fruit trees in the allotment gardens were full of apples and plums. The air smelled amazing and felt like a stark contrast to the white-and-blue police tape that signalled death and darkness.

They didn't say a word to each other as they approached the cottage. They didn't have to.

When they stepped into the little house, Sara turned to Jörgen.

"What did Tobias do to make someone want to put him through this?"

"Well, he must have done something. Something horrible," Jörgen said.

"Yes, but what?"

Sara tried to get a sense of the vibe in the small, chilly cottage. But just as expected, she didn't feel anything special. *The people who killed Klingström must have chosen this cottage by chance*, she thought, and realised that she had thought about the perpetrators as more than one. What did that mean?

"There is nothing more to get here," Jörgen said. "The forensics team has done their job."

"I know, but sometimes you need to go back to the crime scene to see things from a new perspective."

Jörgen didn't answer but probably agreed with his boss.

"I wonder what they were thinking and how they got him here? And why they chose this place to start with? First of all, they had to know that the allotment gardens even exist. Then they had to find the right cottage and finally get the victim here somehow. What do you see here?"

"A strange but probably quite thought-out crime. This place is pretty deserted in the autumn. Some might come here to pick winter apples after the cottages have been closed for the season. But if they do, I assume it happens during the day. They must have come here after dark. And they probably checked out the area beforehand to make sure the cottage they chose was actually locked up for the season. Otherwise, it would have been too risky," Jörgen said.

"I just thought about something," Sara said. "If the perpetrator or perpetrators picked this place, it was probably familiar to them. Have we looked into the people who own the allotments around here?"

Jörgen stared into space for a second.

"No, the thought hasn't even crossed my mind. How clumsy."

"None of us thought about it." Sara stroked his cheek.

"No, but it's my job to think about things like that," Jörgen said, and looked embarrassed.

"Let's think about it now, then."

Sara ducked under the police tape. They headed back to the police station. It was so obvious that Jörgen was in a hurry that Sara couldn't help laughing.

15

Samira walked up and down the streets in Lund. She didn't know what to do. She definitely didn't want to go home. Her phone kept ringing, but she didn't answer it. It was her mother. Samira didn't want to speak to her at all. She tried calling Tobias again and again. Why wasn't he picking up the phone?

She turned her phone off and decided to make a stop at Espresso House. She bought a coffee and found a table in the back. She sat there for a while and then decided to check her phone again. She dialled a number and after just one ring, a light voice answered her call. It was all it took for Samira to start crying.

"Elin," she sobbed.

"Samira, where are you?"

"I'm at Espresso House, by the station," she forced herself to say.

"What are you doing there?"

"I can't go home. Something has happened. And I don't know where Tobias is."

"Come to my house. I'll meet you halfway," Elin said.

When Samira met her friend halfway to her home, the injuries from her fall down the stairs weren't visible in the dark. Elin hugged Samira and stroked her back. Comforted her. Samira relaxed in her arms and allowed herself to be comforted. Then they started walking in silence. Samira walked close to her friend and slipped an arm through hers.

When they walked into Elin's flat, Samira hung her bloody sweater on a hook in the hallway.

"Can I borrow a sweater?"

Elin looked at her as she stood under the hallway light. She touched the tape on Samira's forehead and gently stroked her swollen nose.

"Of course. Come with me," Elin said. "Let's have a cup of tea."

Once they were sitting next to each other on the sofa, Samira braced herself. She had decided to tell Elin. But Elin started talking before she had a chance to do so.

"I have to tell you something."

"What is it?"

Samira held her breath.

"My parents know Tobias's parents. My mum called me today. Tobias's father had called her and told her that . . ." Elin stopped talking.

"Tell me."

"Tobias has been murdered," Elin finally said.

"What? Murdered? What do you mean?"

Samira's whole body turned into a knot. She refused to believe what she was hearing. It simply couldn't be true.

"I don't know. I truly don't know."

"What if . . ." Samira didn't finish the sentence.

She leaned against Elin, whimpered, and wiped her nose with the back of her hand. Elin stroked her cheek slowly and gently.

"It's all my fault," Samira said. "How could they?"

"Whatever happened, it's not your fault. But I'm not sure I understand what you mean."

"I know they know I was seeing Tobias. My father was furious."

"So? Are you saying they murdered Tobias?"

"No. Well, yes . . . No . . . I don't know."

"Why would they murder Tobias? What is it you're not telling me?"

"Culture," was all Samira could say. She didn't have it in her to explain further.

"Come here," Elin said, and put a hand on Samira's arm. "You need to rest. Let's lie down on the bed. You don't have to tell me anything. I'm here for you."

Samira stood up and followed Elin to the bed. They lay down next to each other. Samira appreciated the respite.

"We'll get through this together," Elin whispered, and stroked Samira's cheek. Her breath felt warm against Samira's neck.

16

It was a dark night and the air was cool. *Autumn*, Sara thought as she walked up the stairs to her front door. She was home alone. Her twin daughters, Klara and Bella, had gone to Tanzania on a volunteer trip. They were staying with Alexandra's parents. Sara had known Alexandra for years. She had fallen in love with a Swedish man and moved with him to Sweden from Tanzania. In her home country, she had been abused, locked up, and deprived of her money. But she had given birth to two daughters. And she had finally managed to escape her abusive husband. Johannes was with Josefin. Josefin, who had been forced to stand there while Rodney Ritger held a knife to her throat. Rodney, who had shot himself with Sara's weapon.

Sara wasn't thrilled about her son's relationship with Josefin. It wasn't that she didn't like the girl, but Johannes had slipped into the role of therapist. And he wasn't mature enough for that. He was always annoyed now and not at all as happy as before. She was worried about him, but knew all she could do was be there for him when he needed her. At least she thought so, although she still wasn't quite sure if it was the right way to go. She had been overjoyed when Johannes had agreed to see a therapist and she never asked him about what they talked about during their meetings.

"It's not easy being a mother to a teenager, especially not under these circumstances," her friend and therapist Louise Malmberg had told her, and given her a hug the last time they saw each other.

When Sara walked in through the front door, she surprised herself by placing her shoes neatly on the shoe rack. She giggled to herself as she walked into the kitchen. She started the kettle and prepared a couple of sandwiches. Then she walked into the living room and put the sandwiches on the coffee table. Sara made herself comfortable on the sofa and called Anders.

"Hi, honey."

"Hi, what are you up to?"

"I'm preparing for a case. The main hearing starts tomorrow. It's boring. I'd much rather be with you."

He whispered the last sentence, stroking her with his words.

"I've got a lot going on at the moment, but can I see you Saturday?" she whispered back.

"Yes," he said.

She could hear he was smiling. She loved his smile.

They said their goodbyes and hung up. Anders was careful in his approach. He was afraid that she would push him away if he wasn't.

17

Rita paced back and forth in her flat. She was restless and frustrated, and it was far too early in the morning. Her knee had been hurting for days, so she couldn't go for her regular runs. She filled the coffeepot with water and as she poured it into the coffee maker, she spilt some of the water on the floor. She cursed the construction of her coffee maker before starting it.

Her refrigerator was empty except for a dried-out cheese wedge, some cream cheese, and an egg carton containing one lonely egg. It looked pathetic. She promised herself to get some groceries that same night and sat down to enter a shopping list on her phone. She got up and found some crispbread in the cupboard. She topped it with the last of the cream cheese and a slice of the dried-out cheese wedge before pouring some coffee into her huge mug. It had a picture of Lisbeth Salander on it. Then she sat down by the kitchen table again. She scrolled through the news on her phone. In the middle of an irritating article about no-go zones, a Facebook message popped up on her screen. Rita opened it and read it.

Do you remember me? We met this summer together with a group of idiots on Klostergatan. I would really like to see you again. Feel free to get in touch with me if you want! All the best, Linda Andersson

It took Rita a while to figure out who the message was from. But once she did, she instantly felt excited. Suddenly, she wasn't restless anymore.

She wrote a hasty reply when she realised it was already 7:30 a.m. She had to get dressed, brush her teeth, and cycle to work!

It's so nice to hear from you. I don't have time to talk right now, but would love to see you. I'll write to you again after work. Rita.

18

Sara and Rita arrived at the police station at the same time. They parked their bikes in the bike stand.

"Hi!" Rita said, and hugged Sara so tightly that she almost got the wind knocked out of her. "You look great in that coat."

Sara looked down at her old coat and laughed. "Thanks! You seem happy?"

"Yes, actually. Do you remember when I went to dinner with Andreas von Bahr and a group of his friends this summer? That time when I got so pissed off that I left the restaurant with a redheaded woman who shared my rage?"

Sara thought about it for a while.

"Well, it rings a bell . . ."

"The redheaded woman's name is Linda, and she contacted me this morning," Rita told Sara with a smile on her face.

Sara laughed, slightly baffled by Rita's enthusiasm.

"Great! So, are you planning on seeing her again?"

"Yes, I haven't had time to schedule anything yet, but I'm looking forward to it. I really liked her."

Rita didn't seem to notice Sara's raised eyebrows. They walked into the police station and up to their floor. Jörgen and Torsten were waiting for them in the conference room.

"Where is Jonny?" Sara asked.

"On the toilet," Torsten answered just as Jonny strolled into the room.

"Let's go," Sara said, and waved her hand at an annoying fruit fly. "Tobias Klingström has been found murdered in a cottage on an allotment. It's not that late into the autumn season yet and some of the cottages in the allotment gardens are still in use, which means the perpetrator consciously or unconsciously took quite a risk by picking the location. The victim has been subjected to brutal violence, but there are things that tell us the perpetrator or perpetrators have acted in a deliberately calculating way. For example, there are clear signs of torture. I mean, you don't pull someone's nails out in blind rage. The victim seems like every mother-in-law's dream. Kind, full of empathy, social, loyal, friendly, and wise. It makes me suspicious. Nobody can be as perfect as this guy has been described. I'm sure there is something more to him. Why else would someone want to kill him in this ruthless and sadistic manner?"

It was a rhetorical question and they all nodded.

"Did we get any help finding the girlfriend, or have we maybe even found her?" Sara asked, and turned to Jörgen.

"Yes, I think I know who she is. Tobias Klingström's parents didn't know her surname, but they knew she lived in Hörby and that she studies medicine at Lund University. I looked up Pakistani names in Hörby and found the name Khan. Also, there is a student called Samira Khan who studies at Skåne University Hospital. I assume this is our girl."

"I mean, don't they throw acid in women's faces in Pakistan?" Jonny said, and for some strange reason, he looked quite happy with himself.

"Yes, it happens there and in some other countries, unfortunately. But what are you trying to say, Jonny?"

"I mean, it gets me thinking about honour culture," he said, and grinned in a way only he could.

"It's a theory to consider, I guess," Sara said, and turned to Jörgen. "But we need to know a lot more about the family before we even start to make assumptions like that."

As always, Jörgen sat in front of his computer with his back hunched and his eyes close to the screen. Sara reminded herself to send Jörgen to an ergonomics expert who could teach him how to sit correctly. And maybe she should advise him to get blue-light blocking glasses too. He looked up at her from behind the screen.

"Ali Khan is a car mechanic. His wife doesn't work. He has no record. We have never had anything to do with them before." He straightened his back slightly. "And yes, I'll look into the rest of the family," he said without being asked.

"Where do you think we should question Samira Khan? Should we ask her to come to the station or is it better to see her at the university hospital?"

Sara turned to her colleagues.

"I think we should try to be discreet about it," Rita said. "Let's call her. And then we'll question her wherever is most appropriate. Probably here."

Sara noticed that Rita was still looking happy. Her voice sounded more cheerful than usual.

"Hmm," Torsten said, "it's important that we don't jump to conclusions here. We have no idea what her family is like and how tied they are to the ways of their culture."

Sara nodded.

"You're right. Let's not jump to any conclusions. But we have to question the girl. We'll see what it leads to."

19

Samira woke up with a pounding headache. Her body felt stiff. She instantly thought about Tobias. Dead. Murdered. She started crying again. Elin wasn't next to her anymore. She lifted her head from the pillow and looked around the room. Empty. It didn't matter. Life was meaningless. Tobias was gone.

Elin walked in through the front door with a bag in her hand.

"Fresh bread from the bakery," she said, and smiled supportively at Samira. "I'll make you some tea."

"I'll be right there," Samira said quietly. Her voice sounded hoarse as she had been crying all night. In Elin's embrace. Inconsolable. And she had told her friend everything. Now she was crying again, but she had made her mind up. She had to find out what had happened.

"You have to go to the police," Elin said with her back turned to Samira in the cramped kitchen. "You have to. And you need protection from your parents. The police can help you with that."

"I'll go to the police because I want to find out how Tobias died, not because I need protection. I don't need anyone to protect me."

When she looked up at Elin, she realised how angry she had sounded. Elin, her friend who had been lying next to her all night like a security blanket. She looked away and then she stared at her feet. "I'm sorry," she said, and walked over to Elin to give her a hug. "Sorry. It hurts so much. Tobias is gone. Gone forever."

"I know. It's okay. I understand. And I'll always be here for you."

"I loved him."

Elin stroked Samira's thick braid. "Beautiful Samira," she whispered. "Kind Tobias."

"It's horrific, Elin. So painfully horrific. What am I supposed to do?" Samira whimpered. "I just want to die."

20

Rita tried calling Samira Khan over and over again, but she had turned off her phone. She decided to leave the girl a voice message and hoped she would get back to them when she heard it.

"I'll pop out to get a salad," she shouted as she walked past Sara's office. Sara looked busy with something. She nodded, but didn't say anything.

As Rita walked down the stairs, her phone rang. It was Sara.

"There's a girl in reception who wants to speak to us. Could you go get her?"

"Yes, but I was just about to—"

"Forget about lunch. It's Samira Khan."

"Holy crap, speak of the devil . . ."

Rita walked into reception and spotted a young woman with a black braid and a headscarf loosely draped over her hair. The braid was so long that it wasn't fully covered by the headscarf. The young woman's eyes were red and she held a tissue in her hand. She wiped her nose with it a couple of times. *Poor girl*, Rita thought, and approached her. She reached out her hand. The young woman, who looked like she was in her early twenties, stood up and took Rita's hand without looking at her.

"Samira Khan," she said quietly.

"Rita Anker. If you come with me we'll go somewhere a bit more private where we can talk."

They took the lift up to the right floor and just as they had taken their seats, Sara entered the room.

21

How was he murdered?"

The young woman's question lingered in the air like a speck of dust. Rita looked to Sara for support, even if she didn't really need it. She knew what to say.

"We can't tell you, Samira," she said calmly. "But we would appreciate it if you could tell us how you know Tobias."

Samira stared into space.

"We can't tell you because of something called 'confidentiality of investigations.' It means we can't talk about details that concern the investigation to anyone other than the people working on the case," Sara clarified. "For us to do our job and find whoever did this to Tobias, it's important that we know as much as possible about him."

Rita smiled at Sara, grateful for her help.

"Okay, I understand." Samira bit her lip and closed her eyes. Rita saw she was doing her best to keep it together and decided to help her out.

"How long have you two known each other?" she asked.

"Since this spring."

"How did you guys meet?"

"At a party at my best friend Elin's place. She has known Tobias since they were children. Or, her parents are close friends with his parents. He is . . . was a bit older."

Samira started crying. Quietly and with clenched jaws. Rita gave the young woman a moment and thought that she looked like a little girl as she sat there with tears streaming down her face and teardrops dripping from her nose. Rita nodded to Sara, who turned around to grab a box of tissues from a shelf on the wall behind her. She handed it to Samira, who took a tissue and wiped her eyes and nose with it. Rita felt ready to ask another question.

"What did you think about him? What was your first impression?"

"I fell in love with him right away. He was kind and sensitive. Thoughtful. And so handsome."

Samira kept telling them about Tobias and it sounded as if she could have talked about him forever. Rita thought that perhaps she felt as though she were keeping him alive with her words.

After a while, Rita interrupted the girl and did her best to keep a neutral expression on her face.

"If someone had threatened Tobias, do you think he would've told you about it?"

"I don't know, but he doesn't have any enemies," Samira answered. "Everyone loved him, I know that for a fact. He was the nicest man I've ever met."

"How do you know everyone loved him?"

"Elin told me. And he mentioned he had a lot of friends."

"How many?"

"I'm not sure. I never met them. The only time I saw any of his friends was at Elin's party that night. She had a whole bunch of friends over. He knew one of them, but I can't remember his name. I think they were good friends though."

"How come it was only the two of you whenever you met?"

Samira hesitated.

"Because we liked to spend time together alone," she finally said.

"But hadn't it been quite natural for you to see each other's friends from time to time?"

Samira hesitated again. She looked at her hands and then she looked at Rita.

"Yes, maybe. But we liked being alone."

Rita decided to leave it.

"Did Tobias meet your parents?" she asked instead, and noticed a twitch in the corner of Samira's mouth.

"No, he didn't."

"Was there any reason why he didn't?"

It looked like the question took Samira by surprise because her mouth twitched again. Once again, she hesitated.

"It was never a good time."

Rita wasn't sure how to move forward and glanced at Sara.

"How do you mean?" Sara asked, and reached her hands out towards Samira.

Samira sighed. Gave in.

"My parents are very traditional," she said calmly. "They don't want me to have a boyfriend at all. And in the end, they want me to marry someone who shares my background—a man from Pakistan."

Rita stayed silent for a while. She wasn't sure how to handle the situation. They were closing in on a sensitive subject and she didn't want to put too much pressure on the girl. If she did, there was always the risk that Samira would lose confidence in the police—and especially in Rita. It would be very unfortunate.

"What would happen if they found out you were seeing a Swedish man?"

"They would get upset," Samira answered without hesitation.

"How upset?"

"Very," Samira said through clenched teeth.

"Could you describe what you mean?"

Rita waited.

"I don't know. They would probably ground me." Samira looked down.

"But you're a student. Would they stop you from studying?"

"I don't know. No, I don't think so."

Rita braced herself. "Is there any reason to believe they knew about your relationship?"

Samira's reaction made Rita cautious. The young woman suddenly looked scared—a bit too scared. But she quickly gathered herself.

Rita looked at Sara, who clenched her jaws. Then she looked at Samira again.

"No, not at all," Samira said, and suddenly she seemed defensive and almost aggressive.

Her slender body looked tense. Rita felt bad for her and decided that the interrogation was over. She realised they wouldn't get further at this point.

The girl in front of her radiated desolation and sadness. *Not that strange, maybe,* Rita thought after saying goodbye to Samira Khan in the reception area.

'That girl is definitely not telling us the whole story," Sara told her when she came back to the office. "We'll have to do some digging here, or what do you say?"

"Definitely."

22

Samira wrapped the headscarf around her head, making sure all her hair except for the end of her braid was covered underneath the fabric. She picked up her phone and opened the camera in selfie-mode to have a look at herself. Her dark eyes were red, so she took out her eyeliner and painted her upper and lower lash lines black. Now she looked more like herself. But her eyes were deprived of all joy. There was nothing she could do about that.

Her head felt as if it were physically spinning from all her thoughts. But she had made up her mind. She didn't know what else to do. It felt like she didn't have a choice but to go home. They wouldn't stop until they found her. And how hard would that be? The only place she could hide was with Elin, and they knew her. She had no idea what she should do next. Her brain wasn't functioning and her thoughts refused to make sense. She got off the bus and walked slowly towards her home. Everything had been so great. All that was left now was chaos and uncertainty—and rage.

She slipped in through the door and closed it silently behind her. All her nightly escapades had made her a master at sneaking. She threw a quick glance at the shoe rack and the coat hooks. Her father's shoes and jacket were missing, which meant her mother was the only one at home. Samira relaxed slightly. Her mother was sitting in the kitchen with a cup of coffee in front of her on the table. Her hand was stirring the hot drink manically.

When Samira put a hand on her shoulder, she flinched and spilt some coffee on the table. She turned around to look at her daughter. She frowned and her eyes were filled with disappointment and anger. *Maybe she is scared too*, Samira thought.

"Where have you been?"

"At Elin's place," Samira said in her native language for once.

"Your father is furious. What have you done?"

"What have *you* done?"

Her voice broke.

"*We* haven't done anything. You're the one who has done something. You've disappointed us and brought shame on our family. Do you understand what you've done?" Her mother stood up and put her hands on Samira's shoulders. "Samira, do you understand what you've done?"

"You're the ones who did something. He's dead!"

She stared at her mother. And then she started crying. She screamed through her tears. She screamed for her beloved Tobias.

It was impossible to tell what Samira's mother thought or felt.

"Go to your room. We'll see what your father has to say when he gets home."

23

We have a lot of people to interrogate. Tobias's friends, for example. And I'm convinced we should keep an eye on Samira Khan. We need to find a way to question her parents. Something isn't right. Samira is twenty-three years old and a med student at Lund University. She has been a student for two years. Her parents are modern in that way, but as far as we've understood things, they would never accept her having a Swedish boyfriend. The cultural pressure is incredibly strong and honour culture is a real issue, at least back in Pakistan."

Sara waited for her colleagues to react.

"I'll try to come up with a strategy when it comes to Samira's parents," Torsten said. "I actually attended a lecture the other day about the clan vis-à-vis the state. Very interesting. I took a couple of notes, but I'll tell you more about it later."

"Interesting," Rita said. "I would love to hear more about it."

Everyone nodded.

"Another thing I find a bit strange is how Tobias Klingström is described as a saint. He seems to be perfect in every way. No flaws," Sara continued.

"It could be the truth," Jonny said. "Maybe he's one of those people who loves everyone and is loved by everyone in return."

Sara smiled. What happened during the summer had really changed him. He was calmer now. Kinder and more pleasant to be around.

"I guess that could be the case, but most likely he is a human being like everyone else—with flaws and all. What did you find out about him, Jörgen?"

"He worked in Lund up until two years ago when he suddenly got a job in Hörby."

"Suddenly?"

"Yes, that's what it looks like. *Abruptly* might be a better word for it." Jörgen gave his boss a serious look.

"Do we know anything about why he took this new job?" Sara asked.

"No, not much. But something must have happened. I'm not sure why, but he was relocated to Hörby for some reason. Back in Lund, he worked with youth welfare. In Hörby, he was responsible for children's health plans. A bit different as far as I can tell."

"Jonny," Sara said, and pointed at him. "I want you to contact Tobias's old boss in Lund."

Jonny gave her the thumbs-up and the little gesture made Sara feel good.

Overall, she was happier than ever. To be able to collaborate with her old colleagues on cases like the present one was great. Even if they all had other cases, it was still much better to work together than to work with a new team. They knew each other well. *It's easier to deal with what's familiar,* she thought.

24

Sara walked with brisk steps onto Byggmästaregatan, followed it down to Bokbindaregatan, and took a left. Then she took a right onto Hantverksgatan. She slowed down and looked at the beautiful houses that lined the street. She dreamed about someday buying a house just like one of them. They had big, beautiful gardens in the back and she couldn't stop herself from getting on her tippy toes and having a look behind the garden gates. Every summer, roses grew all over the front of the houses. The street she walked on was particularly quiet.

She came out on Bryggaregatan and took a left. At Fjelievägen she took another left and picked up the pace as she made her way back towards the police station. The walk took a bit over an hour and helped clear her head.

Lunch was over and the reception area was quite empty. Sara said hi to the staff and walked up to her office.

She sat down and called Torsten, who was with the medical examiner at the hospital. As always, he had walked to his meeting. He kept his body in great shape, but no gym in the world could tempt him to stand in front of a mirror, flexing his muscles. Running and biking were what he was into. Next summer, he would bike with Team Rynkeby to Paris. Sara admired his determination.

He picked up the phone, but he didn't even allow her to speak before he presented her with his suggestion.

"What do you say? Should we just go over to Samira Khan's parents and talk to them? Not as an interrogation, just an informal conversation."

"I was just going to suggest something similar. Great minds think alike." Sara laughed.

"Great, see you soon."

"I hope the medical examiner can give us some new leads," Sara said before hanging up. Then she dialled a new number.

"Hi there," Rita said. She sounded happy.

"Where are you?"

"I'm on my way to David Ljung, a friend of Tobias Klingström. He lives in Professorsstan. On Professorsgatan, more specifically. He is running an advertising agency from his house. I'll call you after."

"Okay. Torsten and I will go to Hörby when he returns from his meeting with the medical examiner. Just so you know."

Sara reached for her iPad and made a list. The Khan couple, Anna and Karl Klingström, Tobias Klingström. A question mark after each name. Then she wrote down Tobias Klingström's name in the middle of a piece of paper and scribbled down other relevant names around his. Finally, she drew arrows between the names to illustrate how they were all connected. She had done the same on the whiteboard earlier.

She sighed. It was probably better to leave the task for the analysts. They were better at it than she was, and more efficient.

25

Jonny sat in the waiting room in Kristallen, the enormous building in which the Lund municipal office operated. The social services head office was located in the same building. He was waiting for the social services director.

He picked up his phone and scrolled through Facebook. Nothing on there caught his interest. He decided to see if he could find Tobias Klingström's profile. To his surprise, the victim's profile showed up right away. He clicked on it and scrolled through the messages on Tobias's wall as he wondered if Jörgen had already gone through them. *Oh well, it doesn't matter*, he thought. He noticed that Tobias had close to a thousand Facebook friends. His timeline was full of hearts from both women and men. Jonny scoffed. Nothing of interest.

"Welcome," a voice said, and made Jonny lift his gaze.

A very elegant woman was standing in front of him. He stood up and took her hand.

"Jonny Svensson," he said, and bowed like a schoolboy. He felt slightly embarrassed, but at least he hadn't curtsied.

"Astrid Karpe," the woman said.

They walked together to an office where there were two armchairs. She pointed to one of them as she sat down in the other.

"I understand you want to talk about Tobias Klingström," she said, getting straight to the point. She looked right at him, and even though he felt like looking away, he forced himself to meet her gaze.

"Yes, I have some questions. Could you tell me a little bit about him?" he asked, and tried to sound confident, although something about the woman's posture made him feel insecure. Jonny blushed. He couldn't believe it, but his face felt warm so he knew it was true. He was indeed blushing.

"Well, he was a very pleasant man. Everyone liked him. Friendly, thoughtful, helpful, and ambitious."

"So, all positive then," Jonny said, sounding more sarcastic than he had intended.

"No, actually. Not in here."

"Not in here?"

"No, not among us."

"How do you mean?"

"Someone actually reported him. I can't tell you more than that."

"Oh, I'm sure you can," Jonny said, sounding more authoritative all of a sudden.

"No, I can't. It's confidential."

Her rudeness made Jonny lose his newfound confidence. All at once, he wasn't sure if she had the right to keep the documents from him, so he decided to let it go for now.

"I guess I'll come back with a warrant then," he said, standing up, realising he sounded like an actor from an American movie. *I guess I'll come back with a warrant*, he thought to himself and blushed again.

"Yes, I guess you'll have to do that," Astrid answered. She didn't even bother to stand up. "I'm sure you'll find your way out."

Jonny turned his back to her and walked away without a word. He instantly regretted interrupting the interview like that. He could've steered the conversation in a different direction. Before he walked back into the police station, he popped into the bathroom in reception. He splashed his face with some cold water.

26

Torsten and Sara sat in the car. Sara was driving. It was 4 p.m. Jonny had looked defeated when he came back from his meeting with the social services director. The medical examiner had confirmed what they already knew. Tobias Klingström's throat had been slit, but before that, someone had cut him badly in the genital region and pulled his nails out. The crime scene had been wiped clean of DNA. Normally, they would be able to find DNA anyway, even if it wasn't always possible to analyse it. But this time, they hadn't found a single trace. The cottage was clinically clean. According to the medical examiner, they could at least guess what the knife looked like. Not much to celebrate.

Rita wasn't back yet. She had been out questioning Klingström's friends.

Jonny had been assigned the task of contacting Tobias's parents to ask them why he had left Lund for Hörby.

"Let's take it easy, right?" Torsten told Sara as she navigated the heavy traffic on Norra Ringen. It looked like there was even more traffic heading towards Lund, though, and she was grateful they were driving in the opposite direction. She took the exit towards highway E22 at the roundabout and stayed in the left lane.

"Yes," she said without looking at her colleague. "It's just a conversation. We'll have to be careful. We don't want to create more problems."

When they got to the highway, she could finally relax; she glanced at Torsten.

"Hey, how are you?"

"I'm great," Torsten answered. "Veronica is here and she's staying with me for a week."

Sara could hear the happiness in his voice. He deserved to be happy.

"That's great, Torsten," she said, and raised her hand for a high five. He took her hand and held it.

"You truly have a big heart," he said.

There wasn't a lot of traffic and they soon made it to Hörby. Sara knew the little town well, even if she had only been there a couple of times to visit the famous market.

When they approached the house where Samira's parents lived, Sara started questioning if they were really ready for the interview. After a while, she made up her mind.

"Let's not do this," she said to her colleague. "We don't know enough about this. I think we should call in an expert."

Torsten glanced at her. "No, you're probably right."

She parked the car on the side of the street and looked at the house where the Khans lived. Then she nodded, made a U-turn, and started driving back towards Lund.

"Do we have any resources like that in our district?" Torsten asked.

"I'm not sure, but I think so," Sara said. "Let's look it up when we get back."

27

Samira had curled up into a little ball on the bed and now she was lying there, staring at the wall. Her eyes were red, and tiny drops of sweat glistened along her hairline. She felt feverish and chilly, even though she was sweating.

She heard the door to her room open and pretended to sleep. She breathed as quietly as she could to hide the fact that she was awake—and to hide how scared she was.

A warm hand stroked her hair, and when she smelled the oil and gas, she knew it was her father.

The hand disappeared, and shortly after, she heard the door close again.

A while later, she heard voices from the kitchen. It was her parents. She tried to hear what they were saying, but couldn't. She decided to walk up to the door and place her ear against it to hear better. She knew it was a risky move, but didn't hesitate for a second. She had to know what they were saying.

"What are we going to do, Najima?" she heard her father say.

"The question isn't what we're going to do, but what have you already done, Ali?"

The question cut like a knife. Samira flinched.

"I haven't done anything. It was Sanju. You know . . ."

"*Karo-kari,*" her mother said. "Will it happen to Samira?"

"Not as long as I can stop it."

Her parents were silent for a while. Samira heard a chair being pulled out and someone turning on the tap in the kitchen. Then someone started the kettle.

Tea, she thought, and felt thirsty. There was nothing to drink in her room. She had to manage without it.

When the water in the kettle had stopped boiling, she heard her father singing a poem from their home country. He had sung the same song to her many times when she was a child. It was about a beautiful girl who was about to be married off to a man, but who ignored her parents' wishes and ran away instead. Later, she was found dead and her father grieved her death. Samira felt tears streaming down her face. She licked her lips. Her tears tasted like salt. And grief.

Then her parents started talking again.

"They won't find you honourable if you stop it," Samira heard her mother say. She imagined how she sat there with her hands clenched in her lap and her eyes like cold, grey metal. "Everyone thinks Samira is a whore. You know that. Are you going to let her continue her studies?"

"Yes, but she'll be home right after school. Where was she before?"

"At Elin's place."

"She can't go there anymore."

Samira closed her eyes and exhaled. She sneaked back to bed and pulled the duvet over her head. She didn't want them to hear her crying.

28

Sara walked towards the allotment gardens. She didn't feel like going there, but the late afternoon was sunny and beautiful and the air smelled amazing, and it felt easy to breathe. She needed to see the crime scene one more time. The sun was about to set.

They had contacted an expert in honour cultures, Agneta Johansson. She was a fellow officer working in Malmö and she had a lot of experience. It was always easier to talk to a colleague. She had agreed to come to the station the following day to give them some advice before their interview with Samira's parents. No evidence pointed in their direction, but still, Samira Khan's behaviour made it look as if she was under a lot of cultural pressure. Even if they didn't have anything to do with the murder, their daughter could still be in danger.

Samira had told them herself that they would be furious if they knew she had been in a relationship with a Swedish man. Still, something felt contradictory about the whole situation. Why would they let her study medicine alongside Swedish men on a daily basis if they were so oppressive?

So many questions. Not enough answers.

What had happened at that social services office and why was the social services director so reluctant to let them know about it? Why had Tobias Klingström been transferred to Hörby? How come someone had reported him if he was such a saint?

So many questions. Not enough answers.

Sara opened the gates leading into the allotment gardens. The air smelled like apples and decomposing plants. Dirt. She thought about Anders. They had finally found time for a date and were planning to meet up that Saturday. She was looking forward to it.

When she arrived at the little allotment garden owned by the Bruhns, she stopped.

The sun had set and Sara moved silently towards the cottage. She stepped inside and realised she could barely see her hand in front of her in the dark little house. She considered turning on the light but decided not to. *It's a bad idea to attract attention*, she thought. Sara used the flashlight on her mobile phone to light up her surroundings. The cottage had one room with a small kitchenette and it was empty except for a couple of the owners' things and some simple furniture. The forensics team had done a thorough job.

She suddenly heard a loud slamming noise, which made every single hair on her body stand up. Then she spotted the cat sitting on the bench outside the house. It had tipped over a bucket. Sara sighed. *I can't believe I let that spook me*, she thought.

She kept shining her flashlight around the room and, all of a sudden, she noticed something shiny under the kitchen counter. Sara pulled out a pair of plastic gloves from her pocket and got on her knees to take a closer look. There was something there. A bracelet.

29

Sara held up the bracelet. She had asked the whole team to return to the station. It was late at night and they had all agreed to come—although very reluctantly. Ove Ovesson was there too.

It was clear her team would rather be somewhere else, but Sara saw how their eyes lit up with excitement when they saw what was in her hand.

"A bracelet. Yes, I know, stating the obvious," Torsten said as if he was trying to dismiss the laughs that never came.

Sara nodded.

"It has an inscription in a foreign language on it. I'm guessing it's written in Urdu. I found it under the kitchen counter in the cottage where Tobias Klingström was found murdered. Which is where the crime took place, right?" she said, and turned to Ove Ovesson.

"Yes, definitely. There is nothing to suggest the opposite. All evidence tells us that's where he was murdered. Blood, nails, well . . . everything, really. I'll take that bracelet," he said, and held out a plastic bag. Sara dropped the bracelet in it and took her plastic gloves off.

"You talked to Tobias's friends today, Rita. What did they have to say?"

"Well, they all speak very highly of him. The same goes for that guy on Professorsgatan. David Ljung. The thing is that I get a bad feeling about him, as if something isn't right. He works in advertising. He's an art director. But there was something cold and distant about him. He played golf with Tobias. But they've known each other their whole lives. I'm not sure what it is, but I feel like there is something there."

"Well," Torsten said, "most people have something to hide. It doesn't necessarily have anything to do with Tobias Klingström's murder."

"No, of course not. But we still have to look into everything that seems odd," Sara said, defending Rita's observation.

"Of course." Torsten smiled to show he wasn't looking to start a discussion. Not that anybody thought he was. Torsten was professional through and through.

"Agneta Johansson will pay us a visit tomorrow. She's an expert in crime related to honour cultures. I've called her in as support to guide us in our approach to Samira Khan and her family. Torsten and I were on our way over there today, but we changed our minds. We don't want to step into something we don't know anything about."

Rita clapped her hands. "Can we go home now?"

"Yes, it's about time," Sara answered, and started packing up her stuff. She was excited about their progress. Even if they were still moving slowly, every step in the right direction was a success.

30

They sat at M.E.A.T. in Kattesund. Rita's cheeks were rosy and Linda Andersson had a big smile on her lips. Rita's hands were constantly moving and Linda had to move glasses, plates, and breadbaskets out of the way to save them from crashing onto the floor. But Linda didn't mention it. She just kept moving stuff out of the way. Rita liked it. *Attentive and kind*, she thought.

"Isn't it lovely to get to know new people?" Rita said.

"Yes, especially if they're called Rita Anker," Linda said with a big smile on her face. Rita blushed. *How silly*, she thought. *Why didn't I just say it was nice to get to know her?* She looked at Linda and realised how beautiful she was. Her skin looked like porcelain.

Linda reached her hand out and it brushed against Rita's.

"I'm gay. I'm a lesbian."

"I like it when people tell it as it is." Rita laughed to hide how baffled she was.

"Maybe it was impulsive of me to blurt it out like that," Linda said, and gave Rita an inquiring look.

Rita shook her head.

"I only laughed because I like your honesty."

Linda crossed her arms over her chest.

"It's not that strange, is it? To tell someone you're gay?"

"No, of course not. And I like you a lot, so it doesn't matter. I was overjoyed when you contacted me," Rita said, and reached for Linda's hand.

Linda laughed and untangled her arms again.

When the staff had turned off the lights in the restaurant and Rita and Linda reluctantly had taken their jackets and left the venue, Rita's face was aching from all the laughing. They hugged each other goodbye. To her surprise, Rita felt butterflies in her stomach when Linda slipped into her arms. Linda was almost a head shorter than she was and her breasts were soft.

Rita kissed her on the cheek. When she left, she was overcome by an unfamiliar feeling. What was going on?

31

When Samira woke up in the morning, everything felt surreal. And she felt guilty. She hadn't called Elin, although she had promised. Instead, she had turned her phone off. She realised she had to be careful now, especially considering her parents' conversation.

Samira got out of bed and turned on her phone again. Ten text messages from Elin. Worried messages followed by angry ones—followed by even more worried ones.

"Elin," Samira heard a confused and tired voice say at the other end of the line.

"It's me."

"Samira," Elin said, and exhaled.

"I don't have it in me to talk to you. I don't want to talk to anyone."
She heard Elin gasp.

"What happened? I was so worried. I was about to call the police, but I wasn't sure what to do."

"I came home, talked to Mum, and went to bed. I have to go to school now. But I just wanted to tell you I'm okay. I'll call you later."

Samira tried to sound more confident than she felt, but she wasn't sure if she was pulling it off.

"Are you sure you'll be okay? You know I'm here for you if you need me."

"Yes, and yes," Samira said.

"I'll call you later this afternoon."

"Talk to you later," was all Samira could say.

Samira sneaked out of bed. The flat was silent. It was 8:30 a.m., so she knew her father was at work. But where was her mother?

She walked into the kitchen. It was empty, but there was a note on the table.

You can continue your studies but you will return home straight after your last lecture. We have a copy of your schedule and know when you're done for the day. Those are the rules from now on.

The note was short and written in Urdu. Samira felt a shiver down her spine. But she knew what the deal was.

And she knew what they had done.

32

The police station was bustling when Sara came in. She had slept well and although it wasn't yet 8 a.m., she had even made time for a short run before work. The sky was blue. *What a day*, she thought, and couldn't wait to start working on the murder investigation.

The whole team met up in the conference room. The analysts had compiled a detailed chart of all the people relevant to the investigation. Sara hung it up on the whiteboard and read the names of Tobias Klingström, his parents, and his closest friends. Those close to the victim had nothing but great things to say about him. Sara decided to put a pin next to David Ljung's name. Then there was Astrid Karpe, who had been Tobias's boss when he worked in Lund, and Samira Khan, as well as her parents and a couple of her relatives who lived in or close to Hörby. Samira didn't have a large family, but considering the honour culture they seemed to live by, Sara and her team needed to look into each and every family member. If nothing else, they had to do it for Samira. That was all they had for now, except for the old Bruhn couple. Their names were written in the periphery and there was nothing suggesting they had any relationship whatsoever with the victim.

Elin Eriksson, her parents, and her younger brother's names were also scribbled down on the edge of the paper.

Sara wrote the word *bracelet* on the whiteboard. Then she drew a line from it to Tobias Klingström and wrote *for my lover* next to it.

"This is what we have so far," Sara said. "The text on the bracelet translates as 'for my lover,' just like I've written here. My guess is that the bracelet belongs to Tobias Klingström and that it was a gift to him from Samira. Another possibility is that the bracelet belongs to someone else. The murderer, for example. It can't be that hard to find out. Jörgen, please take a photo of the bracelet. Other than that, the cottage was wiped clean. So, no traces."

He nodded.

Sara kept drawing lines between different people and, somehow, all the lines touched on a common point—Tobias Klingström. But except for the fact that everyone knew Tobias Klingström, Sara and her team still didn't know how they were all connected.

"And, Jonny, I understand that Astrid Karpe refused to give us the files revealing why Tobias Klingström was transferred from Lund to Hörby. She said it was because of confidentiality, right?"

Jonny rubbed his beard.

"Yes, and I wasn't sure if she had the right to refuse, so I let it go."

"They are forced to break confidentiality when it comes to crimes with a minimum sentence of one year in prison. This applies even if the files contain information not solely connected to the person in question. That's what Prosecutor Baum says. So, we're getting our hands on those documents. With or without her permission. But I'll call her after the meeting."

"She won't give them to you," Jonny said, shrugging his shoulders as if he couldn't stop himself.

"You might be right. In that case, I guess we'll have to fight it out," Sara answered with a raised eyebrow. She put her hands together. "It looks like Tobias Klingström was a very well-liked person, maybe even loved by most. But there is something more to it. I might have mentioned it before, but I'm convinced that I'm right about that."

"I think everything points to the Pakistani family," Jörgen Berg said. "Although there isn't anything to suggest they haven't integrated into Swedish society." He paused for a second. "But on the other hand, I'm not sure if cultural pressure like this has anything to do with integration. Either way, I'm convinced you're right when you suggest something is going on underneath the surface here."

Sara nodded.

"Oh, by the way, weren't you supposed to look something up about the allotment gardens?"

"Yes, you wanted me to look into the owners of the other cottages to see if we recognised any names," Jörgen said, and stared at the computer screen.

"And?" Sara drummed her fingers on the table.

"I've compiled a list of the owners, but nobody seems familiar so far. Some of the official owners might very well have handed their allotments over to their children or grandchildren without registering it though, which means we might not have the correct information yet. Sorry, I forgot to tell you."

She lifted her hands and waived them dismissively.

"Then we'll wait until you have all the information," she said, and tried to pick up the conversation where she had left off. "So, how should we approach the Khans? I don't want to risk creating new problems. I think the best thing to start with is to ask Samira Khan to come to the station again. We need her to explain to us what it means to live in an honour culture. That way, we might avoid looking stupid. If she wants to tell us, of course . . . And also, Agneta Johansson will be here soon. In an hour. Maybe we should talk to her first. We'll need her expertise."

33

She rushed into the classroom and received an angry look from the professor. The look quickly changed from angry to intrigued. Samira sat down, apologised, and looked at the table in front of her to hide her face.

After the lecture, the professor approached her.

"How are you, Samira? You look so tired and sad."

"I didn't sleep well."

She did her best to sound normal.

"Nothing else?" The professor studied her closely.

"No, nothing else."

The day moved slowly and she had a hard time focusing. Martin asked her if she wanted to have lunch and she accepted his invitation, even though she wasn't hungry at all. She found him so kind and knew he really cared, so she went with him to the cafeteria. She had some tea. Martin looked at her. It was hard to tell if he was worried or curious. Maybe both.

"What's up? Tell me," he said.

"It's nothing. I just didn't sleep well. The exam is coming up. I'm probably stressed about it."

Samira ran a hand across her face and pinched her cheeks to regain some colour.

"Are you sure?"

Martin locked eyes with her and made her feel uncomfortable. She nodded, but didn't say anything. She didn't have it in her to repeat herself. For each time she was forced to say that everything was normal but that she hadn't slept well, it would be harder and harder to keep a straight face. She knew that.

"A family friend passed away," Martin said as they left the cafeteria.

Samira looked away. *No, no, I don't want to,* she thought. She couldn't deal with other people's grief. Not right now. But there was no way out. She had to say something.

"How sad. How's the family? How's Elin?" she heard herself say without managing to sound very interested.

"It's tough, of course. He was young. Thirty-something," Martin said. "Sorry, I didn't mean to bother you with this."

Samira pushed her chin against her chest and pulled her headscarf down to try to hide her face while she walked slightly behind him.

"No worries," she whispered.

"No," Martin said, and didn't speak again until they got back to the university.

She felt him staring at her all day, but he didn't approach her again. Still, she felt it. She felt his gaze following her. His eyes piercing her. Her chest felt tight and she sat through the rest of the lectures without being able to see or hear a thing. Not even the lab work made her snap out of her haze. *Tobias. Mum. Dad. The police.* Her head was spinning.

34

Samira walked briskly across the gravel and rounded AF-borgen—the iconic students' house in Lund. She flinched when she saw Elin and her brother Martin sitting on a bench next to the building. They were both drinking coffee from paper cups. Elin brought her cup to her mouth but froze when she saw Samira.

"Hi there, I wasn't expecting you," Elin said, and made space for Samira on the bench between her and Martin. Samira hesitated and wasn't sure what to think. Did they look guilty? She straightened her back and looked at Elin. Then she looked at Martin.

"How are you?" Elin asked, and sounded a bit too cheerful for someone who wasn't hiding anything.

"Like I deserve."

She crossed her arms in front of her chest.

"Martin and I were just talking about how hard it is to study."

Elin laughed.

That laugh was forced. She's lying, Samira thought, and wanted to leave. But at the same time, she wanted to stay. She wanted to ask what they were talking about. They were probably talking about her. Martin looked away. She knew she was right. He looked uncomfortable and suddenly excused himself. He leaned over and kissed his sister on the cheek. He stroked Samira's head with one hand before he left.

"I take it you've been talking about me?" she said to Elin, still with her arms crossed.

Samira studied her best friend, who hesitated for a second before appearing to make up her mind.

"You're right. We talked about you and your situation," Elin said, and gave Samira a pleading look.

"I knew it," Samira replied, and blinked a couple of times. She relaxed her shoulders and at once felt relieved.

"Well, you know I'm always honest with you," Elin said.

Samira nodded.

"But I didn't know what to do, I felt so lonely," Elin said, "I can't handle being the only one who knows what you're going through. And I mean, Martin is my brother and if I can't tell anyone else, I thought I could at least tell him. He knows you too. And we're basically the same. Almost."

Samira nodded again and relaxed a bit more. She placed her hands on her lap.

"*What* did you tell him?" Samira asked, emphasising the first word of the sentence.

"I told him that you and Tobias knew each other, that you were a couple. That's all I said."

Elin looked down and drew circles in the gravel with her right foot. Tiny circles.

"It's okay," Samira said after a while.

"But he promised not to tell anyone. Not even our parents."

Elin's eyes pleaded. Samira didn't say anything. Nothing really mattered. Tobias was dead. He was gone. Forever.

"What did Martin say?" she asked finally.

"He thought it was horrible. And he said it explained your reaction when he mentioned Tobias earlier today."

Samira was lost in the confusing world she lived in now. She wasn't sure what was true, who had done what, or who she could trust.

"And I told him that you stayed at my place yesterday and that your parents are threatening you. Sorry, I know I shouldn't have said that."

"No, you shouldn't have," Samira said through clenched teeth.

"But what was I supposed to do?"

"Nothing, you're supposed to be my friend. That's all I need."

Samira looked away. She felt tears welling up in her eyes.

"But hey, shouldn't you go to the police?"

"Stay out of it."

Samira's chin trembled but she didn't want to cry, so she got up. She walked away without a word—and without even looking at Elin.

35

If it were up to Sara, she would have wanted Torsten to interrogate David Ljung. But instead, she had asked him to call the social services director and make her change her mind about the documents she had refused to give them. Therefore, it was up to her and Jonny to talk to David.

They agreed to walk together through Lund City Park in an attempt to process what had happened there that summer. In a way, the murder investigation that started in the park had brought them closer. Years of strain between the two of them had culminated during the investigation and turned their relationship into a better one.

Jonny has lost some weight, Sara thought, and smiled to herself. He moved with more urgency and seemed less lazy in general. Also, he didn't fight her as much anymore. She wondered if he had stopped smoking. When she thought about it, he hadn't smelled of cigarettes in a while.

"Isn't it nice that autumn is finally here?" Sara said.

"It's not my favourite season. It tends to make me depressed."

Sara was pleasantly surprised by the way he opened the door to conversation. It didn't happen very often.

"Oh, that happens to me in the spring," she said.

"Hmm."

"I hope we can get David Ljung to tell us more than he did when Rita questioned him. She's a great interrogation officer, but she didn't manage to get much out of him at all."

"Yeah. Do you mind if I smoke?" he asked, and pulled a pack of cigarettes out of his pocket.

So, he still smokes, Sara thought, realising it was none of her business.

"Wasn't it strange that Agneta Johansson couldn't give us better advice about the Khan family?" he asked, and lit his cigarette. He inhaled the smoke and blew it out in the shape of a circle.

"Yes, you're right. I had expected a lot more, but maybe we need to talk to another expert. I know one in Hörby. I met her in another context but I heard she's really good at what she does. She's from Iran, but I don't think that matters."

"Sounds good," Jonny said as they walked towards Mejeriet. He stopped abruptly. "Do you see those flowers?"

Jonny pointed at the rhododendron bushes. Sara turned towards them. The ground was covered with withered roses, a teddy bear, and some burnt-out candles.

"I haven't seen that before, but I guess I don't really run past here anymore," she said. "This summer was hard on all of us."

"Yeah," he said, and started walking again.

Sara had to run to catch up with him.

They walked up Stora Södergatan, crossed Stortorget, and continued along Kungsgatan. They stopped for a second to have a look at the interesting and expensive furniture and lamps in Zimmerdahl's shop window. The store only opened on Saturdays, but you could always call or email the owner. A bit further down the street, they walked past the door to the Swedish Wine Association's basement venue. Sara thought it would be nice to know a bit more about wine. Nobody seemed to be in there and all the lights were turned off.

"Do you know anything about wine?"

"Not at all," Jonny answered. "I'm a beer guy."

"Yes, of course you are," Sara said, and nodded at his waist.

Once they got to Biskopsgatan, they crossed the road and walked over to Sölvegatan before heading down a couple of streets lined with beautiful houses. It was a nice walk and it gave them a chance to talk. Jonny told Sara more about his life and his family than he'd ever done before.

She was surprised by his willingness to open up about himself. And glad.

Twenty minutes later, they made it to David Ljung's house. They rang the doorbell, both intent on getting him to share more information with them this time. Maybe Rita just hadn't asked him the right questions. He was one of Tobias Klingström's closest friends, after all, and it was time to push him a bit more. Rita was convinced there was something there. Torsten's words echoed in Sara's head. *Most people have something to hide.*

<h1 style="text-align:center">36</h1>

Samira opened the front door. She was exhausted. Too exhausted to be scared. All she feared was finding out what her parents had done.

Ali Khan was waiting for her in the hallway.

"I have to study," Samira said, and she was just about to sneak past him when he grabbed her braid and pulled her back.

"You don't make the rules around here," he said, and pulled harder. "I'll let you study, but this Christmas you're going to Pakistan."

"No way," she exclaimed.

As always, she answered him in Swedish. As always, to distance herself from him. But this time she was more scared than usual. And Tobias's death still pained her. It made every cell in her body ache.

"You have no choice. You've shamed us. You don't make the rules, do you hear me? And if you don't listen to me, I won't allow you to continue your studies. You're filthy. You're a whore."

Samira swallowed.

"I hate you. For all you've done. For everything you represent. I'm going to be a doctor. I won't let you take anything more from me."

She freed herself from her father's grip, ran into her room, and locked the door behind her. She was scared. But she didn't have anything more to lose. If she was going to die, she was going to die.

Nothing more happened. It terrified her. She prepared herself for the worst. But everything was silent and calm until someone opened the front door. Low voices. Footsteps entering their home. Mumbling, male voices mixed with her mother's voice that was calm one second and upset the next. She couldn't hear what they were saying. Who was that? Was it Sanju?

37

Torsten called the social services director. He was determined to get his hands on those documents.

"Astrid Karpe," a deep female voice answered.

"Hi there. My name is Torsten Venngren and I'm with the Lund Police."

"Hi, what can I do for you?"

Torsten didn't think Astrid sounded very eager to help at all, but he ignored her tone.

"We need the documents you're withholding regarding Tobias Klingström's transfer to Hörby."

The woman at the other end of the line was silent for a while.

"They're confidential," she said assuredly.

"Yes, that's what you told my colleague, but it doesn't really matter here," Torsten said. "This is a murder investigation where the perpetrator risks prison for more than a year, which means confidentiality can—and must—be broken."

"Oh, is that right? I don't agree."

"Maybe you don't," Torsten said calmly. "But the thing is, you don't have to. We're getting those documents whether you like it or not."

"I need that confirmed," she said, "by a prosecutor."

"That won't be necessary. My request is enough. If you don't like it you can call my boss, Chief Inspector Sara Vallén."

Suddenly, it went quiet at the other end of the line, and he realised she had ended the call.

He called her again, but this time she didn't pick up. Torsten called prosecutor Åke Baum to explain the situation, and the prosecutor quickly sent over a warrant. One that wasn't necessary, but as he was in charge of the investigation, he didn't mind sending one anyway.

Torsten called a secretary at the social services office and asked for the fax number. Then he faxed the warrant to the social services director's office.

Within a couple of minutes, his phone rang.

"This is Astrid Karpe," said the woman at the other end of the line. "You can pick up the documents tomorrow. I'm going home now."

"Wait . . ." Torsten exclaimed, and realised she had already hung up.

He cursed at the social services office in general—and the social services director especially. It wasn't like him, but he was frustrated and couldn't help himself.

38

Sara rang the doorbell to the advertising agency that operated out of David Ljung's home. The house was palatial and opulent and she tried to figure out what style it was. Patrician? Art Nouveau? She realised she had no idea. She knew the words but didn't really know what they meant. She giggled to herself and decided to ask her step-father, Sven-Åke, some other time. He would know for sure. Jonny looked at her and shook his head. Sara didn't say anything. They listened for footsteps and soon enough, they heard someone walk across the floor on the other side of the door. A beautiful woman with pale skin and dark hair tied back in a knot opened the door. She gave Sara a curious look that turned slightly sceptical when her eyes wandered over to Jonny, whose clothes still fitted him poorly even if he was looking much trimmer than he had in years. He hadn't bought new clothes to fit his new figure yet. He always forgot things like that. Sara regretted not being more supportive when it came to that area of his life. But she also suspected there was something about Jonny's gaze that provoked a sceptical reaction from the woman in front of them. His eyes radiated authority and superiority and his approach appeared suspicious and invasive.

Sara held out her hand and the woman shook it elegantly. It was somewhat of a contradiction to the way the woman looked, acted, and dressed. She was wearing a black leather skirt and a see-through blouse with ruffles and lace. Sara couldn't help noticing the black bra that contained the woman's plump breasts underneath the blouse.

"Sara Vallén, Lund Police Department." She nodded towards Jonny. "This is Jonny Svensson, my colleague."

"Camilla Brink," the woman said. "Is something wrong?"

"It depends on how you see it," Sara answered. "But we'd like to talk to David Ljung."

"I don't actually know where he is. He's been missing since last night. I haven't seen him since."

"When was the last time you saw him?"

"It must have been around half past three, I think. He said he was going golfing."

"And you haven't heard from him since?"

"No, it's very strange. He normally calls me. Especially if he has meetings planned."

"This isn't a planned meeting," Sara said.

"Oh, okay. Well, maybe he's up to something else then. I'm not always here," she added. "I'm studying to become a journalist and I'm just helping David out with some copywriting now and again."

"Can I leave my card with you? And could you please ask him to contact me as soon as he's back?" Sara said, and gave Camilla her business card.

"Sure," Camilla said. "I'm certain he'll be back eventually. Worst case scenario, I'll leave him a note."

"Thanks."

Sara and Jonny left the house and hurried back to the office. This time, they took a shortcut through the pedestrian tunnel under the central station.

39

Torsten Venngren and Rita Anker were on their way to Hörby to meet with the municipal office's expert in honour cultures.

Aidah Iskander-Svensson was waiting for them in reception and they followed her up the stairs to the social services office.

"Coffee?" she asked, and showed them into a conference room.

Rita noticed how beautiful the woman was. Her jeans were tight and her behind was small and pert. Her posture was good and she maintained eye contact. She came across as confident—a safe pair of hands.

Both Rita and Torsten nodded, and she walked away. They could hear the coffee machine, and the woman returned shortly with two steaming cups.

"We work hard at communicating information about the ways of Swedish society and the laws that apply here, but people from countries ruled by an honour-shame culture tend to lack faith in the government and authorities. Therefore, it's a slow process to change their attitudes towards women and power structures in general. It's hard to gain their trust."

"And what do you do if you suspect someone is living under that kind of cultural pressure?" Rita asked.

"There are no easy ways, you have to remember that," Aidah said.

Rita nodded and looked at Torsten. This wasn't their area of expertise.

"It's important to understand how hard it is to break free from your family's expectations and traditions—and from oppression. If we find the situation acute, we move swiftly. If it's a situation that's less urgent, we move slowly and think carefully about our every move. In each case, we conduct a threat and risk assessment. I'm sure you do something similar?"

Torsten nodded.

"We use tools called Sara and Sam."

Aidah smiled.

"Women and girls carry the honour for their families but other than that, they aren't worth much," she explained.

Rita wondered how much cultural pressure Aidah Iskander-Svensson had experienced in her own life.

"It sounds contradictory," Aidah said, "but in these cultures, it's not at all."

"Isn't it hard to get these girls to leave their parents?" Rita asked.

"Yes, incredibly hard. It's not like moving away from home. If they accept a new identity and protected housing, they're not allowed any contact with parents, siblings, or other family members. You can probably imagine how hard that is, especially for a young person."

"Yes, I guess it's like completely losing your identity," Rita tried.

"Exactly. Not something you would want to do if you had other options, right?" Aidah said, and raised her eyebrows. Rita thought she looked friendly but slightly superior. Torsten smiled.

"No, of course."

"Worst case, they're never able to return to their old life again. These people are experts when it comes to finding their girls." Aidah sized them up as if she was trying to determine if they understood what she was saying. Then she put on an information film about honour culture and about their work to fight the oppression of girls and womenand in some cases, boys and men. When the movie ended, she packed up her computer.

"Our most important task here is to make sure the girl isn't found out, and to make sure her parents don't take her out of the country before we have time to act. It has happened before," she said, and raised a finger. "I need you to set up a meeting between me and Samira Khan so I can assess her situation. The sooner the better. And I advise you not to interrogate the parents until the girl is safe. As long as you don't have enough evidence to lock them up, that is," she continued, and gave them a serious look.

"We're doing our best. Thanks for meeting with us and teaching us about this," Rita said, and stood up at the same time as Torsten.

After the meeting, they drove back to Lund. The silence in the car spoke for itself. They both had a lot to think about.

40

Rita and Torsten brought a fresh autumn breeze from outside with them into Sara's office. Torsten hadn't even taken his scarf off before he started talking.

"We've now been told how to best approach the Khan family. We were advised to talk to Samira again and try to get her to tell us about her family. We were also advised to let you and Rita do the interview. Or one of you. But not one of our male officers. We should also try to get her to agree to meet with Aidah Iskander-Svensson. She knows what to do in these situations and is in direct contact with other important resources and people."

"Great, I look forward to hearing more about how to approach the family later. Did you get any advice on what questions to ask and how to ask them?"

"Yes. Most importantly, we were told not to bring the parents in for questioning before we know the girl is safe. Otherwise, they might take her out of the country if we approach them. Rita knows what I'm talking about."

Torsten gave Rita a friendly look. Everyone knew he was the best of them all when it came to interrogations, but his humble nature was probably his finest quality. Rita smiled at him. Sara felt a flutter inside when she saw how well her colleagues worked together.

"Excellent."

"Also, Jörgen has talked to Tobias Klingström's parents, Anna and Karl. They confirm the bracelet belonged to their son," Rita said. "We ran into Jörgen as he was on his way home. Apparently, his wife is sick and he needs to take their dog out for a walk."

"Oh, a bit early for that, maybe, but sure. Is he coming back?"

"He didn't know, but he was taking the analysts' chart of people connected to the victim with him. He said he would study it. So, he'll be working either way."

"I suggest we go to the university tomorrow morning to meet up with Samira," Sara said, picking up their previous conversation.

"Sure," Rita said, and walked towards the door with Torsten. She turned around in the doorway. "Torsten and I will plan the interrogation."

"Great," Sara said, and returned to her documents.

A moment later, Jonny came into her office.

"Did you hear anything from David Ljung?" he asked.

"No, not a word. Maybe you can try to get hold of him again tomorrow? Could you call him or pay him a visit?"

"Sure thing. That's what I'll do."

41

Samira lay in a foetal position on the bed with her back to the door and her chin tucked into her chest. She tried her hardest to stop crying but couldn't. She cried like a child.

She heard the door creak as her mother walked into the room. She sat down on the edge of the bed and stroked Samira's hair. Samira knew her mother didn't have any power to change what was happening, but it was still nice to feel her comforting hand on her head. She allowed herself to feel like a child. She turned around and rolled into a ball again. Judging by the look on her mother's face, Samira understood her face was puffy and her makeup smeared all over the place. But she didn't care about fixing it. Samira's mother gently ran her hand underneath her daughter's eyes. She licked her index fingers and removed some of the smudged mascara next to her eyelashes. And then she nodded. "That's better."

Samira stopped crying.

"I haven't done anything," she whispered. "I don't know what to do, Mum."

"We've given you all that you need and more. And still, you've put us in this difficult position," her mother said calmly.

"I'm a prisoner," Samira said in Urdu.

"Your father has decided that you're going to Pakistan this Christmas."

"I don't want to go to Pakistan." She looked at her mother with tears in her eyes. "Why do I have to?"

Her mother shook her head but didn't say anything.

"I'll die. I can't go," Samira pleaded.

"There is nothing I can do. You know that. And you won't die."

"Yes, I will. You might as well kill me. I refuse to go there."

"You must."

"I won't," Samira said, and tried to look confident. She knew she didn't.

Her mother shook her head again and stroked her daughter's cheek. Then she left the room without a word.

42

Samira had reluctantly agreed to meet with Sara and Rita at the police station after Rita told her they would have to show up at the university if she didn't agree to come and see them. That option had been out of the question for the young woman and she had promised to come to the station on Byggmästaregatan. They had let her pick a time for the meeting and she had suggested 4 p.m.

Sara spent the morning trying to find David Ljung and finally tracked him down in his home office. He looked surprised when he saw Sara standing outside his door with her badge in her hand. But he opened it for her and invited her in.

She stepped into the hallway and was blown away by what she saw inside. The house was gigantic with high ceilings and marble floors. Above their heads, a bright modern lamp hung from the ceiling. David showed Sara into the kitchen—she had never seen anything like it before. The marble floors continued into the kitchen and she saw straight away that the equipment and appliances were of top quality. The refrigerator and freezer were bright red while all other appliances were black. In the middle of the enormous room, there was an island with a stove and an oven. A fully stocked knife stand stood on the island. Sara noted that they were all top-notch Global-brand knives. The kitchen looked like a picture from a magazine. *Overly lavish and not very welcoming,* she thought as she stood with her mouth gaping, knowing deep down that she was probably just jealous. She realised her mouth was open and closed it.

"What do you think?" David asked, and smiled when he saw Sara's face.

"Fancy," Sara admitted. "But that's not why I'm here."

Camilla, whom she had met the day before, stepped into the kitchen and shook Sara's hand. Sara looked at the two of them and noticed that Camilla refused to look at David Ljung, who suddenly looked tense. Camilla's face was slightly flushed and there was an irritated look in her eyes. Sara waited.

"I apologise—we've had a bit of a disagreement," David Ljung said awkwardly.

"Are you kidding? I wouldn't call it a disagreement," Camilla said, obviously not willing to cover up their fight.

David shook his head and asked Camilla to go back to the office.

She looked furious, but turned around and left.

"We argued about me not letting her know where I was when I was away for a day. It made her worried. But I was visiting Tobias's parents and it got really late. Before that, I met up with some friends. As you probably understand, Tobias's death has been hard to deal with. Hard for all of us close to him."

Sara didn't answer but gave David Ljung a sad look. Of course nothing would be the same again after the murder of a close friend. It would have been stranger if he hadn't been upset.

"I understand you and Tobias were close," she said to start the interview.

"Yes, he was the best guy I've ever met. Very loyal to his friends. We've known each other basically our whole lives. Our parents know each other, but I guess that's not unique for a city like Lund. People move in and out, but the few of us that live here long-term, we stick together."

I've heard that one before, Sara thought, but kept a straight face.

"You mentioned he was loyal to his friends. How was he with those who weren't his friends?"

David flinched.

"Well, I mean . . . he was a loyal person."

"Loyal to his employer?"

"I guess."

"Loyal to his clients?"

A twitch appeared underneath his right eye—gone as quickly as it had started.

"Yes, he liked his job. He liked helping people in need. I could never do it myself," he said. A drop of sweat glistened in his hairline.

"Do you know Samira?"

"Nope, who is she?"

He looked genuinely surprised.

"I thought you knew," Sara said, and studied him. As far as she could tell, he had no idea what she was talking about. Apparently, he had no idea his best friend had a girlfriend.

"No idea," he said firmly.

Sara decided it was time to move on.

"Do you know why he transferred from his job in Lund to the social services office in Hörby?"

Another twitch. He looked away.

"I think he wanted to change location. It's never good to work close to home when you do what he does."

The answer came a little too quickly. He was hiding something and they would soon find out what it was. Rita was getting the documents from the social services administration in Lund as they spoke.

Sara continued the interview but got nowhere. Whatever she asked him, he had an answer to her question or denied knowing anything about it. All she had to go on was the nervous twitch underneath his eye. Not much, in other words. But she knew the truth would surface sooner or later.

When Sara left, she felt as if she had taken a step in the right direction after all.

43

Rita received the documents. She wanted to read them right away but decided to wait until she met up with Sara back at the office. It took all her willpower not to open the envelope and have a peek. She laughed at herself and hurried back to the police station.

She had to wait for an entire hour for Sara to return from the interview with David Ljung, and before they looked at the documents, Sara wanted to talk about her meeting with Ljung. They both felt he was hiding something, and whatever it was would probably have a negative impact on Tobias's reputation if it surfaced.

They opened the sealed envelope with Sara's name on it. It hadn't been easy for Rita Anker to persuade the receptionist to give her the documents, and it wasn't until she threatened to report her that she handed the envelope over. Rita wasn't proud of her methods, but what the hell was she supposed to do? She explained it to Sara, who shrugged her shoulders as if it wasn't a big deal.

In the envelope they found a so-called Lex Sarah report—a report that care providers are obliged to file if they suspect mistreatment—as well as a letter from Ann-Britt Karlsson, the mother of a girl called Jannice Karlsson. As they looked through the rest of the documents, they found a response letter to Ann-Britt Karlsson, written by the social services director.

They read it carefully and found out that the social services office had reported itself for not handling a self-harming girl's case professionally.

There was also an internal investigation report and an action plan in the envelope and they quickly realised they had found the explanation for why Klingström had been relocated.

Ann-Britt Karlsson's handwriting was hard to read and her letter was riddled with spelling errors, but the mother accused Tobias Klingström of not investigating her daughter's need for care, even if she showed clear signs of self-harming. The letter also mentioned that Klingström had behaved very inappropriately towards her daughter and ended with a promise of reporting him to the police.

The response letter made it clear that the social services office would make sure the issue was handled correctly and advised Ann-Britt not to report the case worker for the sake of her daughter.

"I wonder if these accusations are true," Sara said.

"Even if they are, it's not very likely that the mother who wrote this letter killed Tobias."

"No, I don't think that for a second. But at least we've found out why Tobias was relocated. I'll ask Jörgen to check if Ann-Britt Karlsson ever reported Tobias."

"Shouldn't he have stumbled across something like this when he looked into Tobias's criminal history?"

"No, my guess is this wouldn't show up in his record at all, as misconduct in the workplace normally isn't reported with a named suspect. It depends on what the reported crime is, of course. But she probably never reported anything. Let's check though."

Sara got up and headed towards Jörgen's office.

44

Samira let the girl in reception know she had arrived. It was just past 4 p.m. She knew she would have to catch the 5:15 bus home; otherwise, they would come looking for her. Worst case scenario, they wouldn't let her continue her studies. She didn't know what to do. Should she run away? Should she stay? The threat of being sent to Pakistan that winter hung over her head like a menacing black thundercloud. Anxiety made her thoughts race back and forth.

"Welcome," the tall blonde police officer said. It was the same officer she had met the last time she was there. Was her name Rita?

Samira stood up and followed her.

Sara got up to greet Samira and Rita when they stepped into the office. Then she pointed at the chair across the table from her. She noticed how petite the young woman was. Her big, almond-shaped eyes reminded her of the eyes of a deer. They were very dark. Her eyebrows were neatly plucked and just as black as the long braid that peeked out of her headscarf. Although she appeared small and fragile, there was something proud about her. *Petite, strong, proud and fragile,* Sara thought to herself. *And very sad.*

"We've met before. As you might remember, my name is Sara Vallén. This is Rita Anker. We're very glad you could make it here."

Samira looked at them but didn't seem interested in what they had to say.

Or am I wrong about her? Sara thought, and noticed that Rita looked just as pensive as she felt. Samira's headscarf had slipped back slightly, revealing her hairline.

"I notice you have a cut on your forehead," Sara said. The girl quickly ran her hand across the taped-up wound.

"I tripped down the stairs at home," she said. "I was running for the bus."

"Okay. And how did you trip?"

"I tripped on my own feet."

It sounded like a feasible explanation and Sara decided to let it go.

Rita pulled out a photo from a folder and put it down on the table.

She slid the photo over to Samira. It was a photo of the bracelet. Samira wiped a tear from the corner of her eye.

"That's Tobias's bracelet. I gave it to him," she said.

"Thanks, then we know for sure," Sara said, and put the photo away. "We would like to know a bit more about your and Tobias's relationship."

"What exactly is it that you want to know?"

"How you guys were doing, what your plans were for the future . . . well, stuff that gives us a better idea of what your relationship was like."

"We never talked about the future, really. We just spent time together. We didn't see anyone else. I've already told you about who he was. I'm not the one who killed him."

"So, you guys kept to yourselves?" Sara asked, and ignored the rest. She wasn't sure if she was asking the right questions, or even how she should ask them. She felt like she was walking on thin ice and feared that she would fall on her backside at any second. Or maybe even fall into a hole in the ice.

"Yes."

Rita jumped in. "And why was that?"

Samira looked at her and shook her head. "I've already explained that. My parents don't know I have a Swedish boyfriend. They don't want me to have sex before I get married. It had to do with tradition and culture. My parents were raised in Pakistan. That's how you live there."

Rita glanced at Sara, who stared back at her in a way that made it clear she wasn't sure what to say either. Sara held her breath and braced herself when she saw that Rita had made up her mind.

"What would you say if I suggested that your parents were behind Tobias's murder?"

The young woman stared at Rita, shocked. She obviously hadn't expected the question.

"They would never do that. They're not murderers," she said firmly.

Rita couldn't take her question back so she decided to keep pushing. Sara realised she was still holding her breath so she exhaled and inhaled again.

"But if I was right, I assume you would also be in danger? Right?"

"I'm not in danger. My parents are conservative, but they would never kill me."

"Maybe they wouldn't, but what about your other relatives?" Rita tried.

"No, I said."

"I think we have to talk to your parents anyway," Rita said provocatively.

"Why? They haven't done anything."

Rita kept going like an elephant in a house of glass. Sara needed to stop her.

"Is there any reason why you need to be concerned for your safety?" Sara asked as softly as she could.

"No." Once again, Samira sounded very certain and crossed her arms in front of her. She checked the time and squirmed in her seat. "I need to go. My bus leaves in a couple of minutes and I can't miss it."

"Okay, you better hurry then," Sara said, and stood up. She was convinced there was more to the story but knew that now was not the time to dig further. There was no point. She thought about Aidah's advice and realised they had to approach the girl in a different manner. But they had to move fast. They had to build trust, and right now, it felt like an impossible task.

45

ow we know why Tobias Klingström moved to the social services office in Hörby. We can also assume that was what David Ljung was trying to hide from us." Sara drew a line on the whiteboard and turned to her team. "There was a mother who accused Klingström of not helping her daughter when she needed help the most. She also stated that Klingström had acted inappropriately towards the girl. One can only assume this inappropriate behaviour was of a sexual nature. However, there is nothing about this in our records and no report of misconduct in the workplace." Sara took a step back and looked at the whiteboard. Now they had tied yet another person to Klingström—Jannice Karlsson. There was a cross drawn next to her name.

"Is she dead?" Jonny asked, as if the cross could possibly mean anything else.

"Yes, she took her own life a year ago," Rita answered.

"She had been self-harming for a long time, but maybe that whole thing with Tobias Klingström pushed her over the edge?" Torsten suggested after reading the documents.

The atmosphere in the room turned sombre, but Sara continued the briefing.

"Could we be dealing with an honour killing here?" Jonny asked calmly.

Rita nodded. "Samira Khan says her family would never do anything like that, but I'm not sure she's convinced. Either way, she seems scared of them. What I find strange, though, is that I would have assumed that Samira was the one they would've killed if this was an honour killing. But according to Aidah Iskander-Svensson, who is an expert in the area, it doesn't necessarily have to go down that way. I also spoke to Agneta Johansson, who confirms this. Both of these experts agree that Samira now risks falling victim to *karo-kari*—honour killing. Or she might be forced to marry someone back in Pakistan."

"But shouldn't we do something to protect her, then?" Torsten looked upset.

"Yes, but we can't protect someone who doesn't want our protection," Sara answered, and looked him in the eye.

"We have to be able to do something, right?"

"Yes, we'll question her parents. If nothing else, it'll make them realise we're on to them."

"Is that really the right way to go?" Jonny asked. "Isn't the cultural pressure in these situations stronger than the fear of being caught by the police?"

"From what Aidah has told me, the cultural pressure is strong; you're right about that. But we might also be able to convince Samira to come with us and accept our protection. It all depends on how it goes when we interrogate her parents. Other than that, I don't really know what to do, but we can't just leave it as it is. Either way, we have all the reasons in the world to keep an eye on the Khans. Samira's parents could very well be the ones behind Klingström's murder." She turned to the whiteboard. "Do we have any other leads? What about Ann-Britt Karlsson? Not very likely considering the brute force used here, right?"

She put the cap on the whiteboard pen to signal that the meeting was over. Then she left the room to the sound of chairs being pulled out around the table.

46

When Anders stepped in through the door, she was instantly filled with a warm feeling. She threw herself at him. He picked her up and kissed her for a long time. *Oh, what a lovely feeling,* she thought.

"You're wonderful," he whispered into her ear.

"You're more wonderful," she said, and laughed. "Dinner is ready."

"It can wait."

He was right, it could wait.

Anders and Sara sat in the tub. She was holding a glass of wine and swirled the red liquid round and round to release the aroma. She placed the glass under her nose and inhaled.

"This is delicious," she said after tasting it.

"Yes." Anders looked at her with eyes full of love. Immediately, she realised something. *If I lose him, I don't know what I'll do,* she thought. She was obsessed with him.

He ran his index finger along the inside of her thigh and looked up.

"How is your case going?"

Sara shook her head. "No, let's not talk about that. I don't want to ruin our night talking about work."

He laughed and waved his hand until he spilt some of his wine.

"Okay, let's not talk about it. You're right."

"Why don't you tell me about you? I want to know more. Much more."

"Oh . . ." he said, and thought about it for a while. "I did this test years ago. You know one of those personality tests combined with some kind of skills test. It was interesting. I've always been convinced that my biggest strengths are maths and logic. It turned out I was wrong all along. Apparently, I'm better at language. It really took me by surprise."

Sara threw her head back and laughed. "That sure is interesting. Isn't it funny how you can have such a twisted self-image? I've experienced something similar. Tell me more."

"That's why I decided to become a lawyer. My plan initially was to become an engineer."

"I can see why. You're great with technical stuff. I've seen it with my own eyes . . ."

"Yes, but maybe more on a hobby level. What I like most is tinkering with my bike. Speaking of bikes, don't you want to start biking with me?" He winked at her and smiled.

"You're so sweet. I love you."

Sara's words took her by surprise.

Anders looked nothing but happy.

"And I love you," he said. "Come here."

Sara turned around and made herself comfortable in front of him with her back against his chest and his hands cupped over her breasts. It was amazing. Truly amazing.

47

Sara opened her eyes and looked at the man next to her. He was sleeping deeply and snoring a little. She didn't mind. She was awake and alert. She slipped out of bed and started making breakfast. She felt happier than she had in years.

Johannes wasn't home, and although she would have loved to see him more often, she enjoyed her time alone with Anders.

Unfortunately, she would have to go to work even though it was Sunday, but not until later. She was expected to meet up with her team at 1 p.m., so she still had plenty of time. They would probably have time for a walk before that.

When he got up, breakfast was served. She had heated some bread in the oven and it smelled wonderful.

He kissed her neck and inhaled her scent. "It smells amazing and I'm starving," he said, and reached for the coffee.

"Me too. I'm starving too, I mean."

"And you smell amazing too." He smiled.

After breakfast, they headed outside. The air had the scent of rain. They walked towards Lund Cathedral but didn't go inside as there was a service being held. They walked side by side, enjoying life and each other's company.

When they reached Bantorget, Anders stopped in front of Grand.

"Do you want to grab a coffee before work?"

He took her hand and walked her up the stairs. Then he opened the heavy entrance door and urged her to go inside.

Grand was and had always been one of her favourite places. It breathed history, ballroom dancing, and establishment. Not that she felt at home in any of those contexts, but the sense of history in the building tickled her imagination. The lounge was full of people. Some ate brunch, others had coffee. A couple had just ordered two glasses of champagne. They looked like they were in love. Maybe they were newlyweds?

She turned to Anders again. The coffee tasted delicious. She realised that she still didn't feel as full of joy as she should. Suddenly, a completely different feeling washed over her. She felt guilty and wondered if Anders could tell. Everything was so perfect. She should feel happy, and she *did*, but although her surroundings were so warm and cosy, the grey sky outside filled her with melancholy. Something didn't feel right and she wasn't sure what it was.

As she walked back to the police station, her footsteps felt heavier than she had expected them to after such a lovely morning. Anders had gone back to the house to get his things. He also had some work to do. Considering the way her emotions kept changing, it was probably for the best. She crossed Bantorget and walked along Trollebergsvägen up to Byggmästaregatan. *I'm losing it*, she thought to herself. *Who wants to be with someone as emotionally unstable as me?*

The streets were almost empty. *People are probably snuggling up in their homes, if they aren't all having coffee at Grand*, she thought.

For some reason it felt good going to work on a Sunday. The wind tugged at her clothes and hair and slapped her in the face, but after years of living in the south of Sweden, she was finally used to it. It didn't even bother her anymore. Especially not on a day like this one.

As she approached the police station, she started thinking about work and everything still to be done. She decided the best thing to do was to help Samira Khan get in touch with FemCenter—the women's shelter in Malmö—and realised this meant they had to ask Samira to come to the station again. Then she decided to contact Aidah to ask for her support.

The others were waiting for her and even Jonny smiled when she walked into the conference room.

"Wow, that's quite the determined look on your face," Torsten said, smiling.

Dear Torsten, she thought.

"I agree," Rita said, and put the palms of her hands together as if she was about to start clapping—which she obviously wasn't.

Sara told her team how worried she was about Samira Khan and how she wanted to use Aidah to help the young woman.

"I'll reach out to Aidah right away. Then we'll contact Samira tomorrow," Sara said, and picked up her mobile phone.

She stepped outside and had a long chat with Aidah, who confirmed their decision was the right one.

After the call, Sara told Rita that Aidah would be ready for a conversation alone with Samira the next day.

"Aidah said it was best if we started there. She'll also work on a threat and risk assessment to determine what kind of danger Samira is in when it comes to her family and the cultural pressure she is under. We don't want to risk talking to Samira's parents before we know she's safe. If we do, she could end up disappearing—one way or the other. And if something happens to her, we'll have another case on our hands. It's unfortunate, but this is the way we'll have to work."

They spent the rest of the afternoon mapping Tobias's last days alive, which wasn't as easy as they'd hoped. Torsten and Jörgen organised the documents explaining Tobias's relocation to Hörby and after a while, Torsten entered Sara's office.

"We've tried to interpret every sentence of Ann-Britt Karlsson's letter, but I think it's probably best to talk to her. I'll call her to schedule an interview."

"Great. We need to talk to anyone who is connected to the victim."

When they said their goodbyes at 6 p.m., things felt good. Sara couldn't wait to get home to Anders. Love had pushed her anxious indecisiveness to the side.

Sara and Rita walked together for a while, with Rita walking next to her bike. It was windy outside and they wandered along close together, talking about life, love, and grief. Peter Matsson felt like a distant memory, even if it had only been a couple of months since

Sara had convinced herself that she was in love with him. *You live and you learn*, she thought without feeling bitter. At the same time, she wasn't completely sure if she had learnt anything, but she didn't tell Rita. Instead, she decided to focus on the fact that things felt good in her life now.

48

Sara had always hated Mondays. Or, more accurately, she had always hated the nights leading to Mondays. This Sunday night hadn't been any easier than other Sunday nights. She wasn't sure what to do about Anders and her past. She felt drained of all energy and knew the only way to regain it was to get out and move. She had been so busy with her new relationship that working out had become less of a priority than usual. The fact that she had an all-or-nothing mindset wasn't news to her. As she unlocked her bike, she reminded herself that she biked almost every day. Even if work wasn't very far away.

When she stepped into the station, Rita came running.

"I've talked to Samira Khan. She didn't seem excited about it but she'll be here at noon during her lunch break. That was the only time she could make it. I called Aidah Iskander-Svensson and asked her to be here by 11 a.m."

"Super, Rita. Thanks."

"And by the way, Ann-Britt Karlsson is on her way to see Torsten."

"Also, super."

"Wow, someone is in a great mood," Rita said sarcastically.

"Just let it go."

Rita gave her an inquiring look and for a moment, Sara felt like telling her friend about her conflicting thoughts. But then Rita shrugged her shoulders and the moment was over. Maybe it was all for the best.

Sara went into her office and took off her coat, scarf, and hat. She had always hated wearing a hat. Her hair simply wasn't made for it. Nor was her face.

"You're so bloody vain," her ex-husband used to say to her when they were still together and their marriage was crumbling. He had been annoyed with everything she did or said back then. And she had been annoyed with him in the same way. Oh well, that was a long time ago. Now they were finally on speaking terms again.

She called Åke Baum, who was in charge of the preliminary investigation. She needed to share some information with him after the weekend. She heard a commotion at the other end of the line, followed by cursing.

"Hello," Baum answered the call, almost yelling.

"Well, I guess that's one way to take a call," Sara said, laughing.

"I walked right into a shelf. I'm sorry. But you know how it is when you hit your head or stub your toe. Something snaps and it makes you so much angrier than when you hurt other parts of your body."

She laughed again and told him about the conversations they'd had about Samira Khan's parents and how they were planning to help the girl.

Åke Baum sounded satisfied with the information and asked her to continue working as they were.

"No suspects yet?"

"No, but we have a couple of ideas. First of all, we're not sure about Tobias Klingström. We feel as if he might have been hiding something, and we're wondering who he was behind his perfect facade. Secondly, we're focusing on Samira Khan and her family. We'll keep digging. I'll get back to you as soon as I know something."

"Sounds good. It's been a bit more than a week so we still have some time before things start getting cold."

"I think we've come quite far considering we haven't had much time yet."

"Sure, sure. But I'll talk to you again later," Baum said, and hung up.

49

Ann-Britt Karlsson sat in a chair across from Torsten. She was skinny and looked old—older than she was. Torsten knew she was about to turn forty soon, but she looked at least ten years older. Judging by her grey skin and the fine lines around her mouth, he assumed she was a smoker. And she reeked of alcohol. *Poor soul*, he thought.

He told her why she was there. Her helpless and nervous appearance made his heart ache. He forced himself to act professionally and distance himself from his emotions.

Ann-Britt Karlsson answered all of Torsten's questions. She didn't scream or cry. Although she seemed willing to help, she came across as being more confused than anything else.

"Jannice had problems," she said. "She skipped school a lot and the principal called me about it more than once. But there was nothing I could do."

"Why did she skip school so often?"

"She cut herself all over her arms and even on her face."

"Why do you think she did that?"

"I don't know, but she didn't do it to kill herself. Her therapist said her soul was hurting. And I guess that's the truth."

"So, she didn't cut herself to end her life?"

"No, not back then anyway. But I don't really understand how these things work," she said. "I drank instead, to forget."

Torsten noted that she used the past tense of the verb.

"Tobias Klingström was assigned to take on her case. What happened after that?"

"That bloody idiot. He probably thought with his cock."

"What do you mean?"

"He tried to trick her into having sex with him."

"How did you find out?"

"Jannice told me, of course." She looked at Torsten as if she was trying to make out what kind of man he was. "That's all men care about."

"Maybe you're right."

The woman told him about her daughter. How she had felt worse and worse. She had killed herself a couple of months before she would have turned eighteen.

To make up for the woman's lacking sense of chronological order, Torsten had to ask questions. It was simply easier if he asked the questions in the right order than to let her tell the story freely. Jannice had come home one day and told her mother about the social worker who didn't want to give her the help she needed. She had been offered treatment, but she never showed up to it. The girl was feeling worse and worse, and Ann-Britt couldn't understand why. But six months before her daughter took her own life, Ann-Britt had written to the social services director about how poorly Klingström had treated her. She also accused him of making sexual advances. She had wanted to go to the police, but as she was sure they wouldn't believe her, she didn't. Also, the social services director had advised her not to.

After talking to Torsten for almost an hour, Ann-Britt started to squirm in her chair and her answers became shorter and less forthcoming. Torsten was happy with the information he had managed to get from her and knew they would have to keep digging. He let her out of the office and sat down to write a report about what the woman had told him.

Things were never easy, and that was something he had got used to a long time ago. In a way, that was what he loved about his job as an officer. He had nothing better to do anyway. He didn't have a wife anymore and his daughter lived in London. It was what it was. He straightened his back and kept writing his report.

When he was done, he went to Sara's office. Sara was sitting at her desk with a woman Torsten assumed to be Aidah Iskander-Svensson. She smiled and said hello to him. Her skin was pale like the whitest of porcelain and her eyes were big and black. Her nose was straight and proud and her plump lips framed a row of perfect white teeth. There was something elegant about her that blew his mind. He caught himself with his mouth slightly open and closed it immediately. At that moment, Jonny walked by the office but turned around and left the moment he saw Aidah. Torsten smiled to himself. Jonny had always been uncomfortable around beautiful women.

50

Rita and Sara left Samira alone with Aidah. It felt safe.

Aidah and Samira had talked for more than an hour when they finally left the room. Sara walked down to reception with Samira, who was heading back to uni.

Aidah looked satisfied when she sat down with Rita and Sara.

"She is struggling to know what to do, which is very common. I've given her my phone number and told her she can call me any time. I'll keep working on helping her come to a decision, but she'll need some time."

Apart from being filled with grief about losing her boyfriend, the conversation with Samira had made it clear that the girl was worried about her future. Once again, Aidah explained that leaving your parents and accepting protection and a new identity was a long process that didn't happen overnight.

"Her head is full of questions about what would happen if she left her family, and she will have more questions as time goes on."

Rita felt impatient.

"But did she say anything about suspecting her parents of being involved in the murder of Tobias?"

Aidah shot her a sad look.

"You have to understand that this is a massive deal and very difficult. But I'm sure she suspects her parents or other family members to be involved somehow. She hasn't expressed it explicitly, but I've worked with this for a long time and I'm pretty good at reading these girls. It's important to realise that families who live outside their home countries are still very much affected by what their family back home thinks. They aren't completely free. They are still tied to the old ways."

"But do you think the parents are guilty here?"

"I can't say. For me, the most important thing is to understand the girl. If I don't, I can't help her. I'll meet with her again later today. She's catching a bus from Lund central station and I'll be meeting up with her outside the hospital to walk her there. It'll give us a chance to talk."

"Did she tell you anything more concrete?" Sara asked.

Rita noticed that her boss was also starting to feel impatient, although she was trying her best to hide it.

"As far as I can tell, they've found out about her relationship with Tobias Klingström. Now they're threatening to put her on a plane to Pakistan. My guess—and it's a qualified guess—is that they're planning to force her to marry someone down there. As I mentioned before, women carry their family's honour. They don't have much value in other situations. I've started on the threat and risk assessment. We'll see where I land with it, but I think the risk of her being taken out of the country at one point sooner or later is high. I'm doing my best to get her to accept help and protection."

Sara thought about what Aidah had just told her.

"What do we do?"

"Nothing, for now. Let me handle the communication. I don't think she has anything to tell you that is relevant to the investigation—at least not yet."

"What happens if she accepts a new identity?" Rita asked Aidah.

"She won't be able to continue her studies and she'll have to change her name, as well as cut all ties with everyone from her old life. Taking on a new identity will have a huge effect on her life. Every part of it. No exceptions." Aidah looked serious. "The world she has lived in for all of her life will never be the same again. To be able to live a normal life and continue her education, she'll probably have to move to another country."

"Damn," Rita said, and gasped. "It sounds horrible. Poor girl."

"You're right. But it's worth it to stay alive. Also, she's young and things can still turn out great for her in the end. Her biggest loss will be her mother. As I understand it, she's very close to her. Even if it often looks as if the mother is as tough as the father, that's normally not the case. The mother has no control at all over her husband or the other men in her family." Aidah stood up. "Well, I have to go back to Hörby now. But as I said, I'll meet with Samira this afternoon. She seemed to really want to see me. I'll be in touch."

Aidah turned around in the doorway. "I'll be putting together that threat and risk assessment. If Samira is okay with it, I'll show it to you. And by the way, I advise you to tread very carefully now. This whole thing is almost more than a young woman can take. The fact that she is even standing up at this point is admirable."

"Of course. We'll stay in the background," Rita said. She felt an immense amount of respect for the knowledge Aidah possessed. And once again, she couldn't help wondering what she had been forced to go through in life.

51

Samira had a lot to think about, but she couldn't focus. She sat next to Martin in the classroom while the professor in obstetrics held his lecture. She listened to every word, but everything the professor said mixed in with her own thoughts about the future. She was hurting. Martin glanced at her now and again, as if he was trying to figure out what was going on in her mind. Samira pretended not to notice, but she knew that everyone could see that she was miles away.

What should she do? She had far too many questions and not enough answers.

When the lecture was over, Samira left the hospital and found Aidah waiting for her outside.

The two of them walked together towards the central station.

"Do you want to tell me what you're thinking? What are you afraid of? And what do you think might happen? Do you have a lot of family in Sweden?"

Samira clearly felt that Aidah was pressuring her to share her story. But it was also clear that she felt respected by her.

All at once, the floodgates opened and Samira told her everything. She told her how nice her family was, but how hard it was not to be allowed to live her life the way she wanted to. She told her how her parents had encouraged her to study as they had never had the chance to do so themselves; how they were controlled by the rest of their family—even though they lived on the other side of the world. She told her about the few other family members she had in Sweden, that they were all close to each other and how they were all controlled by cultural pressure.

"I don't know what I would do without my mother," Samira said. She lowered her head and buried her chin in the winter scarf she was wearing over her headscarf.

"Yes, I know what you mean," Aidah said as she stopped to hug Samira.

With her face hidden in Aidah's jacket, Samira finally mustered up the courage to say what she had been thinking for days.

"I think they had something to do with what happened to Tobias."

She cried. Again. How could one person produce so many tears?

"Yes, you might be right."

What had she done? Had she just ruined her parents' life?

"No, they can't be guilty of this," she said, changing her mind.

"That might also be true, but you told me they had figured out that you and Tobias were together."

Samira nodded.

"Dad has decided to send me to Pakistan this Christmas. I know he wants me to marry someone back there."

"That's probably the case," Aidah answered. "There are strong forces behind these decisions. I understand that you're scared and filled with anxiety. Only you can decide what to do here. Nobody can force you to go to Pakistan, get married, or leave your family. What's important to understand is that the forces controlling your parents' actions are conditioned by culture, not by themselves as individuals."

The bus came and Samira got on it. She had made up her mind and knew what had to be done. It was the worst moment of her life.

52

Aidah called to tell Sara about the conversation. She informed her that Samira was now in the process of deciding what to do next.

"I can't tell you everything that she said as she has to give me her permission about what and what not to share with you. I didn't get a chance to ask for permission as she had to jump on a bus, but I think she'll be ready to make a decision any day now. Until then I ask you not to contact her parents. Or do you have enough evidence to put them away?"

"No," Sara said honestly, "we don't have any evidence at all. We'll hold off for now. In the meantime, we'll keep gathering information about them."

Sara gathered her colleagues and repeated what Aidah had said. She also told her team that she expected them all to hold off for now.

"We still don't have any evidence suggesting they had anything to do with this," Torsten said. His wide-open eyes and the tone of his voice told her he was irritated. Sara didn't like that side of him at all. But she knew herself and her trigger points well enough to keep her feelings in check.

"No, that's exactly what I said to Aidah. Has something happened? Why are you irritated?"

"Things aren't moving forward. We don't even have a suspect yet."

"Of course things are moving forward. For example, we're figuring out that Tobias might not have been as angelic as everyone describes him. And we've established a suspicion of Samira living in a family controlled by honour culture. I would say that's progress. But now I want you to tell us what you found out during the interrogation of Ann-Britt Karlsson."

Torsten took a deep breath and told the rest of the team about Ann-Britt, as well as what had happened at the social services office.

"Now we have something concrete to go on," Sara said. "We need to talk to David Ljung again, as well as Klingström's bosses. His closest bosses, that is."

"Yes, but can you really trust someone like that mother?" Jonny wondered. He also seemed irritated.

"Of course."

Torsten ran his hand through his curls, forcing them back. One of his fingers got caught in a knot and he pulled it out with a frustrated grunt. He didn't let that side of him show very often.

"We'll keep digging. Rita and I will go to the social services office in Lund. Jonny, I want you to talk to David Ljung. Torsten, talk to Tobias's boss in Hörby. It's enough if you call her."

Jonny nodded. Torsten too. Jörgen didn't need instructions.

"I'm going to call Baum with an update," Sara said while she and Rita left the conference room. Sara felt grateful that her job took so much of her energy that there wasn't much left to think about her own worries. Even if she felt tired and sad most of the time lately, she didn't have time to think about that while she was working. So that's what she did. She worked.

53

Visiting Tobias Klingström's boss didn't offer them any new information. But she did confirm that Jannice Karlsson had been in a pretty bad condition, that she had been self-harming, and that she had been assigned a new social worker after the relocation of Tobias Klingström.

Rita and Sara set up a meeting with the new social worker, who didn't really give them anything new to go on either. However, the social worker was genuinely upset about the girl's suicide and seemed to blame herself. The two officers both got the feeling that she was angry. She asked if it was okay to get back to them if she remembered anything that might help the investigation. Sara sensed there was something she wanted to say, but didn't want to talk about while at work.

"Call me anytime," Sara said, and handed her a business card.

As they left the office, Jonny called to complain. He couldn't get a hold of David Ljung.

"Golfers . . . They seem to live on a different planet than the rest of us," he scoffed. "The chick that works with him promised to let us know as soon as she gets hold of him. He isn't picking up his phone, which he never does when he plays golf, according to her."

Just as they ended the call with Jonny, Torsten called.

I wish they would wait until we meet up back at the station, Sara thought, feeling exhausted.

"Tobias's boss in Hörby confirmed the reason for him relocating there.

But she couldn't imagine such a good person treating a girl like that. That's what she said. She only had nice things to say about Klingström." When Sara didn't answer him right away, he said, "Oh well, it is what it is. People generally want to believe the best of the people around them. I guess that's a good thing."

"Yeah, I guess. Let's talk more back at the station," Sara said.

"Is there something wrong?" Rita asked, and put an arm around Sara's shoulders as they walked back towards the station.

"No, not at all. I'm just worried about the investigation," Sara answered, glancing at the train tracks. "And then there is Anders."

Rita stopped.

"Anders? Has he done something bad?"

Sara tugged her arm.

"I can walk and talk at the same time," she said, and smiled. "And no, on the contrary. He's the most lovable man I've ever met. But I'm worried about myself. I'm worried that I'll scare him off."

Rita stopped again.

"And how would you do that?"

Sara pushed her.

"With my mood, my inner demons . . . I'm worried about how he will react to it all. We don't know each other all that well yet. I love him, but I can be horrible. You know that."

Rita put her hands on Sara's shoulders.

"No, you're never horrible."

"Yes, I can be. When I'm scared of losing someone I tend to push them away to protect myself. To avoid being abandoned. And when things from my past surface, I tend to become cold and mean."

"I see . . . Couldn't you just tell him then? Rip the plaster off, I mean?"

Sara laughed. To her, her laughter sounded more like a bark.

"It sounds so simple, but it really isn't. What I've been through is enough to scare anyone off."

"I guess you're right. But do you have a choice here?"

Sara didn't answer. Instead, she pointed to her temple and moved her finger in circles as she rolled her eyes.

Rita laughed and gave Sara a friendly push.

"I'm pretty sure you're the daft one here," she said, and hooked arms with Sara.

54

Jörgen was searching the internet for anything connected to Jannice Karlsson. *There must be something interesting on here considering this girl's age,* he thought to himself. But there was nothing to find. Then he came up with what he thought was a brilliant idea to search the web for the phrase "young people and mental illness." After a while, he found a blog belonging to a young woman who wrote under a pseudonym. What caught his attention was that it hadn't been updated for a while. He crosschecked the date of Jannice's suicide with the date of the last published blog post. The blog hadn't been updated since her death.

He looked for his colleagues but they all seemed to be out of the office.

He double-checked what blog host had been used to publish the blog. Blogspot.

He called up the company's IT technicians and asked if they could help him track down the writer behind the blog.

"If you give me the address, I'll see what we can do."

After the call, he read the transcript of the interview with the social worker who had handled the girl's case after Tobias. He found her phone number and cleared his throat as the phone rang.

"Hi, my name is Jörgen Berg and I'm a colleague of Sara Vallén and Rita Anker. I would like to ask you a couple of questions about Jannice

Karlsson. I'm sure you need to call back to validate this number. Do you have a pen?"

Jörgen gave the woman the switchboard number and she called back right away.

"Jannice obviously wasn't doing so well," Jörgen said. "What was she like before she ended her life?"

"Broken," the social worker said. "And her relationship with her mother seemed complicated. They didn't fight much, but her mother was an alcoholic—or, I guess she still is. She had no other adults around whom she could trust."

"Was there anything that indicated that she was about to take her own life?"

"It depends how one sees it, I guess. She did cut herself, but that doesn't always lead to suicide."

"Did you ever get the idea something else had happened? Apart from her situation at home, I mean?" Jörgen heard the woman at the other end of the line hesitating for a moment.

"We know Tobias Klingström was relocated because of the letter Ann-Britt Karlsson wrote," he said to encourage her to talk.

"I don't know too much about it because of confidentiality within the administration, but something felt off about the whole thing. I'm pretty sure I'm not the only one who thinks so."

"What was he like, Tobias Klingström?"

"I mean, everyone loved him. We're not even sure if what the mother wrote was true. I can't imagine that he would've hurt Jannice. Maybe he couldn't help her in the right way though. But I know she was offered treatment. I don't even think she went there. Maybe once or twice. Then she was gone."

"Yes, I understand Tobias was well-liked," Jörgen said, "but the truth is that everyone has things they don't like about themselves that they try to hide. This could be the case here."

"Maybe," the woman said without sounding convinced.

"Why do you think Jannice didn't show up for her treatment?"

"Well, there were probably many reasons. But if you ask me, I think more in-depth efforts and resources might have been needed to help Jannice. I don't think she had enough self-insight to help herself. Also, she didn't trust society."

"Right, I see. You might be on to something here."

Something isn't adding up, he thought after hanging up the phone. Something about Tobias felt fake. Why would a mother accuse him of not doing his job and acting inappropriately when her daughter had just killed herself? For money? Not likely. She didn't even go through with the police report.

There were still so many questions to answer.

It was getting late and he packed up his things. He wrote Sara a note and put it on her desk. Then he remembered he still hadn't looked into the owners of the other allotment gardens. Note to self.

55

Although she wasn't in a great headspace, Sara was happy with the progress they had made so far. The investigation kept moving forward. Now they had the opportunity to stop a forced marriage. She hoped everything would go as planned. All the way.

She walked briskly towards Lund city centre. She was meeting up with Johannes and his dad, Göran, at a tapas restaurant for food and a little chat. She checked the time and realised she was early, so she decided to stop at Saluhallen.

She stepped inside and inhaled the scent of exotic spices, baked goods, and food from the restaurants. She made her way through the crowd and the busyness of the place reminded her of the market halls she had visited in cities like Paris and Barcelona. There was something special about those places. Something genuine. She wasn't sure what it was.

She stopped by the cheese counter and looked at the amazing selection. After a while, she made her way back past people who were enjoying their food with glasses of blood-red or golden-yellow liquid in their hands. She felt much happier and managed to push away her negativity. She really didn't have much to be sad about. She smiled to herself.

A few minutes later, she arrived at the restaurant at Lilla Gråbrödersgatan. She was excited to see both Göran and their son. The three of them hadn't sat down together since the tragic and traumatic events of the summer when Johannes had been a murder suspect and her relationship with Peter Matsson had affected them all. It had taken a toll on her girls, Johannes, and Göran. And it had brought the traumatic events of her younger years back to the surface. The trauma that had taken years to recover from had returned to her like a kick in the gut—literally—but once again her therapist, Louise Malmberg, had helped her through it. And meeting Anders had given her new hope when it came to love and life, and had helped her steer away from the constant threat of anxiety, panic, and depression. She had emerged from the situation—stronger than ever. As she thought about it, she realised her anxiety was back. Maybe not right there in the restaurant, and maybe she wasn't back to square one—but it wasn't good. She knew that much. It was back so clearly that it was affecting her relationship with Anders. Not constantly. But now and again.

She forced herself to forget about it and focus on Johannes instead. She was worried about him, just like Göran was. Louise had recommended he should talk to a therapist and he had agreed. It had been good for him.

"But right now, it feels like he's more focused on helping Josefin than helping himself," Sara had told Göran over the phone.

He had agreed with her and they had decided to set up a meeting.

Sara stepped into the restaurant, which had been a record shop in a past life. She enjoyed the vibe and decided to bring Anders there for their date that weekend. As long as she was still in a good mood by then, of course.

Göran was waiting for her and they sat down in the bar and ordered a glass of wine while they waited for Johannes.

"We can't stop him from seeing Josefin, obviously," Sara said to her ex-husband.

"Of course we can. He hasn't turned eighteen yet."

Sara grinned.

"Are you saying we should lock him up?"

"If we must."

"You're kidding, right?"

"Of course," he said. "Did you buy it?"

"It's been a long time since we were married, Göran. Maybe I can't read you as well as I once could," she laughed, just as Johannes walked in through the door and took off his jacket.

"Can I get a beer?"

"I don't think so," Sara and Göran said in unison.

"Oh, come on . . ."

Sara got up to hug him. He kissed her cheek.

"You're almost eighteen," she said, "but you won't get a drop of alcohol from us until you are."

He looked at his mother and smiled at her in a way she couldn't quite interpret.

"Hi, Dad," he said, and hugged Göran.

Sara turned to the head waiter, who guided them up to the first floor and showed them to their table. A moment later, a waitress came over with a couple of menus.

It took them a while to place their orders.

"I'm hungry like a wolf," Johannes said.

"For a change . . ." Sara said sarcastically, and stroked his cheek gently. She noticed that he needed to shave.

"By the way, it feels great sitting here with the two of you," Johannes added.

He tucked into his food as if he had never eaten before. As they were having dessert, Sara decided that it was time to talk to her son about his relationship with Josefin. She wasn't sure how to start. Luckily, Göran beat her to it.

"How are you and Josefin doing?"

To both of their surprise, Johannes didn't instantly respond defensively. He put his spoon down next to his plate and looked at them.

"Well, it's been pretty tough. I thought I would be able to help her, but I've understood that I can't. I want to break up with her, but I'm afraid that it would push her over the edge."

Johannes looked to his parents for support and guidance.

"I have a suggestion," Sara said.

Göran nodded.

"Your mother is good at these things," he admitted.

For some reason, her ex-husband's kind words moved her.

"Thanks," she said. "Well, I actually have two versions of the same suggestion. Either we'll set up a meeting with Josefin and her parents where we can talk about your feelings and fears. Then you can explain how you can't play the role of Josefin's therapist and that doing so isn't good for you. At the same time, you can express how scared you are of what might happen if you end your relationship."

Johannes looked horrified.

"Or?"

"Or I'll reach out to Josefin's parents and tell them how you feel. You'll break up with Josefin on your own, but her parents will be there, ready to support her through it. What do you say?"

"I don't like the first suggestion. It sounds way too dramatic somehow."

"I agree," Göran said, and crossed his arms.

"The other suggestion sounds better, but could both you and Dad talk to Josefin's parents in that case? It's important to me that they understand how much I care about Josefin. But I can't do this. It's all we ever talk about. We never really enjoy our time together. All I do is listen to her and comfort her."

Sara shook her head.

"I can't believe they haven't contacted a therapist."

"They have. But Josefin says she likes talking to me better," Johannes said, and shot his parents a sad look.

"That's not good at all," Göran said. "Your mother and I will contact Josefin's parents. And you'll break up with her. It's tough, we know. But you have to do this for your own sake."

"Deal," Johannes said.

They finished their food and hugged each other. Johannes went home with Sara.

56

Samira came home and went straight to her room. She didn't say a word to her mother. She needed to think. After a while, Najima came into her room and sat down on the edge of the bed.

"I need to study," Samira said without looking at her mother.

"We need to talk."

"About what?"

"About you. About your future." Najima stroked her daughter's back with warm hands.

Samira stood her ground and didn't crack, which surprised her slightly.

"Did you know I talked to the police?" she said provocatively.

"What? Why?"

"Because they wanted to talk to me."

"About what?" Najima said, raising her voice.

Samira didn't answer; she just kept her gaze focused on the wall in front of her.

"You're lying," Najima said. Then she stood up and walked towards the door.

"I don't want to go to Pakistan," Samira whispered.

Her mother shook her head and left the room.

Samira heard the front door open followed by the characteristic sound of her father's shoes brushing against the doormat. She heard him hang his jacket by the door.

"Is Samira home?"

"Yes, she's studying," her mother said.

Samira let out a relieved sigh.

She heard her father walk into the living room and sit down in the big leather armchair. He turned on the TV. Samira knew he was tired. He always was.

When Samira had finally finished her studies for the day, the flat was silent and dark. Her parents were asleep. She sneaked into the bathroom, brushed her teeth, and washed her face. When she eventually went to bed, she lay silently in the dark, trying to relax while her head kept spinning. After a while, she managed to fall into a dreamless slumber.

When morning came, Samira sat down to have breakfast with her mother and father for once. She didn't speak, but she sat there. She tried her hardest to make sense of the chaos in her head but did her best not to let it show on the outside. She didn't want to put her life at risk.

Her father barely looked at her. But she decided to be brave.

"Why are you sending me to Pakistan this Christmas?" she asked, trying to sound as neutral as possible.

"Because," Ali answered.

"What is it that you think I've done?"

"We don't think, we know," he said without looking at her.

Samira braced herself.

"What is it that you know?"

He turned his head towards her and she looked at him. When he finally met her gaze, she looked into his eyes without flinching. He looked away for a second. She knew that he despised her as much as he loved her. She knew she had brought shame upon the family. For loving Tobias.

"You know," her mother said.

"And what have you done? You've . . ."

She couldn't even say it. Suddenly, she was filled with hatred and a wave of sorrow washed over her.

Samira stood up so abruptly that her chair fell over. She rushed out of the kitchen, reached for her jacket, and left her headscarf behind. She slammed the front door, ran down the stairs, and left the building.

57

Jörgen told Sara about the blog and about the conversation he'd had with Jannice's new case handler the day before.

"I think she wasn't quite sure what to think about that guy—Tobias."

"Rita and I met with her yesterday and I felt like something was bothering her. I think she blamed herself for the girl's death somehow."

"Yes, but according to her, the girl wasn't getting enough help and needed more resources. I think she was talking about therapy. Either way, I think we should keep looking into what really happened between Tobias and Jannice Karlsson."

"Yes, but how? They're both dead."

"But her mother isn't. And neither are Tobias's friends. They might be able to fill in the blanks."

"Of course, good idea. Let's deal with it first thing today. And I hope you'll be able to get your hands on the IP address for that blog. Most youngsters have a blog today, and it might actually be hers."

Jörgen nodded and smiled.

"Hey, by the way. I'll look into the allotment garden owners today."

"Fantastic," Sara said, and gave him a thumbs-up. "Did you see Jonny, by the way?"

Jörgen shook his head.

"I'm sure he'll be here soon."

Just as he said that, Jonny came into the kitchen, sounding out of breath.

"I mean, this is so strange. I just received a text message from an unknown number, but it was signed off with the name David Ljung."

"And what did it say?"

"It said, 'I'm on holiday but will be back in a week.' Why in the world would he tell me that? How did he even get my number?"

"Strange," Sara said as her eyelid drooped.

Jörgen laughed.

"You might wanna shake your head and get that eyelid under control."

"Gosh, I can't help it," she said as she shook her head.

Jörgen smiled at her in a way that made her feel slightly embarrassed. She suspected that he had a crush on her. A secret crush.

"Maybe Camilla gave it to him?" she said, and turned her head away to hide her blushing cheeks.

"Yes, that might be the case. I'll look into it. But it sure is strange."

"Let's meet up in the conference room. I'll call Åke Baum and invite him too," Sara said, feeling more like herself again.

Her whole team sat in front of her in the conference room. Sara noticed that Rita looked tired. Torsten and Jonny seemed alert and awake though. As always, Jörgen sat in front of his computer and Sara could see how curious Åke Baum was.

"We have no suspects, but at least we've got a couple of leads," Sara said.

Rita stared out the window.

"Rita?"

"Yes," she said, "I'm with you."

"We're looking into the possibility of this being an honour killing. We're sure Samira is experiencing a lot of cultural pressure and we're worried that it could end with her being forced into a marriage against her will. We're working multiple angles to find a solution. We're also investigating Tobias's work history as a case handler with social services in and around Lund. It's hard to get anywhere when it comes to this lead though. Partly because both Tobias and the girl, Jannice Karlsson, are dead. Partly because nobody we talk to can seem to give a straight answer. We've searched Tobias's home but his computer was basically empty. Well, except for the usual stuff like email and Facebook. Nothing looked suspicious."

Sara looked at Jörgen and gave him a nod.

"I've found a blog online that might belong to Jannice. A lot of girls have blogs nowadays. I haven't gone through the whole website, but I plan to do so today. We aren't sure if it's hers yet, but I'm in the process of tracking down the IP address. Also, I'm looking into the allotment garden owners today. We might find something there that will point us in the right direction."

Sara reminded herself again to make sure he saw an ergonomics expert. Jörgen's back looked more and more crooked each time she looked at him. It wasn't great.

"Thanks, Jörgen. Jonny?"

Jonny told everyone about the text message. It was baffling. They would have to look into it.

"Åke?" Sara turned to the prosecutor. "Do you think we should bring in Jannice's computer, if she had one? Wouldn't that make things easier?"

Åke Baum turned to Sara and nodded.

"These honour-related crimes are hard to deal with, but I've heard what you have to say. We can't force the girl to leave her family if she doesn't want to. However, I think we should put surveillance on her parents and their flat. For the girl's sake. She could be in danger and we can't risk it. Do you have enough resources for this?"

"Well, I guess we'll have to make it work," Sara said, gesturing impatiently with her hands.

Åke Baum smiled and for the second time in the same day, Sara started blushing and turned her back from her colleagues to hide it. She wrote something and drew a couple of lines on the whiteboard. Then she could face them again.

58

J onny ignored the fact that he could use the exercise and decided to take the car. After all, he had lost a bit of weight lately. He patted himself on the stomach and laughed.

It wasn't exactly easy to drive around in Lund. He cursed and muttered. The city was full of one-way streets and it wasn't permitted to drive on certain streets during the day. He was happy he lived in Malmö. Malmö had become rougher lately, but at least the traffic was okay. The problem there was more about people shooting each other. The escalation of violence in the city was bad, but at least it didn't affect him in his day-to-day life. There were no shootings on his street.

"The criminals are taking over the world," he once said to Torsten as they worked a case in Malmö.

Torsten had hummed without saying anything.

Jonny rang the doorbell to David Ljung's house. The young assistant opened the door.

"You again?"

"Yes, I need to talk to you."

"Sure," she said, and opened the door to let Jonny in.

He followed her into the magnificent kitchen. She pointed to a chair and the coffee machine. The coffee machine looked expensive, just like everything else in the house. Jonny took a seat and nodded to accept the offer of coffee. He realised how out of place he must look in the immaculate home with his baggy, scruffy clothes. The woman looked both elegant and vulgar. A strange combination.

The coffee machine made a buzzing sound and she served him a double espresso in a little cup. Even the coffee made him feel awkward.

"Thanks," he said without looking at her.

"What do you want to know now?" she asked with a sparkle in her eye.

"I wonder if you gave David the note with my phone number?"

"Yes, I did. But then he left again. He hasn't told me what's going on, so I have no idea what he's doing."

"I got a text message where he told me he had gone on holiday and would return in a week."

"What?" Camilla gave Jonny a puzzled look. "Well, he hasn't told me about any holiday. What's he doing? I can't work here alone, and I definitely can't cover for him. This isn't like David at all."

"Maybe he just left on a whim. Is he an impulsive guy?"

"Yes and no. He normally keeps everything in order, but lately, he's been acting quite strange and has been doing things that are quite out of character. Maybe it has something to do with his best friend being murdered, but what do I know?"

"Yes, it could be an explanation, of course," Jonny said. "But has he done anything particularly odd?"

"You mean like going on holiday without telling me?" she said with a sarcastic smile on her face.

Jonny thought she looked funny and had to stop himself from laughing.

"Well, yes . . . Or something else?"

"I don't know. This is definitely the strangest thing he's ever done though."

"Does he have a girlfriend? Or maybe parents I could talk to?"

"Girlfriend," Camilla said, and winked. "I guess that would be me. But I'm not really his girlfriend. I'm more of a when-it-suits-him girlfriend. His parents are dead."

Camilla pulled back her long hair and shaped it into a creative hairdo. Jonny couldn't figure her out. Her whole persona was a contradiction to him. Elegant and beautiful, but tastelessly dressed. *Or maybe her clothes are modern,* he thought, and realised he was staring at her. He worried that she would think he was interested in her and looked at his hands instead.

"How long have you two known each other?" He looked up again.

"Ten years or something. I was very young when we first met. Fifteen, I think."

"Did you guys start an intimate relationship at that point?"

Jonny heard how stupid his question sounded and noticed that it made Camilla awkward. Embarrassed, almost.

"Well, I wouldn't call it a relationship."

Jonny changed the subject as he knew he wasn't the best person for that kind of conversation. *I better leave this to Rita,* he thought. He continued the interview but when he felt like he had reached a dead end, he decided to call it a day.

"Well, that'll be all for now," he said.

Camilla walked him to the front door and just as she was about to close it behind him, he remembered something.

"Camilla!"

She opened the door again.

"Yes, what now?"

"Do you know if David has more than one phone?"

"I'm not sure. Why?"

"He texted me from a new number," Jonny said, and walked up to her. He picked up his phone and showed her the message.

"I don't recognise that number," she said. "But he could have mobile phones I'm not aware of. There are things I don't know, you see."

Jonny studied her and noticed a coldness he hadn't seen before. He nodded, turned his back to her, and left. The door closed behind him.

59

But isn't it bloody strange that he goes on holiday without telling her?"

"Yes, definitely. But I didn't want to poke around in the girl's love life and thought it was a better idea to let Rita talk to her about it. It was something about the way she spoke about their relationship that felt odd to me. She let it slip that she was only his girlfriend when it suited him. At least that's how I interpreted it. And that it all started when she was fifteen. Maybe there is something there? Maybe they have that in common, Tobias and David? Sex with minors? Or something else, maybe? Something more than normal sex, I mean . . ."

Sometimes Jonny could really think outside the box. Sara gave him the thumbs-up.

"I'll ask Rita to follow up. We might be on to something here."

Sara realised her heart was beating faster than normal. She could hear her pulse. She loved moments like this, when things started to fall into place.

"I need to talk to Aidah and find out what's going on with Samira. I need to know if she has heard anything. Can you talk to the surveillance unit and see if they have any news, Jörgen?"

"Sure, I'm on it."

Torsten walked into the room and nodded towards Jonny.

"Jonny and I are going back to the social services office. We need to talk to the director. I've read those files over and over again and I need to straighten a couple of things out. It feels like there is more to the story and I think she knows more than she's telling us. And then we'll go to Ann-Britt Karlsson to pick up Jannice's computer if she had one. I'll interview Karlsson again as well. I need her to give me more straightforward information. I hope she's capable of that."

"Good," Sara said. "I don't understand why these people keep so much to themselves. Why can't they just tell us how it is?"

"Well, I guess they're scared of incriminating people close to them."

"But they're dead. What harm could it possibly do?"

"Honour," Torsten said. "Honour is important to people. Even if it means different things in different cultures."

"You're right, as always."

Torsten the wise. Torsten the beautiful and kind, Sara thought.

60

Samira made up her mind. In the middle of a lecture. She stood up, left the classroom, and stepped out into the crisp air. She took out her phone.

Aidah answered immediately

"Hi. I've made a decision."

Aidah didn't say anything. It annoyed Samira slightly.

"I don't want to go to Pakistan and I can't be scared anymore."

"Okay, have you talked to your mother?"

"Yes and no. I can't tell her much, but I think she understands."

"I think so too," Aidah said. "Let's meet in Malmö. Can you make it here on your own or do you want me to pick you up?"

"I don't know." Samira hesitated. She really didn't want to go to Malmö. Every time she'd been there before, she had felt unsafe.

"I'll pick you up. Go to the bus station, I'll meet you there. Call me when you're there and I'll stay on the phone with you until I come to get you."

Thirty minutes later, Aidah arrived at the bus station and Samira jumped into the passenger seat. They drove to Malmö, to an address nobody knew about—not even the police. The only ones who knew where she was were the people who worked there.

When Samira walked in, she was met by a woman her mother's age. The woman walked up to her and took her hand.

"Welcome. Are you hungry?"

Samira shook her head.

"A cup of tea?"

"Yes, please."

Aidah stayed with Samira for a while. They drank tea together in silence. Samira tried to find words for what she was feeling. It was too difficult and she stayed silent. She twisted a white napkin between her slender fingers. Then she untwisted it and twisted it again.

After the tea, the friendly woman showed her to her room. Samira still didn't say anything. But she followed the woman and did what she was told.

"I accept my fate," she told Aidah as she was about to leave.

"Yes, but this is not the end. This is the beginning," Aidah said, and hugged her.

"We'll see about that."

61

Jonny and Torsten sat in the reception area, waiting to see the social services director. The receptionist had told them that Astrid Karpe was in a meeting, but that she would be with them shortly.

"We can't wait around for her. We'll leave her a message and tell her to call us. Let's go to Ann-Britt Karlsson instead. She's home. I checked before we left," Torsten said.

Jonny nodded and Torsten walked up to the receptionist.

"Ask her to call us as soon as possible so we can schedule a meeting," he said, and made it sound like an order.

"I will," she answered.

"Tell her it's important."

She nodded.

They got into the car. Jonny drove. They travelled along Fjelievägen, through Trollebergsrondellen, under the overpass and towards Klostergården. Torsten jotted down questions on a little notepad. Silence.

"Vårvädersvägen," Torsten said as they drove along Nordanvägen and took a left onto Vårvädersvägen. Klostergården had been a beautiful part of town once, but its heyday was over. Torsten thought about the girl who had been murdered in Lund City Park. Her parents lived on Sunnanväg. The memory made him shake his head.

The drive took less than ten minutes, parking included.

When they rang the doorbell, the door opened instantly. As if Ann-Britt Karlsson had been waiting for them in the hallway.

They stepped inside and recognised the smell of cigarette smoke. It was a small two-bedroom flat, but it was kept fairly tidy. Torsten noted the lack of dirty dishes on the kitchen counter. The place was furnished in a spartan manner. A couple of figurines stood next to some plastic flowers on the windowsill.

The woman scratched her elbows and Torsten and Jonny glanced at each other when they saw her arms were covered in a rash. She looked grey and tired and it was obvious that she lived on benefits. Torsten couldn't help wondering how a little girl had been allowed to grow up in such a home. It was clear the mother needed both financial and psychological support. He guessed the woman's problems had started way before her daughter's death.

"I hope you understand we need to get some clarity in regards to what happened between Tobias Klingström and Jannice," Torsten said.

"I've told you everything I know," the woman replied, and took a sip of coffee. She hadn't offered any to Torsten and Jonny. And the coffee looked cold. The surface was covered with a greyish film. The woman lit a cigarette.

Jonny pulled a disgusted face and Torsten, sitting next to him, kicked him discreetly. Torsten brushed a lock of hair away from his face.

"I understand if you think you've told us everything you know. What I mean is that we still need to get some clarity when it comes to what you've already told us. I'll ask you a couple of questions."

Jonny pulled out a tissue from his pocket and blew his nose.

"Excuse me," he said, "this always happens in autumn."

The woman in front of them didn't appear to have heard Jonny blowing his nose, or that he was talking to her.

"Okay, ask your questions. I'm not sure what I can help you with though."

"When did Jannice start hurting herself? I mean, when did you realise she was cutting herself, for example?"

"When she was thirteen, I think. And she didn't eat. Sometimes she ate like a horse only to throw it up. I didn't know what to do."

"I understand you have a drinking problem," Torsten said carefully, and glanced at Jonny, who looked horrified.

"Yes. But I'm getting help. I go to meetings."

"Did you accept help back then?"

"Yes, but I fell off the wagon more than once. Jannice's problems didn't make it better."

"When did you contact social services and when was Jannice assigned a case handler?"

"I mean, I've been in contact with them for years. They made me go to the meetings. Jannice was assigned a case handler when she was thirteen, after she started cutting herself. A nice case handler who really tried to help her. Then, when she turned fifteen, that creep Tobias Klingström took over her case."

"And what happened then?" Torsten asked.

"He put a stop to her treatment because she stopped showing up to her meetings. I tried to get her to go, but she just screamed and refused. So, he stopped the treatment."

"And then?"

Torsten was excited to hear more but didn't let it show.

"She told me he tried funny things with her. Sexual stuff."

"Did she tell you more about it?"

"No."

"But you wrote in your letter that he behaved inappropriately. What did you mean by that?"

"I meant that he touched her and tried to have sex with her. All I knew was what Jannice told me, so that's what I wrote. I didn't know what to do, really. I wasn't in a great place myself. I didn't even have the energy to tell social services at first."

"And what happened then?"

"Then some time passed and she spent a lot of time away from home. I thought she was going to school, but they called me to tell me she hadn't been there. A year passed. And she seemed to feel better, even if she had periods where she was sad. At one point she wasn't doing so good so I took her to the social services office, where we ran into Klingström. He told me she hadn't shown up for her meetings and wondered why I didn't make sure she did. I told him he was the one who didn't want her to continue her treatment. He said it was only because she never showed up."

"Why didn't you report him then?"

"Oh wait, I told you in the wrong order. She didn't tell me about the sexual advances until after we ran into him that time."

"Oh, I see. So, to clarify . . . she wasn't doing so good and spent a lot of time away from home. So you took her to the social services office, where you met Tobias Klingström and then, after that, she told you about the sexual advances?"

Torsten tried to smile, but couldn't.

"Yes. And then she told me he wanted to see her."

Torsten and Jonny both listened carefully.

"Oh, where?"

"She didn't tell me. But I forbade her and she became furious with me. Apparently, she thought I would agree to it."

"And when did you report him to social services?"

"It took me a while to come up with what exactly to write. I think she was sixteen when I finally got to it. I don't remember exactly. But he disappeared after that."

It seemed impossible to get the woman to tell them more about what happened to Jannice, but it was obvious something had happened involving Tobias Klingström. What had he wanted from her? Sex? But was there something more?

"Did Jannice have a computer?"

"An old friend gave us one that she used. I don't know how to operate those things."

"We'll take it with us. Maybe it can give us a clue as to what Jannice was up to, or what she was thinking."

"Oh, okay. Sure. I don't use it anyway."

They finished the interview and got the computer.

Once they were back in their car, they remembered the social services director. She still hadn't called them. They decided to drive to the municipal office—or Kristallen, as the building was called. It turned out that Astrid Karpe was in another meeting and couldn't see them until the next day. Jonny used a very sharp tone of voice with the receptionist, who looked miffed.

62

Sara felt defeated and wasn't sure what to do next. The fact that they now had more than one theory to go on didn't make it easier at all. She waited for Aidah to call and give her the go-ahead to at least talk to Ali and Najima Khan. Not that much time had passed, but they had to act. David Ljung still hadn't shown up.

Her phone rang. It was Aidah.

After the call, she gathered her colleagues, who all looked as defeated as Sara felt. No matter how many interviews they conducted, things weren't moving forward.

Torsten had paid Anna Klingström a visit. She was on sick leave and had no idea why Tobias had been relocated to Hörby. All he had told her was that he wanted a change of scenery. That was it.

Sara told her team what Aidah had told her. Samira Khan was at the safe house and they could bring Najima and Ali Khan in for questioning.

The room filled with energy, as if someone had switched on a light switch.

"Finally," Rita said, voicing what everyone else was feeling.

"I've also found a relative to the family. Sanju Mohammed, Samira's cousin," Jörgen said.

Sara nodded.

"We'll talk to him after we've talked to Ali and Najima."

Rita gestured impatiently.

"Why wait? Why not talk to him right away?"

"And say what?"

Rita sighed.

"I don't know. But I get it. Let's wait."

Rita's patience wasn't the best. And Sara understood her. Things had been at a standstill for so long now that she wanted to move as quickly as Rita.

"I'll question Najima Khan," Rita said, and Sara nodded.

"And Torsten will question Ali Khan. I think we should bring them in at the same time so they don't get the chance to speak to each other. Aidah told me Samira is closest to her mother. She also told me Samira doesn't want to share any possible suspicions about her parents with us. So now it's all about keeping her safe. It'll be a long process for her. We can only hope for the best outcome."

Sara called Prosecutor Baum to see if he would give them the go-ahead to bring Samira's parents in for questioning. He hesitated. They didn't have anything on them. But Sara argued that if the two of them had anything to do with the murder, it was necessary to talk to them separately before they had the chance to speak to each other. If nothing else, they were suspected of arranging a forced marriage for their daughter in Pakistan.

"Forced marriage is illegal," Sara pointed out.

In the end, she got what she wanted. Baum made a note of the time. Sara did the same.

She shared the decision with her team and they all cheered.

63

Samira paced back and forth. It was harder than she could ever have imagined. She wasn't allowed to contact anyone. Not even Elin. But she had sent her a text message anyway. A cryptic one. Elin had replied to it with three question marks and a crying emoji. She didn't tell the staff about it. If she decided to change her identity for good, she would cut all ties with her past.

She had to come to a decision, but what would it be? What was the right choice? Was it her parents who had murdered Tobias, or was it her cousin? And if it wasn't her family, then who was it?

Why did they want to send her to Pakistan? Maybe she was imagining things. Were they planning to force her to marry someone down there or did they simply want her to get away for a while? How could she possibly know? If they forced her to get married, she would have to end her studies. But that would also be the case if she accepted a new identity. That's what Aidah had told her.

And what would happen if she refused to go to Pakistan? Samira realised that all she had were questions and not a single answer.

She lay down on the bed and cried into her pillow.

She had been given a new, untraceable phone. Suddenly, it rang. She recognised the number. It was the one Aidah used when she wanted to stay anonymous.

"How are you?"

"This is horrible. I don't know what to do or what decisions to make. I can't study, I can't go outside, I can't do anything."

"Did you try talking to the staff?"

"I've tried, but I can't think of what to say. My mind goes blank. I don't have it in me to tell the story from the beginning. Not even one more time."

"I need your permission to share what you've told me with the police. You'll have to let me tell them anything that might be important. They need to know what's going on and what you know."

Samira twisted her headscarf between her thumb and index finger.

"Promise you won't tell them stuff I'm not sure about."

"I won't tell them anything that's not related to the murder investigation or the marriage."

"Okay, you have my permission. But you know, I want to go home. I want to study. Can't you help me at home instead?"

Aidah was silent for a couple of seconds.

"No, I think you know we can't. We can't move into your house, and I can't watch over you all the time. I'm sorry, it's your decision in the end. But if you stay at home, they will force you to go to Pakistan."

"But how can they force me?"

"There are many ways, my friend."

"How did they even know about me and Tobias?"

"You live in a small town, which means people keep a constant eye on you and everyone else. Don't you have a cousin in Hörby too?"

"Yes. And he's married to a girl from Pakistan."

"He might have seen something . . ."

Aidah kept calm, which made Samira feel both insecure and safe at the same time.

"I guess. But I'll lose my mind if I stay here."

"You will only be there until you've made up your mind."

Samira took a deep breath.

"But if we tell the police Mum and Dad killed Tobias, won't they go to prison? Couldn't I go back home then?"

"Yes, in a way you're right. But if they haven't killed him, or if the police can't prove they did, you're in the same position again. The cultural pressure in honour-shame cultures is strong and, in a way, your parents are victims too. Everyone in your family is. Even if your parents end up in prison, you'll still have to face the rest of your family members. They are just as involved in this as your closest family members."

"Just to make it clear . . . I obviously hope they didn't murder him. I just want to find a way for me to go home. I know you're right. I'll think about it. Can I call you tomorrow?"

"Of course. But I strongly advise you to talk to the staff. They know a lot about these situations. And they'll understand you just as well as I do."

"I'll talk to them. And I'll talk to you tomorrow."

"Great. Yes, talk to you then," Aidah said, and put down the phone.

64

A man with black bushy eyebrows and thick black hair came into the station between two plainclothes officers. He looked angry. Torsten greeted him.

"Why have we been brought in by the police in this manner?" the man asked with almost no accent at all.

"We need to talk to you and your wife," Torsten said in as friendly a way as possible.

"You could have called."

"But now we're talking here instead."

"Where is Samira?"

Torsten wasn't prepared for that question but quickly took charge of the conversation again.

"We'll talk about that later. Please, have a seat."

He pointed at the chair across the table from him in the sterile room. He started the recording and stated their names and the date.

"Do you know a man named Tobias Klingström?"

"Who is he?"

"A young man who worked at the social services office in Hörby."

Torsten noticed a movement in the man's face. A very small movement.

"No, I don't."

He's lying, Torsten thought.

The interrogation went on for over an hour. Torsten pushed every possible boundary. He was an expert interrogator, but he couldn't get anywhere. The man refused to cooperate, and he looked more and more confident.

Finally, Torsten decided to play his trump card.

"We know you want to send Samira to Pakistan to get married."

"What? I mean . . ." Ali Khan seemed rattled.

"That's why Samira is missing. Because she didn't want to go to Pakistan and be forced to marry."

"Where is she?" Khan screamed.

"Please, keep your voice down. Screaming won't help. And, unfortunately, I can't tell you where Samira is. Now I want you to tell me what you know about Tobias Klingström."

It was an order. The man across from him stared at his feet. It was hard to tell if he felt angry, defiant, or defeated. *Maybe everything at once,* Torsten thought.

"She's my daughter," he said.

"Yes, but she's an adult and forced marriages are illegal. So?"

"I don't know anything about that man."

"Well, I think you do." Torsten locked eyes with Ali Khan, as if he could see straight through him.

"I swear, I promise I don't know anything."

"But I know you do. You just don't want to tell me."

The man shook his head and stayed silent.

Torsten realised he couldn't win. For now.

65

Rita sat in an interrogation room with Najima Khan, who alternated between rocking back and forth on her chair and staring at a spot on the wall behind Rita.

Rita started recording the interview. She stated the woman's name and her own name, followed by the date and time. Then she turned to Najima.

"I would like you to tell me a bit about your family," she said carefully.

"What do you want me to tell you?"

"Tell me about your life. What are you up to and how do you live your life?"

"We're a normal family."

"How do you mean?"

"It's Ali and I and our daughter, Samira. She's studying to become a doctor. Ali is a car mechanic and I don't work. We live a normal life."

"I wonder what you mean by 'normal.' What does it mean?"

The woman looked lost for words.

"We get up in the morning, I cook breakfast, and Ali and I sit down together to eat. Samira is usually in a hurry. She has to catch the bus every morning to go to school . . . university. Ali goes to work while I clean, shop, and cook."

"Do you have friends in Hörby?"

"Yes, a couple. They're immigrant women too."

Rita nodded.

"Even if we've lived here for a long time, it's not that easy. It's a struggle for immigrant women like myself to find work. Therefore, I've struggled to learn the language."

"I think you're doing great."

The woman smiled.

"I've studied for years. And I read the newspaper every day. It's a good way to learn the language."

"For how long has Samira been studying now?"

"This is her fifth semester."

The woman talked about her daughter as if she were still at home with her family. Rita thought it was odd, but decided not to remind the woman of the situation for now.

"How's it going?"

"Great. But she's gone now. Where is she? You have her, don't you?"

The woman changed from being submissive to indignant, but Rita relaxed. *Nice*, she thought, *good to get that out of the way*.

"She's fine, but I can't tell you where she is."

Najima refused to give up and kept repeating her question until Rita finally stopped answering her.

"Do you know a man called Tobias Klingström?" she asked instead.

Rita thought Najima looked scared. She was quiet for a while.

"I don't know who he is," she finally answered.

It was obvious to Rita that the woman in front of her knew who he was, but she paused before asking her next question. She let it be silent for a while. Najima Khan stared at something behind Rita. Then she turned towards Rita again without looking her in the eye.

"Why am I here?"

"Did nobody explain to you why you were brought to the police station?"

"No, nobody."

"We want to talk to you as it has come to our attention that you're planning to send Samira to Pakistan this Christmas. Why are you sending her to Pakistan against her will?"

"What's so strange about it? She doesn't have school around Christmas."

"You're planning to force her to get married down there, aren't you?" Rita looked intensely at the woman. Najima Khan hesitated.

"No, she's visiting *family*," she said, and put a lot of emphasis on the last word of the sentence.

"We're quite convinced she is going there to get married."

A tear rolled down the woman's cheek. She shook her head. And stayed silent.

"I understand this is difficult to talk about. I suspect you don't want her to go to Pakistan?"

Rita locked eyes with the woman, who wiped away her tear.

"You're wrong," Najima said firmly. "She's going. Her father and I have decided."

"Would you say the relationship between Tobias and Samira has brought shame on your family?"

"She hasn't had a relationship with that Tobias," Najima answered defiantly.

Rita changed tactics.

"Tobias is dead. Murdered."

"Oh yes? And what does that have to do with me? We haven't done anything wrong. Why would you think so?"

"I never said I thought so, but isn't it strange how Samira is being sent to Pakistan right after you find out she's in a relationship with a Swedish man, who was recently murdered? Don't you see how it looks from my point of view?"

"We have nothing to do with that and we're not forcing our daughter to get married."

"How did you react when you found out Samira had a Swedish boyfriend?"

"I had no idea. So I haven't reacted at all." Rita refused to give up.

"Can you tell me about that time when Samira came home one day only to be welcomed by her very angry father who told her he was going to send her to Pakistan this Christmas and that she wasn't allowed to go anywhere but straight home after her lectures?"

"Where did you hear that?"

"Maybe you could guess?"

"Samira is lying," Najima said, far too quickly. "She's lying."

"Why would she lie?"

Najima shrugged her shoulders. "To punish us?"

"Punish you for what?"

Najima didn't answer the question. She had taken the bait, and Rita felt happy with the progress they had made.

"I didn't mean punish. I meant she might be angry at us."

"Oh, okay. But you did use the word *punish*."

Rita could tell the woman was worried about what she had just said and that she was trying her best to regain her composure.

"Maybe that's what I said, but you have to understand. Sometimes I pick the wrong word when I speak my second language."

"Yes, I understand," Rita said, genuinely empathizing with the woman. "But there is a big difference between being angry and wanting to punish someone. Why would she be angry, then?"

"I don't know. I have nothing more to say to you."

"You could try to explain why your daughter would be angry with you. As we understand it, she is scared of going to Pakistan. Do you know what a forced marriage is?"

The woman nodded.

"But we're not forcing her to get married," she said, and sounded more confident again.

"Well, that's great. But Samira is convinced you are and therefore, she has decided to cut all contact with you. Maybe that could be considered punishment?"

Najima didn't answer. Instead, she looked at her nails as if nothing in the world was more interesting. Rita couldn't help but feel sorry for her. *It must be hard to be so stuck in cultural traditions and norms*, she thought, *especially when the cultural pressure is so strong.*

Rita ended the interrogation and walked Najima to reception, where her husband was waiting for her. Rita watched them as they left. Their backs looked bent.

She shook her head and went up to her office to get her jacket. Now she just had to talk to Camilla as well before she could go home for the night. And it wasn't just any night.

66

Sara took a long walk before dinner. It was already dark. She really needed to get out and it felt great. She walked along the dams that worked like a sewage treatment plant, west of Klostergården. There were still plenty of birds around, and although she didn't know much about birds, she guessed most of them were migratory ones that should have moved to a warmer country already. But it was still warm outside. Maybe that's why they were still there.

She walked out on one of the grassy embankments that separated the dams and sat down on a bench. Her mind raced back in time, into the future, and in every possible direction. There was so much she should tell Anders about herself, her past, who she was and who she had become. She needed to test him. If he couldn't handle it, their relationship would never last. But she knew it would be difficult. She placed her elbows on her knees and rested her head in her palms.

Suddenly, a wave of sadness washed over her when she thought about her father. Why hadn't she been able to consider the difficulties he'd gone through? Why hadn't she understood him? And most importantly: Why had she felt let down by him instead of helping him?

She sighed and looked at the calm water. She wondered why people weren't allowed to swim in it when birds obviously could. Wouldn't people and birds have the same effect on the cleanliness of the water? Didn't birds make the water filthy too?

She slowly got up and walked home while her mind kept racing. It was pitch black outside, except for the streetlights. The air smelled like dirt and leaves. And it was silent. Almost scary. But Sara felt sad, not scared. *There is something melancholic and calm about autumn*, she thought, and smiled in an attempt to make herself feel better.

67

Although it was already quite late when Rita finally came home after a long and pretty intimate interview with Camilla Brink, time had moved way too slowly since she had stepped in through the door. She was really nervous.

All of a sudden, there was a knock on the door. She opened it and was overcome by pure joy when she saw the redheaded woman standing outside.

Linda came inside and they gave each other a hug. Rita was surprised at how natural it felt.

"I've made dinner. Come on."

Linda took off her coat and placed her shoes by the door.

"You don't need to take your shoes off. My father always said only snobs take off their shoes," Rita said, and laughed.

"I want to take them off though; it's been raining and they're dirty," Linda said, and smiled at her.

Rita's kitchen was normally empty and not very welcoming, but today she had managed to make it cosy and lit some candles on the table. Rita handed Linda a glass of wine.

"I want to be honest with you," Rita said. "I'm not sure what I'm feeling here, but I know it feels good. I never saw myself as gay. Maybe bisexual, but I'm not sure. You make me feel warm and happy though."

Linda looked at her.

"You're so beautiful," she said. "Let's see how it goes. Whatever happens, happens, as they say."

"Yeah, that sounds great," Rita said with a laugh, and felt grateful that Linda was so relaxed.

They sat down across from each other. Rita had placed the fondue pot in the middle of the table and now she pushed it to the side and reached for Linda's hands.

"I've been inspired by the eighties tonight. Fondue, I mean. I thought it would make the dinner last a long time as it's so damn difficult to eat."

She laughed again and Linda joined in. It felt wonderful. And strange.

68

When Johannes and Anders stepped into the living room, the floor was covered in documents. It was late.

"Oh, you're working," Anders said.

Sara placed her hands on her thighs and stood up.

"Hi, guys. Nice to see you. You get to cook," she said, and tried her best to hide her ambivalent mood.

Johannes looked at Anders and Anders looked at Johannes with raised eyebrows.

"I suck at cooking," Johannes said.

"Well, I don't."

At the dinner table, Johannes told Sara that he'd already talked to Josefin, although Sara and Göran hadn't been able to arrange a meeting with her family yet.

"I said I couldn't do it anymore. I said it just like that."

"And how did she react?" Sara asked. She was both curious and worried.

"She just said, 'Okay, I understand.' That was all. But I feel bad. What if she's destroyed? What if she kills herself?"

"Do you really think she would?" Anders asked.

"I don't know, but what if?"

He looked at his mother.

"I'll call her parents after dinner. Maybe she needs to let you go to be able to accept help from someone else—a professional. You told me yourself that she didn't want to talk to anyone but you."

Sara felt for the girl and could really see herself in her. It wasn't easy to let go of someone you thought could save you, even if the only way to be saved was in fact to let go of that someone.

"If you could call them, I would appreciate it," Johannes said.

His body language told her he was done talking about Josefin. Sara respected his wishes and changed the subject. She suggested that they visit Klara and Bella in Tanzania that Christmas, but as soon as the idea left her mouth, she regretted it. She simply wasn't sure if she had it in her to take the relationship with Anders to the next step. Maybe never. At least not yet.

Anders gave her a strange look. She tried to ignore it, but couldn't. It felt as if he saw right through her.

Johannes was excited.

"I can't wait to see them," he said, and slammed his knife and fork together so that some of his sauce splashed all over the table. "Let's go! Can we?"

"Yes, it would be great. I need to check with work though. Sometimes it can be tricky to take time off around Christmas," she said in an attempt to try to get out of the trip she had just suggested to the others.

"We'll see if we can make it work," Anders said, and it sounded as if he too was unsure of what he—or maybe she—wanted.

After dinner, Sara called Josefin's mother, who confirmed that Josefin understood it was over between her and Johannes. The woman also told Sara that she and her husband were actually relieved that Johannes had ended the relationship. Now they both hoped that Josefin would finally accept professional help.

After the call, Sara told Johannes that he could relax as Josefin would now get the help she needed. Johannes smiled at his mother.

"Oh, thanks, Mum," he said, and hugged her. "You're the best."

When they had gone to bed, Anders turned to her.

"You're keeping something from me. This isn't the first time you've had a reaction when we talk about relationships. I understand you're struggling with what happened with Matsson. But there is something else. I can see it in your eyes. There is pain there."

Sara thought about it for a while and decided that she wasn't ready. And that he wasn't ready either.

"Can we talk about it another day? I'm too tired to dig around in the past."

"Of course, I just want to get to know you. I can see there is something else there. I'm not going to force it though. Maybe one day you'll want to tell me."

"I love you," she said, and moved closer to him.

She snuggled up in his embrace and tried to enjoy what she had. It wasn't as easy as she thought it would be. After a while, she moved away from him and turned the other way. She didn't realise that he was still awake.

69

When Rita woke up, she felt truly happy. Happy in a way she hadn't felt in years. She turned around and saw the red hair on the pillow next to her. *I'm so lucky*, she thought.

There was no doubt she had done the right thing.

For a long time, she just lay there, looking at Linda—who was fast asleep. Rita thought about everything they had talked about. They shared a lot of views and looked at life in the same way. And yet, they were so different. Rita was physical and powerful while Linda was softer and more feminine. Both of them were full of opinions and joy. Both of them were tough as nails.

Rita didn't want to wake her up but couldn't stop herself from touching her. Linda turned around, wide awake.

"Hey," she said, smiling.

"Good morning," Rita said.

"All good?"

Rita heard the slightly worried tone in Linda's voice. But she knew she wouldn't have to worry for long.

"Excellent, couldn't be better."

Rita laughed quietly as she leaned over Linda and kissed her. Linda kissed her back. Her mouth tasted like red wine and garlic. But Rita didn't care.

When Rita left for work, she was late. *Very late*, she thought, and biked as fast as she could. Slightly hungover, a little bit tired, but happy.

70

The head of the surveillance unit briefed Sara as she was standing in his office.

"Ali and Najima Khan had visitors in their flat. A man and a woman," he said.

Sara listened carefully.

"The women sat in the kitchen while the men sat in what we believe is the living room."

"What did the men do in the living room?" Sara asked curiously.

"They sat in front of the computer and talked to someone on Skype. We sat in an empty flat across from theirs, so we had a good view."

"Excellent," Sara said. "And there were no problems with borrowing the apartment?"

"No, not at all. Anyway, the men seemed quite upset. Unfortunately, we couldn't hear what they were saying, but it was obvious that the conversation got pretty heated at times. It's hard to say what it could mean. But considering the context, there is a chance it was about Samira. But maybe we shouldn't jump to conclusions?"

"Well, we can't be sure, of course. But what could it have been about otherwise? Who did they speak to?"

"Impossible for us to say. But judging by what we could see, there was more than one person on the other end of the call. And judging by their features, they all seemed to be from Pakistan or somewhere close to there."

"What happened after that?"

"After quite a long conversation—probably thirty minutes—they turned the computer off. The two women joined the men in the living room for a while. Then the couple left. As far as we know, the man's name is Sanju Mohammed. He's a relative of Ali Khan. A nephew, I think. And then there was his wife. We think her name is Amira."

"And what about this morning?"

"Ali Khan and his wife had a heated conversation. He was obviously very upset, and she looked scared. Then Ali went to work. One of my guys followed him. Ali arrived at work and as far as we could tell, there was nothing of interest to report."

"He didn't hurt his wife physically?"

"No. No physical violence."

Sara had run out of questions.

"Thanks. We'll keep working on it," she said.

"It's time for me to get some sleep," the head of the surveillance unit said.

"Good night," Sara said, and left his office.

"Torsten," she shouted once she'd got back to her office.

"Yes, what do you want?"

"Briefing," she said loudly, and headed into the conference room. Rita was already there and busy drawing lines between a couple of new names on the whiteboard.

"There is a connection between Jannice Karlsson and Tobias Klingström, as well as between Tobias Klingström and David Ljung. Also, there is a connection between David Ljung and Camilla Brink that reminds us of the connection between Tobias and Jannice. Sexual stuff. The difference is that Camilla is alive and well while Jannice and Tobias are both dead. The relationship between Tobias and Samira doesn't seem to be connected to the other stuff. We're pretty sure about that."

"What did Camilla tell you yesterday?" Sara asked.

Rita put her hands together.

"Well, she's involved in a sexual relationship with David Ljung. Their relationship has been on and off since she was fifteen. He's quite a lot older than she is, especially when you look at it from a fifteen-year-old's perspective. He was twenty-two when they met. There is an age difference of seven years. As I understand it, she's into BDSM. So is he. Could Tobias Klingström have tried something along those lines with Jannice?"

"Didn't I tell you something was off?" Jonny said, clapping his hands. "But where the hell is this David Ljung?"

"Camilla didn't actually know, but she said he had been acting strange lately. Didn't she say the same to you, Jonny? That it wasn't like him to go on holiday without telling her, for example."

Jonny nodded.

"What's BDSM?" Torsten asked curiously. Sara couldn't hold back a giggle.

"SM stands for sadomasochism while B stands for bondage and D for discipline. Bondage is when you tie someone up. It's all about causing pain to someone without hurting them. As far as I know, it's consensual and has nothing to do with abuse."

"Okay. But if it's exercised without consent, then it could really hurt someone."

"Yes, but then it's assault, not BDSM."

Sara looked at the others to see how they reacted to the new information. She saw a mixture of curiosity, disgust, and surprise on their faces. She decided to change the topic and turned to Torsten and Jonny.

"And what did Ann-Britt Karlsson say yesterday?"

"Apparently, Jannice told her that Klingström had made sexual advances, but that she hadn't seen him."

Torsten briefed the rest of the team about what more was said during the interview and then he told them that the social services director was clearly avoiding him and Jonny.

"What the hell," Sara said, and sighed.

"We've given her clear instructions to call us before lunch. I'll give her half an hour. Then I've had enough. After that, I'll call her," Torsten said.

"There is something fishy about this," Jörgen said in an attempt to be funny.

"I smell a whole school of fish," Rita said without showing any signs of finding it funny.

Next, Sara told the team what the surveillance unit had seen at Samira's house.

"I'll try to get authorisation to bug the house, or to at least trace the family's Skype calls. The first option isn't very likely. I'm not sure, but

I think something is up. It's great that we have surveillance in place. We'll hold off for a while as we have nothing to go on—except for Samira's suspicions about Pakistan and Aidah Iskander-Svensson's suspicions about the same thing. I'll talk to Aidah again today. I couldn't get hold of her yesterday."

"I forgot to mention that we've brought Jannice's computer in," Torsten said. "We'll see if we can tie that blog to her."

"Have you read it yet, Jörgen?"

"I've started. I'll let you know when I've read some more. So far, it's all about not feeling well. Mentally, that is."

Sara gave him an encouraging nod.

"And I've finally gone through the records of who owns the allotment gardens," Jörgen said, and smiled.

"Great. And?"

"It wasn't as straightforward as I'd hoped and I still have a couple of things to look into. But I found something interesting.'

"Come on," Rita said, and tapped her fingers impatiently against the whiteboard.

"Well, it seems like David Ljung's parents own one of the allotments. But they're both dead."

Jörgen waited for a reaction from his colleagues. Sara didn't say anything but he could tell by the expression on everyone's face that the information he had just shared with them was very interesting indeed.

71

It's all your fault. You've made me believe that my parents killed Tobias and that they're trying to force me into marriage. But I don't believe it. Not for a second," Samira hissed into the phone.

"No, I haven't made you believe that your parents killed Tobias," Aidah answered calmly. "I understand if you feel uncertain and if you feel like you've overreacted. Or maybe you even feel like I've overreacted. These feelings are normal."

"I want to go home," Samira said with emphasis. She *really* wanted to go home.

"I can't make you stay there, but I'll come to you in an hour. Let's talk about it then."

Samira ended the call, and for some reason, she wasn't angry anymore. She felt uncertain. And she missed Elin. She even missed Martin. He was a nice guy after all. She thought about how he stared at her quite often. Even before Tobias's death. Maybe he had a crush on her? She couldn't help smiling. But then she was reminded of where she was and a wave of hopelessness came crashing down over her. The feeling stayed with her until Aidah knocked on her door.

Aidah walked up to Samira's bed and sat down next to her.

"What am I supposed to do? Tell me, what am I supposed to do?"

Aidah put her right arm around Samira's shoulders and held her close.

Samira started crying. It all felt hopeless.

"I want to go home," she sobbed.

"Let me call Sara Vallén first. You know that officer you've talked to? I want to check that nothing new has happened."

She left the room and when she got back, Samira could tell something serious had occurred. She closed her eyes and expected the worst. She didn't want to look at Aidah.

"What happened? Can I not go home?"

"No, I strongly advise you not to go home at this point. It seems as if they're planning something for you. They had a Skype conversation with what seemed to be relatives yesterday, which can only mean they're talking about two things: how to find you and how to punish you when they do. In your case, I'm convinced they're talking about marriage. Your parents probably have no choice. It's all up to the rest of the family."

"I've seen it happen once before," Samira sobbed. "Not to me, but to a relative in England. It was a super-scary conversation. I was just a little girl, but I heard how they screamed at each other. And I heard the threats. They were aggressive and frightening. I'm not sure what happened, children weren't allowed to take part. But I know I was terrified."

Samira stopped crying. She wiped her tears and blew her nose. Her feelings were all over the place. She looked at Aidah to see her reaction, but she looked just as calm as she always did.

"I'll stay. But can you come visit now and again? Like you have done so far?"

"Of course. Are you going to be all right on your own now, then?"

Samira nodded. She got up and hugged Aidah.

72

Torsten sat across from Astrid Karpe in her office. She looked very uncomfortable and would probably have preferred it if Torsten went to hell. Torsten cut to the chase and asked her to tell him everything she knew about Tobias Klingström.

"No riddles, please. We need to know what happened when Tobias Klingström was relocated. We also need to know if a Lex Sarah report was filed or not. Go ahead."

"A woman called Ann-Britt Karlsson reported him once. I thought her accusations were a bit unclear, but we did submit a Lex Sarah report together with an action plan. This should all be in the files we gave you. These reports are always anonymous. Technically, it's not possible to report a specific case handler. You report social services as an organisation. We had long conversations about the situation and Tobias denied all the accusations. He also said the girl was very provocative, which is apparently typical for people who hurt themselves like she did. He had put a stop to the girl's treatment as she wasn't showing up for her meetings. He had contacted a youth psychiatrist to take over instead. However, we still felt like a transfer was the best thing to do and I don't think she got to meet with the psychiatrist before he was relocated. Jannice was assigned a new case handler and then she died. There is nothing other than the girl's story and her mother's letter about it. The mother wasn't doing great during the time of these events. She was getting along very poorly, actually. We helped her, of course, and we thought she was doing better and better."

"Why wasn't it arranged for Jannice to be cared for?" Torsten asked, and referred to the Care of Young Persons (Special Provisions) Act.

"Tobias didn't find it necessary. He thought the mother would get better, and she did. Also, institutional care like that is terribly expensive. The politicians prefer it when young people with issues can be treated at home instead."

"But what about the girl? How was she doing?"

"Tobias said her condition had improved. You can read about it in our digital records. Then he moved and she got a new case handler. She seemed quite worried about the girl, but she probably didn't have enough resources to do what she thought was necessary. And then Jannice killed herself. She hadn't even turned eighteen when she died, right? Poor girl."

"Yes, she died the year that she was due to turn eighteen. But something must have happened to her to push her over the edge?"

"Yes, that's what I just said. The new case handler was worried. But we didn't think it had anything to do with Tobias. She was self-harming and suffered from both anorexia and bulimia."

"What I find most upsetting here is that you were trying to keep information from us—information that might be relevant to the investigation. Why?"

Torsten couldn't understand what Jonny saw in the woman and why he thought she was so beautiful. He thought she looked boring and plain enough to blend in with the inane wallpaper. Her hands moved nervously across the stack of papers in front of her on the desk. He sighed. It was easy to spot someone who couldn't wait to retire and who was planning to do as little work as possible until that day came. But it didn't stop him from feeling angry. How could a person in her position be so indifferent when it came to people's suffering?

She threw an evasive glance his way.

"I didn't try to keep things from you. I just wanted to make sure everything was done by the book," she said.

"By the book? We were doing things by the book from the beginning."

The woman hummed and got up. Torsten left her office without shaking her hand. He needed to breathe.

73

We're not sure what they're up to, but apparently Ali Khan talked to a male relative over Skype last night. It was an emotional conversation. I think they're planning something," Sara said to Aidah when they sat down together in her office.

"Yes, it sounded serious when I talked to you on the phone earlier," Aidah said.

"What do you think could happen if she decided to go home?"

"I'm pretty sure the family is trying to figure out how to find Samira, and what their actions will be once they do. They could be discussing a forced marriage, or an honour killing. There is no way of knowing. But I think a marriage is most likely."

"I was told there was more than one person on the other side of the Skype conversation. Do you have any idea of who these people could be?" Sara asked, hoping Aidah would have an answer to her question.

"I'm pretty sure they were talking to their relatives and the village council about how to punish Samira, or what needs to happen to her for the family's honour to be restored. It doesn't sound good at all, but Samira is a wise girl. She decided to stay at the safe house when I told her it wasn't a good idea to go home."

Aidah looked at Sara in a way that made her feel awkward for some reason.

"Do you know you're very attractive?" Aidah said as if she couldn't stop herself. "And cool."

To her surprise, Aidah's comment made Sara feel great. But at the same time, it made her feel slightly embarrassed. She ran a hand through her curls and threw a glance up at the ceiling. Then she looked at Aidah again.

"Oh, thanks," she said, and smiled. "And you're incredibly beautiful."

"Oh, stop it," Aidah said, and smiled too.

After Aidah left, Sara went into the bathroom and studied her reflection in the full-length mirror. She ran her hand through her hair again and tried to look at herself objectively. Her eyes looked sharp and alert. Her hair was thick and curly. She was short and in good shape and her body was shaped like an hourglass. She looked powerful somehow. And her outfit looked great. She squirmed in front of the mirror. *Oh well, I might not be as attractive and cool as Aidah just told me, but I'm good-looking enough*, she thought. Next time she saw Anders, she would ask him what it was that he liked best about her. She hoped that the answer would be "everything."

74

Sara was tired when she sat down in her office to go through the case file for the millionth time. There were no DNA traces and no intimate relations between the people in Tobias's life, except the one between Camilla Brink and David Ljung. And they wouldn't be able to talk to David again until he returned from his holiday. It was interesting that David Ljung owned an allotment close to the crime scene. They had to look into that. First, they had to get a warrant to search his home, his office, and the cottage on his allotment.

Samira was safe for now, but for how long? And her parents, what role did they play in it? All they had was a bunch of loose ends. Sara sighed. She called Anders to complain for a bit. He listened to her and comforted her and after their talk, she felt better.

She thought about how observant he had been, and how considerate he was. She caught herself stroking the phone after their conversation, as if she could feel his skin through the warm but emotionless object. Suddenly, a distinct fear of losing him came over her. *I hope I never hurt him*, she thought, although she knew she already had in a way.

Her phone rang again. It was a colleague of hers. Sara took the call.

"Hi there. I've received a tip from a woman," her colleague said.

"Oh yeah, what was it about?"

"The woman who called told me she had something to tell us about the man who was murdered in the allotment gardens. Her name is Marie Jansson."

Sara was interested.

"Yes?"

"She told me about one of her colleagues. They both work for the home care services and, apparently, they work the night shift together. His name is Sanju Mohammed. I've looked him up in our records," her colleague said.

Sara felt impatient.

"Well, you won't find anything there."

"No, that's right. But the woman said she saw him and Tobias Kling-ström together."

"Get to the point," Sara said, and stood up.

"One night, almost two weeks ago, she saw Sanju in the car park out-side the grocery store in Hörby as she was driving past. She saw Sanju put his arm around a man's neck from behind. She thought she recog-nised the man Sanju was attacking as a social worker based at the social services office in Hörby. That's all she said. Make sure you question her. It's enough to do it over the phone to start with. Then we can decide if we need to bring her into the station for a more official interview. In that case, I want you to do a photo line-up."

"Holy crap. We definitely need to ask her for another interview."

"Marie also told me that she confronted Sanju Mohammed, who denied being at the car park. She felt a bit scared, too."

"She doesn't sound too scared if you ask me," Sara said. "I think she sounds brave, calling us about this."

"I think she's mostly scared about him finding out she called the police," her colleague said.

Sara nodded even if she knew her colleague couldn't see it over the phone.

Sara immediately called Åke Baum, who gave her permission to bring Sanju Mohammed in for questioning.

"But make sure you question the woman before you bring him in," he said, "just to be on the safe side. And check if there is any CCTV footage from the car park."

Sara laughed at the obvious instructions. Bringing in a suspect for inter-rogation wasn't something you did if you didn't have enough to go on.

"Got you," she said, and forgot everything to do with David Ljung and allotments. Sara walked out into the corridor and called her colleagues.

The team gathered in the conference room. They were all tired and overworked, but when Sara told them about the woman who had just called in with a tip, they sprang into action.

75

Rita volunteered to call the woman. She was fine with interviewing her over the phone. The others would bring in Sanju Mohammed. The interview was quick and easy. Although Marie had no idea, it was really starting to look as if Sanju Mohammed had a motive to murder Tobias Klingström.

Marie told Rita everything she knew. It was obvious that she was happy to help.

Rita remembered the news articles she had read about Hörby and the strong opinions about unaccompanied refugee children and housing for newly arrived immigrants. She had a feeling racism was a real issue in Hörby. At the same time, she felt frustrated with herself for thinking the way she did. *Stop being so judgemental*, she thought.

She took notes as she spoke to the woman. By the end of the interview, the notes had taken up a whole page. Although Marie didn't have that much to say, what she did say was important.

According to Marie, Sanju worked the night shift too. He was known for being fast, friendly, and efficient. She told Rita he was good at what he did, and Rita felt bad about assuming everyone in Hörby was racist. *Et tu, Brute?* she thought, and reminded herself to tell Linda about it later. As soon as Linda entered her thoughts, she felt butterflies flutter around in her stomach.

While Rita questioned Marie, the surveillance unit in Hörby was collecting footage from the closed-circuit camera in the car park. And there he was. Sanju Mohammed.

76

Two plainclothes officers guided Sanju Mohammed into the interrogation room. He looked very calm. As the whole thing had happened peacefully, there was no reason for violence. The big man had gone with them without a fight.

He sat down on a chair in the cold and sterile interrogation room. Torsten sat across from him, leaning back with his hands on the table. As always, he came across as relaxed and genuinely interested.

"Welcome. I apologise for the rude treatment," he said.

"I don't understand why I'm here," Sanju Mohammed said. His voice was surprisingly light for such a big and powerful man. Torsten didn't normally react to things like that.

"No, I assume nobody took the time to tell you. Allow me to explain."

"Thanks," the man said with a sour look on his face.

"Well, we're a bit curious to hear what you were doing at the car park outside the grocery store in Hörby in the middle of the night, at the same time as another man was there. The man who was there with you is dead now. Murdered. Maybe you can tell me what you were doing there?"

"I've never been there."

"Never?"

"Well, yes, of course. But never at night. I've only been there to do my shopping."

"Strange, because we've seen you on surveillance footage there. In the middle of the night."

"Well, that's impossible." The man pursed his lips. Like a child.

"We also have a witness who saw you there. But maybe you have a twin in Hörby?"

Torsten smiled on the inside. It was always fun to interrogate someone when you knew you had an ace up your sleeve. This time he had both surveillance footage and a witness. It would be hard for Sanju to talk his way out of it.

Sanju Mohammed sighed.

"All I did was warn him. Nothing else."

"Warn him? About what?"

"I warned him about what would happen if he kept seeing that girl . . . or woman."

"What woman?"

"Samira Khan," Sanju said without hesitating.

"Why?"

"She shouldn't be with a Swedish man. That's just the way it is."

"Oh, and how did you warn him?"

"I walked up to him from behind and put him in a chokehold. I might have scared him. But I didn't kill him."

Torsten had to take a second to gather himself. The man in front of him was confessing to threatening another man. It was almost too easy.

"Let's take a break," he said, and left the room. He locked the door and went into the bathroom. He drank some water before calling Prosecutor Baum, who called Sara Vallén.

"He's under arrest," Baum said.

"I'll be right there," Sara added.

Torsten joined the suspect again and told him he was being charged with the murder of Tobias Klingström. Sanju asked for a lawyer and Torsten had to step out of the room to call Baum again. After the call, Sara arrived.

"Something isn't right here," Torsten said. "When I told him he was being charged with murder, he looked so calm. I think I expected him to be angry or at least upset somehow. But nope."

"Yeah, I see what you mean. Either he's our perp and cold as a fish, or he's innocent and knows he has nothing to worry about. I'll come back in with you."

She said hello to the man, who politely stood up to shake her hand without hesitating.

77

He took a moment to think about how to handle the situation. He realised things hadn't worked out great, but he also knew there was nothing he could do about it. It was too late to turn back now.

He picked up his mobile phone and took a picture of the room. To remember how it felt. But what did he feel? Nothing, really. Not even anger.

Then he aimed the camera at the man on the sofa. The sofa was in bad shape. The fabric was so worn out that the padding showed in multiple places. *Someone probably put it down here to get it out of their home,* he thought.

"You know you deserve this, don't you?"

Silence. Not a sound.

"You know there is no going back, right? I can't go back now and neither can you."

Silence. Not a sound.

He sighed and took a couple of steps towards the man on the sofa. And then a couple of steps more. It was dark. He couldn't see much. But then again, neither could the man.

He held up the knife and the flashlight together, just like he had seen police officers do in movies. The light blinded the man. He squinted.

The man on the sofa whimpered and tried to move, but couldn't.

Not at all.

78

Samira hadn't expected Aidah's visit and was glad to hear she was coming. But when she saw the expression on Aidah's face, she felt scared. Her only hope of returning home was disappearing in front of her eyes.

"Come," Aidah said, and guided her into a private room.

Samira followed her, but she could barely lift her feet from the floor. She felt anxious.

"A man has been placed under arrest, suspected of the murder of Tobias. A relative of yours," Aidah said, and waited for a reaction.

"Sanju," Samira whispered.

Aidah nodded by way of an answer.

"The police believe your parents and your family are behind the murder."

Samira doubled over. The pain she felt was too much to handle. She couldn't even cry.

"My life is over."

"No, it's not. We'll make sure you get a good life. Because whatever happens next, we don't know where this will end. And from what I've heard, your family is on the warpath. So, my friend, it's time for us to make a plan."

Samira couldn't answer. Even if she truly thought the pain she was feeling would kill her, she sat down by the table and accepted the pen and the paper Aidah gave to her.

"I want you to rank different things in your life from least important to most important. This will help us guide you in the right direction."

Samira looked at the woman who was telling her what to do. She was acting as if there was anything important left in her life—as if she still cared about anything. It hurt so bad.

"I understand if you feel that everything important in your life has been taken away from you," Aidah said, seeming to read the girl's mind.

"No, there is nothing left. I've lost everything."

"It might look like that now. You're grieving, everything is dark and you've lost a lot. But I guarantee you there is a life out there for you. Let's start with your studies. Do you see the numbered boxes? If you tick box number five, it means something is very important to you. If you tick box number one, it's not very important."

Samira reluctantly ticked a box that showed her studies were very important to her. Important enough to tick box number five.

"Your friends . . . How important would you say they are?"

Samira ticked box number five.

"Do you think you could find new friends?"

Samira nodded.

"Family. How important is your family?"

Samira ticked box number five but changed her mind and ticked box number one instead as she didn't really have a family anymore.

"What made you change from five to one?"

"I remembered that I don't have a family."

"You do. They love you, but they're stuck in old traditions. Do you think you could have your own family one day?"

Samira nodded again. She wasn't sure which box to tick, but went for number four. Then she changed her mind again and finally ticked box number three.

"I don't know anything about the future though," she said, and started crying. A heavy teardrop trickled along her nose and fell onto the paper.

"No, you don't. But the truth is that not a single person your age can see into the future. Life can change quickly and you never know what's around the corner. But you can have a plan."

"Okay," Samira said meekly.

She kept listening to questions and ticking boxes and when they were done, Samira felt relieved.

"So, your studies are important to you? Most important, maybe?"

"Yes, considering how things look now, I guess you're right."

"Let's make a plan for your future, then. It'll be exciting and fun," Aidah said.

Samira thought it sounded bizarre. But she accepted it and let Aidah squeeze her hand.

79

The interrogations with Sanju Mohammed, his wife, Amira, and Samira's parents took a long time. They all denied any involvement in the murder.

All Sanju admitted to was putting Tobias in a chokehold.

Sanju's wife gave him an alibi for the night when he met with Tobias in the car park, unaware that her husband had given them a different story.

"He was home all night," she said.

"That's not right," Rita said. "He told us himself that he was out. I will let your lie slide, but I want you to tell me exactly what he did the following three days. We know he wasn't at work."

"He slept at home every night."

"I'm not only talking about where he spent his nights. I want to know what he was up to during the days."

"He was with me. And I think he went out with a couple of friends one night."

"What night?"

"Maybe Wednesday night? Or Thursday . . . I can't remember."

The woman kept pulling at her headscarf.

Rita wasn't sure if she was telling her the truth or not, but she could sense her tense energy. She gave up. Sanju Mohammed, Ali Khan, and Najima Khan were all placed under arrest because of the risk of them tampering with evidence, and the prosecutor was preparing for detention hearings. They didn't have enough evidence to prove probable cause, so if nothing changed, they would have to let them go in a week.

The interrogations continued. If the three suspects had been tired and worn out before, the slow process wasn't helping. Sara and her team were getting absolutely nowhere. Just as Sanju's wife, Amira, provided Sanju with an alibi, Najima provided Ali with an alibi, and Ali did the same for his wife. But even if none of the family members had actually killed Tobias, they still could have been involved in the murder. Therefore, their alibis didn't mean much. Amira Mohammed was released.

Sara scratched her head and frowned. Rita rubbed her temples and took short breaks only to take notes on her computer.

"How are we moving forward?"

"I don't know."

"At least Sanju is admitting to threatening Tobias Klingström," Rita said.

"And we can probably prove Samira's family is planning a forced marriage. I guess that's something, at least."

"We have to squeeze them harder during the interrogations. No more soft questions," Rita said with a short laugh.

"Samira has decided to change her identity and move to another country. We won't be handling this. And we won't get to know anything more about it. Apparently, her studies were very important to her. Poor girl. What a horrible fate."

"Yes, horrible."

The two women looked at each other and sighed.

Sara sent a couple of officers to search Sanju and Amira Mohammed's home. Rita decided to keep Sara company while they waited to hear from them. When they finally did, it was late. The officers hadn't found anything at all that could be connected to Tobias Klingström. No weapons, no blood, and nothing else.

Sara and Rita both felt hopeless when they finally left the station at 10:30 p.m.

80

Early the next morning, the team gathered in the conference room. Sara had a lot of tasks to delegate. They needed to search Samira's parents' house. And they had to search David Ljung's home and the cottage on his allotment. Åke Baum gave her permission to do so right away.

Sara decided to let her team conduct the searches while she and Jörgen went through the case file, including the virtual diary that Jannice Karlsson had kept. Sara hadn't had time to have a look at it yet.

She sent Rita to search the house in Hörby, together with an inspector, while she sent Jonny and Torsten, along with a couple of uniformed officers, to search the house on Professorsgatan and the allotment.

Right before lunch, Sara received a call from the operations centre. There had been a murder in the Swedish Wine Association's basement venue on Krafts Torg. For a second, she thought about how she and Jonny had been standing right outside the entrance to the basement not too long ago. With her mobile phone pinned between her ear and her shoulder, she called Rita while putting her coat on. She accidentally dropped the phone and cursed. She could hear Rita's voice from the floor, telling her that she would try to make it back from Hörby as soon as she could.

Sara jumped on her bike and arrived at the crime scene before Rita. She was glad to see Sergeant Malva Gran standing by the basement stairs.

First officer on the scene, again, Sara thought as she walked over to her. Malva smiled when she spotted Sara.

"So, we meet again," she said, and reached out her hand.

Sara shook it with both hands. She felt genuinely happy about how glad the young officer was to see her.

"Yes. It's great to see you. The reason for our encounter is a bit grim though. Why don't you brief me before I head down there?" she said.

"A man, still not identified. By the looks of it, he's in his thirties. His throat has been cut and it looks like the perp knew what they were doing. Multiple stab wounds in the genital area. The victim's body is lying half on the sofa and half on the floor. His hands are tied behind his back and well, it reeks of urine in there. It could be our victim's urine. A medical examiner has already been here but he's on his way back to the lab now. The coroner is on his way."

"Come with me," she said, and walked with Sara down the stairs.

Sara wondered how the perpetrator had even managed to lure someone down into the basement. Judging by the marks on the door, it wasn't the first time someone had entered the place without permission—if that was what had happened this time, of course. There was always a possibility that the murderer was a member of the wine club.

"One of the board members of the wine club found our victim when he was coming back to get something he had forgotten to take to a board meeting. Miranda is questioning him as we speak," Malva said. "Miranda Mårtensson, a new colleague," she added when she saw the confused look on Sara's face.

Just as Malva had told Sara, half of the victim's body was resting on the sofa.

They walked closer to get a good look at him.

Suddenly, Rita came running down the stairs.

"You must have driven like a fiend to get here this fast," Sara said, and tried to look stern.

"Yes, I drove pretty fast. But I flashed the blue lights. It was an emergency, right?" Rita answered as she did her best to catch her breath.

Rita gasped and looked at Sara.

"That's David Ljung!" she exclaimed.

Sara gasped too.

They examined the dead body. The victim's head was tilted back, revealing the gaping cut. His pants were bloody in the crotch area. They moved around the room, careful not to touch anything. The forensics team hadn't even shown up yet.

What in the world is this about? Sara thought, and twisted a lock of hair between her fingers.

After leaving the basement, they both remained quiet.

"I don't see the connection here," Rita finally said, and gave Sara a confused look.

"No, we must be missing something."

The young officer, Miranda Mårtensson—who looked fresh out of school to Sara—approached them with Malva to tell them that the man she had questioned was seventy years old and a real wine connoisseur. According to Miranda, the man was convinced it was a burglary as the door had been forced. He had also told her there was nothing to steal in the basement, except for the computer he came back to get. After entering the venue to check for the computer, he had seen a man with his throat slit. He had been shocked by the discovery and called the police right away.

"He saw the computer, but never took it. He wonders if he can take it."

"Not now," Sara said. "Forensics need to look at it first. Thanks for a great handover." Sara gave the young officer an encouraging nod.

Sara and Rita thanked Malva and Miranda, left the crime scene, and jumped into Rita's car after putting Sara's bike in the back. They drove in silence. Both of them tried to grasp what had just happened.

Rita drove along Kiliansgatan, took a left onto Magle Stora Kyrkogata and continued on Stora Tomegatan, Biskopsgatan, and Allhelgona Kyrkogata. She drove past several intersections to Oscarsbron and finally made her way towards the police station on Byggmästaregatan. The roads in the city centre drove Sara up the wall. Although she wasn't the one behind the wheel, she felt frustrated.

"It takes less to drive you round the bend," Rita said, breaking the silence.

Sara nodded.

"I know you shouldn't even drive in town, but it seriously would've been quicker to walk," Rita went on.

Sara nodded again.

81

How are the arrested members of the Khan family doing? Anything new? And how did the search go?"

"The search in Hörby gave us nothing. And Sanju is still admitting to threatening Tobias Klingström, but to nothing else."

Torsten gave Sara a summary of the interrogations, although he hadn't conducted them all personally. And, as always, Jörgen kept the case file in order.

"What about the allotment and David's home on Professorsgatan?" Sara asked with a tone that made the rest of the team curious.

Jörgen stared into his computer, as always. When he realised that Sara knew something he didn't, he looked up.

"We're not done searching Ljung's places," Torsten said. "We've sent officers with strict instructions. But what are you keeping from us?"

"Well, I've got a little surprise for us here," Sara said without smiling. "The murder victim is . . . let's hear a drumroll . . ."

"David Ljung," Jonny guessed.

"Yes," Sara said, clearly surprised. "How did you know?"

"I didn't. I guessed it." Jonny looked pleased with himself.

"Wow," Rita said. "Unbelievable. But why did you even guess that?"

"I guess it's been bothering me that David Ljung has been impossible to reach and that he allegedly went on a trip without telling his girlfriend. Camilla, I mean. And I got a bad vibe from him. It felt like something was off."

"This has complicated things though. Could all this still be related to honour? I don't get it . . ."

Sara went through a thousand scenarios in her head, but she couldn't see the connection. Why would Samira's family murder David Ljung? What was his connection to her? It didn't make sense. But then she thought of something. Something new.

"We need to question Samira again. Surely, there must be a connection here? Maybe Camilla and David Ljung's interest in BDSM plays a role here? What do you say, Rita?"

"You're right, there could be something there."

82

Samira sat in front of the computer, waiting for Skype to start up. She was restless and anxious. What was happening in the world outside her window? She had no idea. She hadn't contacted Elin as Aidah and the rest of the staff had made it clear to her that she couldn't.

"It's not only your safety on the line, Samira. This is about all the other women in this safe house. You're absolutely forbidden to contact anyone while you're here," the woman who was covering the night shift had told her when she saw Samira's phone was turned on. Samira had just received a text message from Elin when she walked in.

Where are you, Samira? I miss you terribly. And I'm worried. And scared. What happened? Why are you missing? Martin misses you too. He talks about you all the time and I don't know what to tell him. Can you please let me know you're okay? I'm worried. You're my best friend in the whole world. Please, write me back! Hugs from Elin

Samira had wanted to answer the message so badly, but the woman had taken the phone from Samira and turned it off.

When Samira had started crying again for the thousandth time, the woman had taken her in her arms in an attempt to comfort her.

"I want to go home," Samira had cried.

"I know . . . There, there," the woman, who was round and warm and motherly, had said.

It had been a while now and Samira still wasn't sure what to do. But in a way it was obvious. Her parents were under arrest. For murdering Tobias. Although she didn't want to believe it, she had suspected it all along. It couldn't be true, even if she knew it was. Even if they weren't the ones who had physically killed him, they certainly had something to do with it.

Deep down she still loved them and knew they were stuck in their old ways. They were convinced they had no choice but to obey the clan. That's what the elders in the village on the other side of the world had told them. She had ruined their reputation and robbed them of their honour. They had killed Tobias for it.

Slowly but steadily, she had grown to hate the old traditions. The traditions that had ruined her life. In every way possible. She wasn't even in pain anymore, but she was overcome by anxiety. And a rage she had never experienced before.

83

Ove Ovesson and Sara were talking to each other in the lab. He was the most thorough person she had ever met. That's why he was perfect for his job. She would miss him the day he retired. And it was only a year or two until then. Sometimes it felt nice spending time with people who had the ability to just *be*. The head of the forensics team wasn't someone who complicated things. On the contrary, he was someone who made people's lives easier. He was quiet and careful. He was simply a nice person to be around.

Her old mentor and boss, Kalle Persson, never returned from his sick leave and retired early. Sara missed him a lot. But in many ways, Ove reminded her of Kalle and she always turned to him when she felt lonely, just like she had turned to Kalle for all those years.

"Most importantly, we didn't find any DNA on David Ljung. We've collected DNA from everyone connected to Tobias Klingström, though we didn't find any at the scene of his murder either. I doubt this will help us now though. The MO differs slightly from the first murder. And more importantly, we're missing a connection to the Pakistani family this time."

"You're right. But David and Tobias were best friends. There must be some kind of connection. It's a shame we couldn't find any DNA on Klingström."

Sara sighed.

"Yes, that's never good. But we do know one thing. Tobias had two phones. We found a second one in his home. His work phone is missing. We're looking through his private one as we speak. It'll be very interesting to see what we find on there. Also, we have his computer. You never know what's on someone's hard drive."

"Yes, so much of a person's life is accessible online nowadays, so there is always something interesting to find. Contact me when you know more, okay? I'll call a meeting as soon as you know something. Now I have to go. But I'll talk to you later."

Ove Ovesson nodded. He stood up and walked silently towards the forensics team's staffroom. Sara smiled when she opened the door and walked down the stairs.

84

Sara made her way to David Ljung's allotment. She wanted to be there herself to look for connections. The small cottage seemed to be out of use. Judging by the state of the garden, David hadn't been there for years. They didn't find anything.

Sara drove to Professorsgatan instead. The house was empty, except for the police officers searching it. Camilla wasn't there. Sara wondered if anyone had told her about David's passing.

She decided to call her later that evening. If her team stumbled across anything interesting or if the forensics team found anything new, she knew they would let her know. It felt nice not to have to do everything herself. She had worked enough for one day.

After a shower and a quick talk with Rita, who seemed distracted and not at all up for a chat, Sara drove over to see Anders. Although she wanted to be with him, she felt anxious and worried about all the loose ends that refused to make sense. What were they going to do with the Khans and Sanju Mohammed?

I'll let it go for now, she thought. *I'll think about it tomorrow when I get to work.*

When she opened the door to Anders's house in Västra Hamnen in Malmö, she instantly felt happy again.

She hurried up the stairs and was just about to open the door to Anders's flat when her phone rang.

It was Ove Ovesson.

"We've found some interesting stuff on David Ljung's phone. And on his computer. But you don't need to come here. I just thought I'd tell you about it."

"Okay, tell me," Sara said. "Give me the short version."

"Are you sure?"

"Yes, definitely. Go ahead, tell me."

"Okay, I'll try to make it short. There were quite a few text messages between David Ljung and Tobias Klingström about BDSM. We also found a bunch of Facebook messages on the same subject. At one point they're talking about a girl they call J. The tone is quite aggressive and they blame each other for pushing things too far. The conversation is pretty hard to follow. There is also a text from an unknown sender. We haven't had time to look up the number yet. The text is from three days ago and was sent by someone called Candy. She wants to meet up with David. It's quite obviously about BDSM. We don't know who this Candy is. But the message was sent the same day David disappeared."

Sara's mind raced.

"I'll get back to the station right away," she said.

"No, stay where you are," Ove Ovesson said. "I'm the only one here and I'm just about to leave too. Let's pick it up again tomorrow. We're still waiting for the DNA results anyway. They said they would get them to us tomorrow. They promised to speed up the process as we have the Khans and Mohammed in custody."

"Fine," Sara said reluctantly.

The date didn't really turn out as Anders and Sara had expected it to. Sara spent two hours on the phone. But when she had finally called the rest of her team with the update, she felt slightly less restless. Anders had lit candles, set the table, and cooked a beautiful meal.

"So, can we eat now?" he said with a smile. He pulled her close and kissed her. She let out a short laugh.

"Sorry, but you know . . . Things are starting to move. Finally."

"I know, but let's sit down and eat. You can tell me about it. It all sounds very exciting."

"Hmm," Sara said, "I'd rather talk about something else. And you know . . . confidentiality."

"Okay," he said, and left it alone.

Sara thought about what Aidah Iskander-Svensson had said earlier and smiled.

"What do you like most about me?"

"Do you mean physically or mentally?"

"Physically, of course," she answered, and smiled even wider.

"Tough question," he said, and frowned.

A row of fine lines appeared across his forehead. *They look nice*, Sara thought, and looked at his eyes. They were blue like ice. Big and beautiful. She smiled at her own thoughts.

"I like it all," Anders said. "Your eyes are beautiful. They're soft and sharp at the same time. Your nose is incredible. It has character. Your lips are beautiful and you look great in lipstick. And you have the straightest teeth I've ever seen. And the wildest hair I've ever seen. I love your hair. It makes me want to be all tangled up in it."

Sara savoured every word.

"More, more . . ." she said, and showed him her teeth just because.

"You have nice legs. 'Nice pins,' as my father would've said. And I like your breasts. Is that enough?" he asked, and smiled at her with sparkling eyes.

Sara winked at him.

"That's more than enough. Now it's my turn." She studied him. "I like how your forehead . . ."

He got up and walked around the table. Then he picked her up and carried her to the bedroom. Once he had laid her down on the bed, she was just about to keep telling him what she liked about him when he pressed his index finger against her lips.

"Don't talk," he said, and removed his finger. The kiss he gave her was more heartfelt than any kiss she had ever experienced before.

85

Sara left Malmö at 7 a.m. and arrived at the police station in Lund fifteen minutes later. She felt refreshed. Happy, even. The building was quiet and empty when she stepped in and shook the rain out of her hair. She went into her office and started her computer.

Her inbox was empty, except for a short message from Rita. The message was signed off with a smiley face and a heart.

Sara walked into the break room, poured herself a cup of coffee, sat down by the computer, and started going through the case file.

Something about the case felt so obvious, but at the same time nothing made sense.

"Something isn't right, here," a voice said behind her.

"Jörgen," she said with a surprised look on her face. "You're here early."

"I couldn't sleep. I'm thinking too much. I realised I might as well go to work. I've been here since 5 a.m. And I've gone through Jannice's computer."

"Talk to me," Sara said curiously, and pushed her locks back behind her ears. She constantly reminded herself that she needed to get a haircut, but she kept forgetting. She realised there was no point asking Jörgen for a hairband as he probably didn't have one.

Jörgen gave her the thumbs-up and went to get his computer. When he got back, he opened the website with the blog. Sara sat down next to him. The blog was called The Secret.

I'm in so much pain. My whole body hurts. I hate myself. The creep wanted to see me again today. He's hurting me. You know, I hate myself when I don't see him and I hate him when I do. Why is he hurting me? I want to die!

Sara could feel the pain behind the words. It was the last post.

Why am I doing this to myself? They locked me in the cage again today. But first, they did something I can't write here. I don't know what to do. He keeps threatening me, saying he'll tell everyone what a slut I am—what a whore I am. But he's the one doing this to me. Disgusting. I feel so bad. Today it's worse than normal. I've cut myself even more. I've cut my arms. And my face. All I want is to die.

Sara and Jörgen looked at each other. It was horrible reading the girl's words. What had happened to her?

Jörgen scrolled to the previous post.

Isn't it rape when someone forces you to have sex with them? I'm just wondering. Today was horrible. He beat me. Whipped me. Locked me in a cage like a dog. He and that other gross man . . . I can't even write what they did to me. But it's so gross. I'm worthless. Completely worthless. I'm a whore. I know I am. But I feel so bad. I want to die.

Sara moved her hand up to her heart. It pained her to hear the girl's words and they brought old demons back to life. Demons that she carried deep inside of her but didn't give much room nowadays.

They kept reading. Post after post. They all contained similar stories and ended with Jannice wanting to die. Jörgen skipped over some parts not to have to repeat himself.

"Here you can see that something has changed. I'm going to read the posts in chronological order from now on. It makes it easier to follow," he said.

I've met the sweetest guy ever. I promise, he's the sweetest guy in the world. He's older than me, but still young. And so kind. And beautiful. I'm so in love. He's the one. I'll never have to meet that creep again now that I have him. Oh, I'm so happy.

"Go on," Sara said.

Oh, I'm so happy with him. He shows me stuff and makes me happy. And he says that he wants to make me happy. He's the nicest guy in the world. I love him. But the creep keeps reaching out to me. He's threatening me. So I think I still have to see him. But I won't write anything more about it. I want to be happy. I want to stop cutting myself. He tells me I'm beautiful. He doesn't mind all my scars.

"So, this 'creep' refuses to leave her alone, even after she's met someone and fallen in love? Who is this fucking maniac?" Sara cursed. She felt angry and sad at the same time. And something gnawed inside of her.

"As far as I can see, the perverted and sadistic abuse continued. It's all extremely degrading. The whole thing is very strange to read, and heavy. I'll print it all out and add the texts to the case file. That way, everyone can read them," Jörgen said. His face looked pained too.

"It seems as if this girl has been subjected to horrible abuse. It's hard to even imagine. How old was she when it started?"

"It looks like she started writing these posts two years ago. It seems as if her death wish grows as time goes on, and in the end, love couldn't save her. She was just about to turn eighteen when she took her own life, so I'm guessing it started when she was about fifteen."

"Bloody hell. We have to look into this. Properly. But if you ask me, these murders seem more connected to this girl than to Samira Khan. Wouldn't you agree?"

"Yes, definitely," Jörgen said. and looked disgusted.

Sara had a feeling they were closing in on what had really happened. It was like a puzzle where all the pieces were finally starting to reveal a picture, even if it had looked impossible to start with.

86

Sara took her computer into the conference room and studied the pictures and words on the whiteboard.

She erased and moved things, rewrote and drew new arrows. She wrote Tobias Klingström's name on the right side of the whiteboard and David Ljung's name on the left side. Then she drew a line between the two of them. She placed photos of Samira, her parents, and her cousin Sanju Mohammed underneath Tobias's name. She drew lines and arrows between their pictures to show how they were connected and then she moved on to David Ljung's side of the board. She drew a line from his name and wrote another name at the end of the line: *Camilla*. Then she wrote the letter *J* and the acronym *BDSM* between the two murder victims. She put down *BDSM* next to Camilla's name too.

Next, she drew a cross next to David's name, where she also wrote down *Candy* and *text message*.

She drew a line from Tobias's name to *Jannice Karlsson* and *The Secret*, as well as to Jannice's mum, *Ann-Britt*. Then she drew a line from *David Ljung* to *Jannice*. The line ended in a question mark. Next, she drew a line between the letter *J* and the name *Jannice*.

She wrote *DNA* between the two murdered men and connected them with a dotted line. She thought about it all for a while. Then she drew another line between *Candy* and *Camilla*. Maybe Camilla was

Candy? It didn't sound completely unlikely. But then she erased the line. The violence seemed too brutal.

She wrote down *modus operandi* next to both victims. Their throats had both been slit and they had both suffered cuts in the genital region. There were a couple of differences between the murders though. Tobias had been stabbed multiple times, which indicated rage. The murder had also included elements of torture as his fingernails had been pulled out. The violence David had been subjected to seemed less emotional and more calculated.

Rita entered the room, gasping for air.

"I've biked like my pants were on fire. I stayed up too late last night and overslept," she said, trying to catch her breath.

Sara glanced at her watch. It wasn't even 8 a.m.

"You're not late."

"What? Isn't it 9?"

Rita looked down at her watch.

Sara aimed a weak but friendly smile her way.

Just at that moment, Jonny and Torsten arrived, breathing normally. They both looked well-rested.

"Did you guys sleep well?" Sara asked them.

"Yes, very," Torsten said. "But I stayed up quite late. Veronica is visiting, you know."

"How nice. It must be lovely having her home from London," she said, and tried to smile.

"I went to bed at midnight, but I also slept well," Jonny said, determined to not be any less important than Torsten. Sara tried to smile at him too, to be fair.

"Look over here," she said, and pointed at the whiteboard. "As you can see, there are still gaps to fill in. But I've been thinking. The letter *J* could refer to *Jannice*. Maybe Tobias and David used her? Jannice was in love with an older guy. This could be David Ljung. Maybe he made her fall for him by being nice to her, only to lure her into what he and Tobias did to her later. Maybe that's why David Ljung was murdered. I think Tobias Klingström was murdered for the same reason. Jannice had a blog where she wrote quite openly about what she went through. She keeps some details to herself, but it's pretty obvious that she has been subjected to something grossly degrading and sexual, with elements of bondage and sadism. As far as I can tell, it was all against her will."

Sara was notably affected by what she had read, although she did her best not to let it show. She raised her hands to her face to hide her emotions, pretending to yawn.

"According to Ove Ovesson, Tobias and David talked a lot about BDSM and they even had an animated discussion over Messenger about using a girl. My guess is they were talking about Jannice. It fits right in with the order of events. On the day of David's murder, he received a text message from someone called Candy. It was about a meeting. I've been thinking . . ." Sara paused and looked at her colleagues for support. Nobody said anything. ". . . the more we investigate this, the less likely it seems that Tobias Klingström was murdered by Samira's parents or cousin. Especially now that David has been murdered too. Or what do you guys say?"

87

Sara and Rita were interrogating Sanju Mohammed. Torsten and Jonny were about to pressure Ali Khan before having another talk with Najima Khan. However, Sara considered if it might be a better idea to let Rita talk to her. Rita was pretty good at getting through to women. Maybe it was because of her intimidating looks combined with her friendly approach. Her size definitely helped.

"Would you please tell us what this is about," Sara said sternly. She didn't feel like being friendly at all.

"I've told you everything I've done, and everything I know."

Sanju looked right at the two women. He didn't waver for a second.

"Yes, but please tell us again," Rita said in a friendlier tone.

Good cop, bad cop, Sara thought.

He told them again about how their family back in Pakistan kept pressuring them and the rest of their relatives in Sweden. Word spread fast among the family members. Samira had been allowed to study medicine and her parents were proud of her. But then they found out about Tobias Klingström. They couldn't possibly accept it, and the family's honour was put into question. It was decided that Sanju had to make sure Tobias never contacted Samira again. He had threatened him, yes. And he had put him in a chokehold. But then he had left him alone. That was all.

* * *

In the other room, Ali Khan told Torsten and Jonny that he loved his daughter, but that he wanted her to understand there were things that had to be considered. And that she should have been grateful to him for letting her study. Yes, he was proud of her. But when he heard she had a Swedish boyfriend, he became very disappointed and his relatives became furious. Samira's cousin was given the assignment to scare Tobias Klingström. Nothing else.

Ali Khan refused to talk about forced marriages and denied any involvement in Klingström's death.

"You have no proof," he said.

"You know nothing about that," Jonny answered.

"Yes, I do. Because there is no proof we did this. That must be it. Otherwise, we wouldn't be sitting here, going over the same questions again and again."

Rita left Sanju Mohammed's interrogation to talk to Najima Khan, who sat hunched over, staring at her hands.

"Yes," she said, finally. "I'm so sad. I miss her. But what can I do? Nothing. Where is Samira? I want to know."

"I can't tell you that. Because even if you and Ali won't hurt her, it's our belief that she can't be in contact with you."

Rita and the woman sat on opposite sides, staring at each other. It scared Rita that a mother could be so cold-hearted and willing to send her daughter off to a strange country to marry someone she didn't love. Maybe an old man or someone who would hurt her for the rest of her life. And even if Najima Khan hadn't admitted to it, Rita knew it was the truth. They believed Samira's story.

"You wouldn't understand anyway," the woman said. She lowered her gaze and stared at her hands again. She was calm and still.

"No, I guess not. But I still can't tell you where Samira is."

88

Elin was meeting Martin to talk and have a bite to eat. She had called him because she felt lonely and worried. She couldn't get hold of Samira and didn't know what to do. She had thought about going to the police, but decided against it. It all felt so weird. Finally, she had called Samira's parents. They hadn't picked up the phone and her call had gone straight to voicemail, which had made her even more worried. She thought about the text message Samira had sent her. It felt like a long time ago now. Samira had written to tell her she was in a safe house as her parents were planning to send her to Pakistan. And she had told her that she couldn't have any more contact with Elin. Then she had sent her three hearts followed by the message: *Don't worry, I'll be fine. But we can't talk to each other from now on. I love you, never forget that. You're my best friend. I love you.*

Since then, she hadn't heard anything. She needed to tell someone. And she couldn't tell her parents. They would ask too many questions. She simply couldn't. But she was sure Martin knew something was going on anyway. He had also wondered where Samira was and why she wasn't showing up to her lectures.

Elin arrived first, but she didn't have to wait long until her brother joined her. It looked as if he had been crying. His nose was red, just like his eyes.

"What happened to you?"

"What do you mean? It's just a cold," Martin said, and wiped his nose with a piece of tissue paper that he pulled out of his pocket.

Elin gave him a stern look. Something was up, she was sure of it.

"You don't look very happy yourself," he said.

"I'm not, but at least I'm not trying to hide it. That's why I wanted to see you. I don't have anyone else to talk to."

"Yes, I assumed that was the case."

He blew his nose again.

Why wouldn't he tell her why he's upset? she thought, and decided to ask him again later on.

Once she had told him about Samira and what she thought had happened to her, Martin softened up. He appeared to visibly relax. He didn't seem to care too much about what Elin was telling him and she didn't actually know much, but she felt relieved telling someone. Martin twisted his napkin into a thin rope and untwisted it again, over and over. The gesture annoyed Elin, who tried her best to hide it.

"I'm convinced it's because of Tobias. I think Samira's parents have something to do with it."

"Do you know so or do you *think* so?"

"Everything happened after Tobias was murdered. Samira started acting strangely. She was scared and came to my place, then she went back to her parents. And now she's missing. She's at a safe house somewhere. She texted me once, but I haven't heard from her since then."

"What exactly happened after Tobias was murdered?"

"Strange things with her parents. They were planning to send her to Pakistan. She thought it was to get married. She was scared. But at the same time, she wasn't. That's all I know."

Martin opened his mouth, squinted his eyes, and shook his head.

"But why would they do that?"

"For dating a Swedish guy. Have you never heard of honour killings? Cultural pressure? Are you stupid? I've already explained it to you. And I think Samira is convinced it was her parents who murdered Tobias. Or maybe not them directly, but her relatives. She does have a cousin in Hörby."

Martin started laughing.

Elin stared at him. She couldn't believe her ears.

"Are you saying those people murdered Tobias?"

"What's wrong with you? How can you laugh at this?"

"Sorry, I didn't mean to. I just find it bizarre that they would kill Tobias just because their daughter is seeing him. Don't you think it's a bit dramatic?"

"That's the thing about these honour cultures. Their traditions are ancient. Of course, we find them bizarre. But for them, it's a matter of survival. Either way, it's nothing to laugh about."

"I apologised already, and I meant it," Martin said, and looked genuinely sorry.

89

She could tell Anders was holding his breath. As if he was expecting the worst. As if he was scared she was about to tell him something he wouldn't be able to handle.

She had made up her mind. She had to tell him. She had a strange feeling that she was about to open the gates to hell. That was why she needed to tell him. She wasn't sure how he would take it. It simply wasn't possible to predict how a person would react when they heard a story such as the one she was about to tell him. She clenched her jaws so hard that they started to hurt.

Her anxiety and the ocean of confused feelings that had been weighing her down lately took on an intensity she hadn't been prepared for. All she wanted to do was run away. She had to put a stop to it. Now.

"Don't look so scared," she said. One of her eyelids started to droop and she could hear the annoyed tone in her voice. His insecurity made her uncomfortable. Maybe it was a bad idea to tell him after all? She decided to take the plunge. Her face was tense, she could feel it.

"Do I look scared? I mean, I'm not scared. Just a bit worried. It's part of my personality," he said, and leaned over the table to steal a kiss from her. Sara didn't give it to him as she was too busy trying to keep herself calm. She felt him studying her.

"I just want to tell you this as it gets to me from time to time."

She looked at him again. His blue eyes didn't look worried anymore. Now he looked sad. His beautiful hands rested on the table in front of him. *He looks like a schoolboy*, she thought.

"Go ahead and tell me. I'm just worried you're about to tell me that you find me boring and don't want to be in a relationship with me. I think you're beautiful and wonderful. I love your hair, your eyelid that keeps drooping, your anger, your energy, your love, your children and well—I love everything about you. And I'm okay with you not being happy all the time."

He tried to smile and she tried to smile back.

"Oh," she said. "No, this isn't about our relationship. It's me. It's about me."

Sara straightened her back and knew she looked strong despite her petite figure. Years ago, someone had even told her she looked striking. And slightly dangerous. Her dark eyes could turn black in an instant when she was serious, angry, or if she wanted something. Her powerful voice made people move out of her way. Sometimes she found it strange that people felt intimidated by her. She was actually a really nice person. But she knew her appearance had given her certain advantages too. When she needed, she could easily make people change direction, sit down, or leave. Her mind raced.

"Okay, I'll tell you now. And don't look so pitiful either," she said. "What I'm about to tell you happened a long time ago."

She had made a decision and she wasn't going to run this time. She thought about Peter Matsson, what he had done to her, and how she didn't run then. But now . . . Why did she want to run *now*? Once again, Sara questioned her own judgement.

Anders gave her an encouraging look.

"When I was seventeen, my father was kidnapped in Uganda. He worked as a diplomat there. It was incredibly traumatic. For some reason, my brother, my mother, and I couldn't reach each other. It was all horrible for my mother of course. She was suffering and tried to hide it from us."

Sara pulled her hair back behind her ears and put a hand on her forehead. She felt feverish. She swallowed and looked at Anders again.

"During that time, I was raped by a mentally disturbed man. It broke me. And for twenty years, I lived with this. Two traumas at the same time were at least one too many to handle. My father was freed eventually, but he was never himself again. He couldn't stand dealing with me and my brother and even if he was back, we only really had our mother. My parents divorced. Dad got sick and died after a while. I've always suspected it was all connected. The two traumatic experiences had nothing to do with each other, but for me, they became entangled as they happened during the same period. It all came back to me in nightmares and constant panic attacks. This has made it difficult for me to maintain healthy relationships with men. For years after all this happened, I didn't feel safe anywhere. It has taken me years to get rid of the feeling of being in danger—and the constant urge to run away."

Sara studied Anders as she told him her story. His face was full of emotion and he alternated between looking angry, upset, and sad. But mostly, he looked afraid. Frightened by the intensity that lived inside of her.

"But sometimes it comes back to me, although it doesn't happen very often anymore. And I've found myself being pulled towards destructive relationships as they're really all I know how to handle. At the same time, these relationships have scared me half to death. Peter Matsson is a perfect example. And somehow my father's kidnapping feels connected to all this, and I've felt insecure, pissed off, and betrayed. And I've been so angry with my dad for letting us down. Although it wasn't his fault."

"How did the rapist attack you?"

The question was unexpected and cut like a knife in Sara's ears. It was as if there was something about that particular aspect of her story that scared him.

"We really don't need to talk about that," she said as her anxiety intensified.

Anders backed off.

"No, you're right. We really don't. But how did your mother react to all this?"

"It destroyed her, of course. But she bounced back. Maybe because she had to. She didn't have a choice. And then they got divorced. She met my stepfather, whom I've known since I was little. He was a close family friend. His wife had left him a couple of years earlier."

Sara had to take a break. At least for a second.

"It took me ages to process all this. The children's father, Göran, saved me in many ways. But you can't save another person, not really. Not if she doesn't want to be saved or doesn't have enough self-insight. Therapy helped me a lot. But there is still stuff that triggers me," she continued.

"I understand," Anders said.

He looked down at the table as he spoke. It made her incredibly angry. Furious.

"No, nobody does!" she exclaimed.

He stood up and walked over to her. He touched her hair and stroked her neck. She tensed her whole body and pulled away from his touch.

"Are you okay?"

"I'm fine," she said as steadily as she could.

"I can tell something is wrong," he said calmly, and stopped touching her.

"I'm just tired. That's all. I've told you."

"No, Sara. There is something else. I don't recognise you."

"You think everything is about you, don't you? You think your feelings are all that matters. My feelings mean nothing to you."

Sara heard how selfish, unhinged, and mean she sounded. She felt like a fly on the wall, watching herself act like an arsehole, but she couldn't stop.

He walked back to his chair, sat down, and stood up again. He looked devastated, but there was nothing he could do.

"If that's what you think, I'm not sure I understand why we should see each other anymore."

He was hurt. She knew it. She had done exactly what she didn't want to do, and she didn't know how to get out of the situation she had created.

"No, maybe we shouldn't," she said, although her harsh words hurt every part of her and ripped her apart.

"I would appreciate it if you could explain to me what I've done that makes you act like this."

She saw the sadness in his eyes. But she couldn't hold back her demons—the demons that wanted to destroy her. She knew she was wrong and that her behaviour was unacceptable.

"I can't," she said without looking at him. It was hard enough for her to deal with her own pain. She couldn't handle his pain too—not right now.

"I can't make you," he said, and left.

She heard the door close behind him and for some reason, she felt relieved. Maybe now her anxiety would go away. But it didn't.

She just sat there—unable to move.

90

After a restless night with only a couple of hours' sleep, Sara decided to go to Malmö to see Samira. She wanted to go alone. Mostly because she didn't want to explain to anyone why she looked like a ghost.

"Hi," Sara said, and reached her hand out towards Samira. "I'd like to talk to you about Tobias."

"Okay," Samira said without revealing what she was feeling.

"Is there anywhere we can talk in private?"

"There is a room over here," Samira said indifferently.

"Great," Sara said, and attempted a little smile. "Are you getting used to this place now?"

Samira shrugged her shoulders.

This isn't going to be easy, Sara thought.

"How are you?"

"As one might expect," Samira answered.

"I understand this is tough, but I need to talk to you about Tobias. My questions might feel unpleasant but they're completely necessary, so you'll have to forgive me."

"It's okay."

"Did you and Tobias have sex?"

Sara studied Samira, who squirmed in her seat.

"Yes," she answered.

"How was it?"

Sara knew the question was strange, but she struggled to find a better way to express herself. She hoped that Samira would understand what she meant.

"It was nice. As if we loved each other," Samira answered, and for a second, Sara thought she could see a glimpse of doubt in the young woman's eyes. But maybe she was only imagining it.

"Did Tobias have any preferences when it came to sex?"

"I don't understand the question."

"I mean, did he prefer anything in particular when you made love?"

"I know what the word 'preferences' means. I just don't see where you're going with the question."

Samira looked miserable.

"What was Tobias into? Did he have a favourite sexual position or did he ever want to try something that you didn't like?"

Sara sensed that Samira was embarrassed. She obviously didn't want to talk about this.

"He wasn't into anything strange, if that's what you're asking," Samira said, and looked at something behind Sara.

"What do you mean when you say 'strange'?"

"I don't know. But it was always very loving."

"Did he ever use violence?"

Sara felt it was time for direct questions. That was the only way she would get a straight answer from Samira.

"No, never," she said firmly. "Never ever. He was gentle and careful. And loving."

Samira stared at Sara, who wasn't ready to give up.

"Did he ever show interest in something called BDSM?"

Samira's jaw dropped. Then she started to cry. She turned her face away and stifled a scream.

"You might not think I know what that is, but I do. Tobias would never be violent towards me in any way! And he wasn't into that stuff!"

She was crying violently now.

Sara stood up and walked over to Samira. She stroked her hair. The long black braid felt dry against the palm of her hand. The young woman cried like a child.

"I'm sorry, I didn't mean to upset you," Sara said while her eyes were tearing up as well.

Samira's whole body trembled, and Sara got a blanket from the sofa and wrapped it around her shoulders. Then she left the room to ask the staff for help. A woman with a motherly appearance followed her back to Samira. Sara leaned forward and stroked Samira's hair once again.

"Sorry," she whispered.

Sara walked out to her car and drove back to Lund. She felt disheartened. *Two failures in 24 hours. Not bad,* she thought sarcastically.

91

Ann-Britt Karlsson was on her way to the cemetery. She was tired. Her life was meaningless. All she did was fight. Fight for her survival, fight to keep her grief in check. *Fight.* A word that described her life perfectly. Her whole life.

The walk to the cemetery felt longer than usual. The air smelled of rain and it felt more like November than the beginning of October. The only way to tell it was early autumn was that there were still leaves on the trees. They were beautifully yellow and orange. She walked past the high-rise buildings near the Arena and through the west side of Stadsparken—past Högevallsbadet. The park was almost empty and the only lights around were those by the beach. Other than that, everything was dark and grey.

Things got busier when she passed Bantorget, where people arrived on trains from their jobs in Malmö, Höör, Helsingborg, and other cities in the area. People who had a job to go to. People with a life to live. She kept walking past Clemenstorget and the little stands on the square. She stopped to buy a rose. A single red rose. It was beautiful.

She entered the gates to the graveyard and noticed that someone must have raked the gravel path recently. She picked up a green plastic vase with a spike at the bottom and walked over to one of the water hoses on the side of the footpath to fill it with water. She grabbed a rake too. The grave was probably a mess. She hadn't visited it in months. She approached her daughter's grave, leaned over it, and caressed it gently. Then she put the rose into the vase and pushed it into the dirt in front of the stone.

She froze when she saw another red rose. A fresh one with a note tied to its stalk. She picked up a stick and used it to turn the note until she could see what was written on it. Something told her she shouldn't touch anything with her hands. The note had a short message written on it in blue ink. *You're the only one for me. My rose.* And then there was a heart. The message made her own heart skip a beat. And then she started crying. Violently. The floodgates opened and she let everything out. Ann-Britt sat down on the ground and caressed the gravestone again. Then she picked up her mobile phone. She still had a little money left on her prepaid phone card. She pulled out her wallet and found the note she had put in there earlier. She dialled the number on the note and pressed the green button. She trembled as she waited for someone to pick up.

"Rita Anker," a friendly voice said at the other end of the line.

92

Sara!" a voice shouted from the corridor. A very excited voice.

"Yes?" Sara peeked out of her office. She had just arrived at the station and taken off her jacket and scarf. She felt as if she was headed down a dark road with no return.

Rita stopped in the doorway.

"What's going on with you? You look like a ghost," Rita asked with a confused smile.

"It's nothing," Sara said without looking at Rita.

"No?"

"No," Sara repeated

"Okay . . . Ann-Britt Karlsson just called. She's by her daughter's grave. There was a red rose with a note attached to it next to the gravestone. The note says, 'You're the only one,' or something like that. She sounded very upset. She didn't know that her daughter had someone who cared about her like that. She thinks the note might mean something. We have to go there."

Sara put her jacket back on, tied her sneakers, and ran after Rita.

Rita drove at full throttle, but Sara chose not to comment on it. She wanted to get there fast, just like Rita.

"Did you tell her not to touch the note?"

"Yes, she hasn't touched it. She just poked at it with a stick. For some reason she felt right away that she shouldn't touch anything. At least that's what she told me. Bloody marvellous."

Ann-Britt had told Rita where her daughter's grave was located and they ran over to it. They were both out of breath when they sat down next to Ann-Britt, who was on the ground with tears silently streaming down her face. *Poor woman*, Sara thought, and put an arm around her shoulders. Rita pulled out a pair of plastic gloves from her pocket and put them on. She took the rose and the note and placed them in a paper bag. Then she looked at Jannice's mother.

"I'll take this rose with me, but I promise I'll replace it with a new one."

Ann-Britt didn't answer Rita, but smiled meekly while she kept crying.

They all stood up and noticed the damp grass had made their trousers wet.

They drove Jannice's mother home. She didn't speak at all in the car, but Sara thanked her when they dropped her off outside her door.

"Thanks for calling us, and great job not touching that note," she said, trying to sound encouraging.

The woman shook the officers' hands and disappeared into the building.

"I wonder who wrote that note," Rita said. Then she drove back to the station.

93

Ove Ovesson entered the room with a sour look on his face. He waved a piece of paper in front of them.

"No matches," he said, "but the DNA on the note belongs to a woman."

"Wow, what? A woman?"

Sara and the others rushed over to look at the results.

"I'll notify Baum," Sara said. "But I don't think this has anything to do with the Pakistani family. This isn't about honour. It's about sex—or more specifically, BDSM."

Sara was sure of it now. They had been looking in the wrong direction from the beginning. Although Sanju Mohammed had threatened Tobias Klingström, which he had admitted to, the evidence pointed away from the theory of the murder being an honour killing.

When Prosecutor Baum heard about both the latest development and the recent interviews with the Khans and Mohammed, he sounded hesitant.

"So you don't have any evidence? All Sanju Mohammed has confessed to is threatening Tobias? Nothing else?"

"No, nothing. All we have are indications. Or, that's at least what we had. These indications might have lost some of their strength now though. If you don't want to go after them for planning a forced marriage, of course?"

"No, I don't. We don't have enough evidence. We're going to have to let the parents and Sanju Mohammed go. And honestly, it was a bit of a long shot to begin with. As far as I've understood things, Khan's daughter is safe now."

"Okay, will you make sure they're released?"

"Yes, of course," Baum said with a dry laugh.

Sara thought he sounded slightly annoyed and realised she had been a bit disrespectful.

"Sorry," she said, "I just wanted to be super clear. I don't want any mistakes. You know what I mean!"

Baum mumbled something and ended the call.

94

Samira sat by herself, looking out at the backyard. She still hadn't recovered completely from the conversation with Sara. She was still in shock. What did she mean by her questions? That Tobias was violent? Towards whom? Why? She had so many questions. But in a way, it gave her something to focus on other than herself.

It was quiet and peaceful. There was no wind and the leaves in the trees didn't even move. She felt as if she hadn't been outdoors for ages. The restlessness she had felt from the beginning had transformed into apathy and acceptance. She waited. Waited for her life to begin again. It felt as if everything had been placed on pause while she remained in the safe house. Time stood still, as well as the rest of the world.

She heard steps behind her and turned around.

"Aidah," she said.

"How are you?"

"Well, how am I? I'm functioning. Nothing else. How are Mum and Dad doing?" Samira tried her hardest not to show how much Sara Vallén's visit had affected her.

"The police let them go. They're still suspected of arranging a forced marriage, but they aren't suspected of murdering Tobias anymore," Aidah said calmly without mentioning the development with Samira's cousin. She didn't want to worry her more than she had to.

Samira flinched.

"Maybe I can go home again!"

"I strongly advise you not to."

Aidah looked at her with a sad expression on her face.

Samira was confused.

"Why not? They didn't murder Tobias."

"We still suspect them of arranging a forced marriage for you," she answered.

Samira sighed.

"But that's not what matters here."

"For you, it matters a lot."

Samira shook her head. She didn't want to understand.

"You're not in charge of my life!" she screamed. Although Samira knew this wasn't about Aidah, she was the one who got to be on the receiving end of her rage. She simply couldn't contain her anger anymore. She slammed the wall with clenched fists. "I hate you, I hate you. If it wasn't for you, I would've been home now!"

95

Once Samira had calmed down, Aidah left the safe house. It was painful to see the girl in such pain.

On the way back to Hörby, her phone rang. The woman who called her spoke quietly, but Aidah knew who she was. She had already looked up the number online. The woman had something to tell Aidah and wanted to see her as soon as possible.

"I'm on my way to the municipal office. I can meet you there in thirty minutes," she told the woman.

"Thank you, thank you so much, I'll be there."

All the way back, Aidah thought about what the woman could want. There were only two possible answers to the question. She either wanted to find out where her daughter was or she wanted to stand up for her. *Let's hope it's the latter option*, Aidah thought.

She parked her car in the staff car park, which was almost empty now. It was late in the afternoon but she didn't care. She wasn't going to miss the opportunity presented to her.

The reception area was closed for the day, so Aidah rushed to the front entrance, afraid of missing her chance. She spotted the short and slightly round woman who was waiting for her outside. When the woman saw Aidah, she lowered her gaze. As if she was ashamed.

Aidah walked up to the woman and opened the entrance door with her ID tag. She let Samira's mother walk into the building first and then she followed her. Najima Khan wore a long coat and a headscarf, hiding herself as best she could. Aidah recognised the behaviour. The fear of being caught. The fear of being seen.

Once they were inside, Aidah introduced herself properly to the woman—Samira's mother—who carefully sat down at the edge of the armchair that Aidah had pulled out for her. She spoke quickly and quietly. After a while, Aidah had to ask her to speak slower and a bit louder. She made sure to use a friendly tone and did her best to create trust while still staying professional.

"I know Samira is at a safe house," Najima said, "but I have no idea where she is. I think you know, but I understand you can't tell me. But I've decided not to let them send her to Pakistan. I want her to come home."

Aidah was surprised by how well the woman had learnt Swedish. Suddenly, she was overcome by sadness when she thought about the isolation many immigrant women faced when they came to the country. For different reasons.

"Yes, Samira is at a safe house, and I'm glad to hear you don't want to send her to Pakistan. But I can't send your daughter back to you as things are looking now. What are you planning on doing?"

"Maybe I can talk to Ali, my husband? He loves Samira. She's his daughter."

"I strongly advise you not to," Aidah said with a serious look on her face. She stroked the woman's hand in an attempt to comfort her. "At least not now."

Najima's chin trembled and she wiped her eyes with the back of her free hand.

"Why not?"

Aidah kept holding the woman's hand. She could feel her pain but didn't let it affect her judgement.

"He might not understand."

"No, he might not, you're right."

Najima's face revealed how powerless she felt. Her round cheeks were pale.

"I've worked with these issues for a long time. I need you to trust me. I'll do my best to find a way out of this, but first I have to conduct something we call a threat and risk assessment. What it means is that I'll investigate your family to determine what risks and potential dangers Samira could be facing by returning home. When I've looked at it, we'll talk again to see what options we have. You and I will meet again when it works for you. And I'll ask a lot of questions. When it's done, we'll see what we can do. I hope you trust me."

The woman nodded and stood up.

"I have to go home now. I don't want my husband to get suspicious."

No wonder her daughter is so intelligent, Aidah thought.

"That sounds wise," she said. "Where is your husband now?"

"He's at work. He had to work late today. He hasn't been himself lately. He doesn't want to be at home. He says he prefers working."

"It's a normal reaction," Aidah said. "This is hard for you two. I know."

When Aidah returned to her office, she sat down to start on the threat and risk assessment. After a while, she picked up her phone. Her red nails tapped against the screen as she opened her contact list and found Sara Vallén's number. The phone rang for a while and then her call went to voicemail. Aidah hung up and decided to try again the next day. She needed to go home to her family.

While she was putting her laptop in her backpack, baffling thoughts crossed her mind about why people tended to make their lives so much harder than they needed to. She sighed. Then she went out to her car.

She sat behind the wheel for a while, thinking about Samira and her mother. Maybe it would all work out for them in the end. It all came down to what she would find in her assessment and what they were prepared to give up.

Aidah turned the key and drove home.

96

Sara decided it was best to see Camilla alone. She needed to ask her about BDSM and try to find out who the mysterious Candy was. Could it have been Camilla who placed the rose by Jannice's grave? Sara didn't want to bring anyone with her. Especially not Rita, as the risk was she wouldn't stop asking Sara what had happened until she gave in. Also, Rita was so incredibly happy. It bothered Sara.

Camilla waited for her in David Ljung's house. They sat down in the luxurious kitchen that felt almost too grandiose for the context.

"Well, simply put, you could say that BDSM combines bondage, discipline, sadism, and masochism," Camilla said.

"Is it dangerous?"

"No, not normally. It's all consensual. Everyone who takes part likes it. And there are rules. For example, you have to stop the moment someone says 'stop.' Respect is important. People who are into BDSM are turned on by the game, but we're careful not to cross any lines."

"But what if things get out of control?"

"Yes, then I guess it can be dangerous. The biggest problem is that there are idiots who take advantage of girls who don't know how to say stop. I know of at least one situation like that. There are probably plenty of these idiots, but they're normally not members of the more organised clubs. Sometimes things get out of control when the different participants aren't aware of each other's limits. And some people like more perverse things, like scat sex. Sex that includes faeces, in other words. Not my cup of tea. I know a guy who was into that. One of David's friends."

"Who? Tobias?" Sara held her breath.

"Yes, Tobias. I've never met him, but he was one of David's childhood friends."

"Tobias Klingström?"

"Yes, that's right. The guy who was murdered. Wasn't David at his parents' house when you came here to look for him the second time?"

"Yes, that's the guy. Are you sure about this?"

"Yeah, I'm sure. David told me. Sometimes I think David was also into that stuff. But he's never tried it with me. And he never mentioned it. But I've always suspected it."

"Was Tobias a member of your club? Or any other club?"

"No, not as far as I know. It would never have worked. David told me he kept himself to himself."

Camilla didn't seem too sad about David's death. Sara tried to understand her, but it was hard. How could she possibly be that calm when someone close to her had just died?

Candy, Sara thought suddenly, but didn't say anything.

"This might be a sensitive question, but I'm a bit curious about your relationship with David. You don't seem very sad about his death, so I wonder what you're thinking."

Camilla looked down for a second. Then she looked up again and locked eyes with Sara.

"If I'm honest, I didn't like him very much. He was a good boss and great in bed. But the more I think about it, the more I realise I didn't really like him as a person. He didn't seem honest. There was something dodgy about him. But of course I'm shocked by his being murdered. I don't think I have accepted it yet."

Sara nodded.

"But what did you like about him, then?" she asked, and knew Camilla could see how curious she was. This was none of her business, really.

Camilla thought about it for a while. Once again, Sara reflected on the contradictory nature of the woman in front of her. Maybe it wasn't only her appearance. This time she was wearing jeans and a T-shirt, an outfit that contrasted sharply with the look she'd had earlier. But she wore her clothes as elegantly as she did everything else.

"Well, I've been with him for so many years that I kind of accepted him as my lover, and as my boss. I guess I never thought about it that much. I guess I would call it a force of habit. And we did have great sex."

"Hmm," Sara said to reassure Camilla.

"But now when I think about it, I realise our love life hasn't even been that great lately. Not for two years, at least. Force of habit, as I said."

Sara looked at Camilla and realised how beautiful she was. Her slender body, her hair and makeup—it was all so perfect that you couldn't help being impressed.

"Do you know anyone called Candy?"

Sara took a chance. And she watched Camilla's reactions closely.

She thought she saw something happening in her eyes. Was she imagining it?

"No, I don't recognise that name. But some people pick names like that. It's part of the game. A good anonymous name. Doesn't give anything away."

"Okay, thanks a lot." Sara stood up and realised her legs were trembling. It was incredibly uncomfortable, but at the same time, she was overwhelmed by the exciting, fizzy feeling she always got when she was closing in on the truth—when she was about to solve a case. The interview had given her some clarity.

She took the young woman's hands in hers and held them hard for a second. Then she put her jacket on and walked out the door into the rain. It was pouring down.

97

Sara returned to the station. She walked straight into the conference room and stared at all the lines and names on the whiteboard. She erased Samira's name as well as her parents' and Sanju Mohammed's. She rewrote their names in the periphery. She stood there staring at the name *Candy* for a while. Could the slight shift she saw in Camilla's eyes have exposed her? Was she the murderer? Or was it a long shot?

Rita came bouncing into the room. She still hadn't gone home. Despite everything, Sara was happy to see she was still there. Rita took Sara in her arms and spun her around on the floor.

"What's up with you?" Sara laughed, and allowed Rita's mood to rub off on her.

"I'll let you in on a secret. I'm in love," Rita exclaimed. "Head over heels in love."

Sara smiled.

"That's a sad smile," Rita said. "What's happened?"

"I think I screwed things up with Anders," Sara explained. She pressed her lips together and gave Rita two ironic thumbs-up.

Rita stroked her cheek. Her touch was light as a feather.

"Silly," she said. "I'm sure you haven't screwed anything up. It's not what you do."

"Let's not talk about it now. Tell me, who are you in love with?" Sara asked, trying her hardest to seem happy and excited.

"Her name is Linda."

Sara raised her eyebrows.

"Are you in love for real?"

"Yup."

"That makes me so happy to hear."

Sara hugged her colleague. She was almost a head shorter than Rita.

"And you're sure you're in love?"

"Very."

They talked for a while, and Sara let Rita describe Linda and the love she felt for her. Sara smiled and listened. Asked a couple of questions. And listened some more.

She felt exhausted.

"I thought about something," she said once Rita had finished talking.

"Shoot," Rita answered.

"I visited Samira to talk to her about Tobias and BDSM. It's pretty obvious that Tobias wasn't violent towards her and that they never had that kind of sex."

Sara took a deep breath through her nose.

Labour breathing, she thought, and smiled when she thought about giving birth.

Rita nodded but didn't say anything.

"Then I went to Camilla, who told me more about BDSM. Something about Camilla's way of describing David Ljung didn't sit right with me. And although she didn't know Tobias, she told me that he liked pushing the boundaries. She told me he kept to himself and had violent tendencies. She even made a comment about him possibly taking advantage of young women—or girls. Obviously, it makes Jannice's accusations seem even more credible."

Rita listened attentively. Her facial expression kept changing as Sara spoke.

"But I'm wondering about Candy," Sara continued. "It seems as if the person who goes by the name Candy lured David Ljung to the basement on Krafts Torg. I might have mentioned it before, but could Camilla be Candy? It's just a thought. I think I saw something in Camilla's eyes when I asked her about the name Candy. But I'm not sure if it was really there, or if I imagined it. I'd love to hear what you think."

Rita inhaled.

"Wow, what if you're right? How do you want to move forwards?"

"That's the thing. We need her DNA. I realised it after I'd already left the house. Maybe we can at least tie her to the note on the rose."

"Ah, I see," Rita said, "but we should be able to get it quite easily. Do you want her to know about it?"

"No, it would be better if she didn't. There is always the risk of her leaving town. Then we might not find her again."

"Let's ask Jonny to go to the house. He can pretend he doesn't know you already went to see her. And then we can ask him to collect some DNA from a coffee cup or whatever. Do you think she's still at David's house?"

"I'm not sure. It didn't look like she had packed up her things when I was there."

"Okay, call Jonny right away, then," Rita said.

"Okay, let's do it. I'll call him."

98

Jonny rang the doorbell outside the house on Professorsgatan. Nobody came to open the door. He sighed.

"So bloody unnecessary," he said loudly to himself.

He rang the bell again. No answer. He grabbed the door handle. The door slid open. *An illegal house search,* he thought to himself before entering the giant hallway.

"Hello!" he shouted.

The house was silent. Completely silent. Jonny walked towards the kitchen. The lights were switched on and he suddenly felt uneasy.

Why were the lights on and why was the front door unlocked? Jonny grabbed his phone and called Sara.

"Hi, this is Jonny."

"Why are you whispering?"

"I'm not sure, but I'm inside David Ljung's house. The door was open. All the lights are on, but nobody seems to be home."

"How strange."

For some reason, Sara was also whispering.

"I'll walk around for a bit, but I'd appreciate it if you got over here. In case something happens," Jonny said quietly.

"Rita and I will be right over."

Jonny found a used coffee cup. He put it in his pocket. *Not very likely David's old cup,* he thought, and assumed it was Camilla's.

He waited for a moment and, suddenly, he heard a noise behind him. He turned around and let out a surprised scream when he saw Camilla standing there wearing leather boots, with leather straps wrapped around her body. She was holding a long whip.

"What the hell are you doing here?" she hissed.

"The-the door was open," Jonny stuttered. "I'll leave right away."

"Get out!" she screamed.

Jonny got out—quickly. Outside, Sara and Rita were waiting for him. To them, he looked as if he had just seen a ghost. Sara put a hand on his shoulder.

"What happened in there?"

"What the hell, the door was open. I shouted, but nobody answered me. I walked into the kitchen and found a used cup. Still nobody around. Suddenly, she was standing right behind me. Bloody hell, she scared the living shit out of me."

"Oh," Sara and Rita said at the same time.

"But you guys don't get what she looked like. She was wearing leather boots that ended above her knees. And she was naked and wrapped up in a bunch of leather straps. And she was holding a whip. I didn't know where to look or what to do, I mean . . ."

Sara laughed. Rita started laughing too, and after a couple of seconds, Jonny joined in.

"It was so weird. I'm in shock," he giggled, while they walked towards their cars.

"Here is the cup. I'm going home. It's late."

Rita took the cup.

Jonny waved at them as they drove off. He had to sit there for a couple of minutes before he felt ready to drive.

99

Okay, something is off about Camilla," Sara said at the morning briefing.

"Go on," Jonny said, nodding towards Sara.

"Last night, I was standing in front of the whiteboard. Once again, a thought hit me that Camilla and Candy could very well be the same person. We've talked about that before. But we don't have her DNA, so after discussing it, Rita and I decided it was a good idea to send Jonny over to collect a sample. I didn't think about asking for a DNA sample when I talked to Camilla earlier."

"So, I went over there," Jonny filled in, "but nobody opened the door. So I felt the door handle and realised the door was open. I walked into the house and found a used coffee cup on the kitchen island. Then all of a sudden Camilla showed up. She was naked except for some leather straps and boots. And she was holding a whip. She scared me half to death. And then she threw me out. Can you imagine how I must have looked in this scenario?"

At least Jonny could laugh at himself. Sara appreciated it.

Torsten and Jörgen's mouths were open and Jonny's laughter spread through the room.

"But in all seriousness, you had no right being there and I totally understand her reaction," Sara said.

"No, I know. I mostly felt stupid," Jonny said. "And she scared me. She looked quite scary, to be honest. I'm not sure if it was her outfit, the whip, or her eyes—or all of it together."

"But at least you found a cup. Let's hope it has Camilla's DNA on it. There is an actual possibility that Camilla, Candy, and the murderer are the same person," Sara said. "That's what hit me yesterday."

"And when will we know if we have a match? Did you ask forensics to hurry up?" Torsten asked Sara, and threw his hands out.

"They said they would let us know as quickly as they could. They're trying to match the DNA on the note with the DNA on the cup. They promised to try to have the results ready by tomorrow. I sent the cup to them last night."

Torsten nodded.

Jörgen hadn't said a word during the whole meeting.

"I've gone through the list of allotment owners. As you know, we didn't find anything in the cottage on David Ljung's allotment. And I don't recognise any other names on the list. To be honest, I haven't found anything of interest when it comes to the other allotment owners in the area. But I'll give you the list anyway, Sara," he said, and handed Sara a document. He had been kind enough to print her a copy before the meeting.

"I think I'll pay Camilla a visit today. Do you want to come, Jonny?" Sara asked, and winked at him.

"Hell no!" Jonny exclaimed, and laughed again.

Sara shook her head and laughed too. It felt good to laugh.

"I'm only messing with you. It would be a horrible idea to bring you there today. I'm going to try to find a way to explain why you entered her house. And I'll have to apologise to her."

Jonny nodded.

"Sounds like a good idea," he said, and smiled.

Sara sat down with the list of allotment owners. Wasn't it quite common for friends to buy allotments in the same area at the same time to be able to share their gardening interests and spend time there together? The problem was that the Klingström family didn't own an allotment, even if they were friends with the Ljung family. But maybe the Ljung family had other friends?

She realised she didn't know how David Ljung's parents had died. How old had they been?

She went to Jörgen's office to ask him and he looked them up on his computer. He didn't say a word while his fingers flew across the keyboard.

"They died ten years ago on the same day. It must have been an accident. I'll see what I can find. At least I can see here that they were almost fifty when they died," he said quickly, and kept staring at the screen.

"Here," he said, and looked up at Sara.

"Yes?"

"They died in a car accident close to Åre. It was winter. They were on a ski trip, and apparently they were travelling together with a couple of other cars."

"Does it say who the people in the other cars were?"

"No, but I can find out."

"Please do," Sara ordered before she left his office.

100

Sara rang the doorbell. It was quiet and the house looked dark.

"Maybe she's at uni," Rita said. "She's studying to become a journalist, you know."

"Yes, maybe you're right. Do you want to go there?"

Rita nodded, and just as they were about to leave the house, Camilla opened the door dressed in a robe. Her makeup was smeared across her face.

"What do you want now?"

"We need to talk to you," Sara said. "And I want to apologise for yesterday. My colleague thought something had happened to you as the lights were on and the door was open."

"Yes, he seemed quite nervous," Camilla said. "Maybe not the best outfit to wear when you find a police officer in your kitchen. I hope he survived."

"He sure did," Sara answered.

Camilla opened the door a bit wider and invited them inside. It was chilly outside and Sara shivered as they entered the house.

"I want to ask you, do you know about David Ljung's allotment?"

"Yes, I do. But he was never there."

"Do you know if David had any family friends with allotments in the same area?"

"Yes, but I don't know their names. I'm pretty sure David told me about some friends who owned an allotment there. I think they were friends of both his and Tobias's family."

"I thought you didn't know Tobias. How do you know this?"

"When David told me his parents were dead, he also told me they used to go skiing with a group of friends once a year. He mentioned a family, but I really can't remember their name. The year David's parents died, he had stayed home. He was twenty and had his own life to live. He also mentioned something about these allotments, although I'm not sure why. He said they had bought them together with that family."

"Can you tell us anything more about this family?"

"I think they had young children. That's about all I know."

"Okay, I'm sure we can find out who they are. As you understand, we need to know as much as possible about David."

Camilla excused herself and told Rita and Sara that she needed to go clean up a little.

Rita started looking through the kitchen drawers for Camilla's phone.

"I don't think you'll find it there," Sara said. "I don't think she'd be stupid enough to keep it where someone could find it. Especially not after the visit she had last night."

"You're probably right."

Camilla came back to the kitchen, looking a bit more put together.

"Where were you on the night David was murdered?" Sara asked.

Camilla gave Sara a curious look.

"Do you have a reason to ask me that?"

"Yes," Sara said without offering an explanation.

"I was at my mum's house. She asked me to spend the night, so I did. Please, feel free to check with her."

"Thanks," Sara said when Camilla gave her a note with her mother's name and phone number.

"Do you think you could help us find the family who owns an allotment close to David's?"

"No, I don't think so. I don't know them and can't remember their surname."

"But if I showed you a list of names, do you think you would recognise it?"

"Well, I guess I could try. I have to get ready for school now though."

"Yes, we'll leave," Sara said. "But hey, by the way . . . Do you own more than one phone?"

Camilla raised her eyebrows.

"No, why would I? I only have this one," she said, and picked up a mobile phone from the pocket of her robe.

"What phone company are you with?" Rita asked.

"Telenor. Why?"

"And what's your number?"

"The same as last time you asked," Camilla said, and crossed her arms in front of her.

"Oh, okay. Can I have a look at the phone?" Rita insisted.

"Sure." Camilla unlocked her phone and handed it over to Rita.

101

Do you think you can find out who Ljung's family friends at the allotment are?"

Sara had gone straight to Jörgen's office when she and Rita returned to the station.

"I can try, but it won't be easy. Maybe we can ask the neighbours on Professorsgatan? They used to live there, right? David inherited the house."

"Good idea, you do that," Sara said.

She sat down in the break room with a cup of coffee and her computer on the table in front of her. But she couldn't focus. She thought about Anders. She thought about the hands that reminded her of her stepfather's and how Anders had described what he liked most about her. She tried her hardest, but she couldn't stop thinking about him.

She got up and brought the coffee and the computer to her office. She spilt coffee on the floor, but she didn't care.

Once she had put everything down on her desk, she picked up her mobile phone and called Camilla Brink's mother. And yes, Camilla had been with her the night David was murdered. Camilla's mother was an open book and the phone call felt bizarre. Camilla's mother knew all about her daughter's sexual preferences. She told Sara she wasn't a fan of it but that she had accepted it as she knew there was nothing she could do to change it.

"Shit!" Sara exclaimed once they hung up.

She called her own mother instead and cried a bit.

"Dear child," her mother said, "you need to let go of the past and move on. Anders is an amazing man—a man you want to be with."

"Yes, I know. I don't know why I'm acting like this. After all these years."

"Let me put it this way instead," her mother continued. "You're the only one who can decide how you want things to be. But remember that love is fragile. It can only take so much. Anyway, I don't have time to talk anymore, I'm playing bridge soon. Bye." Sara's mother ended the call without even giving Sara a chance to say goodbye.

Ove Ovesson stepped into the room and walked up to her.

"Oh my, are you sad? Has something happened?"

Sara looked at him and tried to look as stable as possible.

"Don't worry, I'm just a bit sensitive. I guess I've been working too much."

Ove nodded and gave her a serious look. He didn't believe her. She could tell. But he was too nice to pressure her. She was grateful. He slipped right back into his professional persona.

"So, this is very strange, but the DNA on the cup Jonny brought in doesn't match the DNA on the note from the rose. This is from a man."

"What? Then we'll have to bring in Camilla Brink for a DNA test after all. Immediately," Sara said, and called Baum. Her mind raced while she waited for Baum to pick up. Whose DNA could it be? They knew it wasn't David Ljung's. So, whose was it? And did it still mean that Camilla could be the same person as Candy and therefore—the murderer?

102

"Do I look like a killer?" Camilla scoffed.

"Killers can look a lot of ways," Torsten said without even raising his eyebrows.

"I guess, but I didn't kill David or Tobias," she said with a frown. "Why would I do something like that?"

"I don't know. That's what I want us to figure out, you and I."

"Jesus, this is ridiculous. I didn't like David, but if I had a habit of murdering everyone I didn't like, there would be a lot of victims here," Camilla said, and opened her mouth slightly.

It made her look slightly smug.

"I need a DNA sample from you," Torsten said. "It's quick and won't hurt."

"Go ahead," she said, staring at him.

She opened her mouth wider and Torsten rubbed a swab along the inside of her cheeks. When he removed the swab, Camilla snapped her mouth shut.

"Both you and your mum claim that you were at her place the night David was murdered. But wasn't she asleep?"

"Yes, of course she was asleep."

"So, if you had sneaked out, she wouldn't have known?"

"Of course not. My question is still: Why would I have done that?"

Torsten didn't answer her.

"Have you been living in David's house since his death?"

"No, I haven't been living there. I've been there a couple of times. I guess my plan was to clean up a bit. And get my stuff together. But I never really got to it."

"Have you been eating there? And had coffee or tea?"

"I've had some coffee, but I haven't eaten there. It felt too strange."

"But you've had sex there?"

It looked like the question had rattled Camilla, although Torsten thought she should have been ready for it considering the situation with Jonny.

"Well, yes . . ."

"Who was with you when my colleague Jonny went into the house?"

"It was one of my BDSM friends," she answered, and focused her eyes on something behind Torsten.

"I asked you who it was. Would you please answer the question?"

"It was a guy named James," she finally said. "James Elliot."

"How can I reach him?"

"I can give you his phone number," she said.

"Thanks, that would be great."

She wrote down a number in Torsten's notebook.

"How come the door was unlocked and open that night?"

"I don't know. I usually close the door and lock it. But I guess I must have forgotten."

"Rough interview," Torsten said after telling Sara about it during a break.

"I'm not so sure about this," Sara said. "Did you send her DNA to the lab?"

"Yep, I did it right away."

"Will you call James Elliot?"

"Right away," Torsten said. "We don't actually know if it's Camilla's DNA on that note. I'll make sure to ask if James had a cup of coffee too."

"Yes, good idea," Sara said.

Torsten called James Elliot, who confirmed he had been in the house on Professorsgatan.

"But something felt strange inside that house," James Elliot added, although Torsten hadn't asked him about it. "It made me feel uneasy. I didn't see anyone or hear anything. It was just a feeling."

"Can you describe the feeling?"

"As if someone was watching us," the young man said.

"Can you tell me what you mean?"

"Well, I can't describe it better than that. It was just a feeling I had."

"Did you mention it to Camilla?"

"No, I assumed it was all in my head. To be honest, I didn't want to seem paranoid."

"Did you have coffee or tea with Camilla?"

"I had a cup of coffee. After we had sex," James Elliot answered. Torsten detected both nonchalance and pride in the young man's voice. Or maybe he was only imagining it.

Torsten ended the call and walked back into the room where Camilla Brink was waiting for him.

"James Elliot confirms being with you in the house. But he also told me he felt watched while you were there. Why is that, do you think?"

"No idea, I didn't feel anything like that."

Camilla's gaze wandered across the room and she avoided looking directly at Torsten.

Torsten called Åke Baum, who didn't want to place Camilla Brink under arrest.

"We have nothing to go on here. We can't arrest her for drinking coffee or having sex."

Torsten agreed.

Before he let Camilla go, he scheduled a meeting for her to see Jörgen for another interview the morning after.

103

Jörgen sat across the table from Camilla in an interrogation room. They were going through the list of allotment owners together. She shook her head.

"These names are all so common. It could be any of them."

She stretched out like a cat. Jörgen looked at her without saying anything.

"Do you think the people we're looking for could be on this list though?" he asked once she had stopped stretching.

"When I think about it, I think it was, in fact, one of those super-common Swedish names. Svensson, Eriksson, Johansson. Something like that."

It wasn't very helpful, but Jörgen scratched the names that didn't end in "son" from the list. He didn't use ink, just to be safe. He normally used his computer for everything but for once, he was working with a list on an actual sheet of paper.

He planned to get in touch with everyone on the list whose surname ended in "son." Maybe one of them would know the murder victims' families.

When he dropped Camilla off in reception, he couldn't help feeling a bit sorry for her. He went back to his office to get to work on the list.

Family after family let him down.

"Eriksson," a woman answered.

Jörgen explained why he was calling and the woman listened.

"Yes, we were friends of David Ljung's parents. We studied together back at uni. They died in a traffic accident years ago—probably ten years ago by now. We were going skiing. It was incredibly sad. I'll never forget it." It sounded as if the woman was about to start crying.

"Did you know their son too?"

"Yes, but we lost contact with him as he stopped coming on the trips. He was quite a lot older than our children."

"Can we come and see you?"

"Yes, sure. But why?"

"We're looking into a death and need to straighten a couple of things out."

The woman gasped before she continued the conversation.

"Tobias, you mean?"

"Yes, that's right. Did you know him too?"

"Yes, absolutely. His parents were part of our group. But they normally didn't come on the ski trips. Tobias was also older than our children. And I know he was murdered. Does this have something to do with that?"

Jörgen wasn't sure how to answer the woman's questions, but decided it was probably best not to say too much over the phone.

"It's better if we talk when I can see you," Jörgen said. "Could we come right away?"

The woman snivelled.

"We're not home. We're helping my old parents move and it'll take all night. Could you come tomorrow morning? I can stay home from work," she said.

"That'll be fine," Jörgen told her.

"And I haven't even called Anna and Karl. I just don't know what to say," the woman sobbed.

"Totally understandable," Jörgen said, and didn't know what else to tell her. "Would 10 a.m. work for you?"

"That's fine. I'll see you then."

104

It was dark outside the police station and Sara was planning to go home. There wasn't much more they could do until the result from Camilla's DNA test came back. She had been analysing the case file for hours but couldn't get anywhere. Maybe they would get some clarity in the morning when Jörgen had talked to the allotment owner who knew both victims' families.

She put on her warm coat, grabbed her purse, and started walking towards the exit when her phone rang.

"Chief Inspector Sara Vallén speaking."

"Hi, my name is Elin Eriksson and I would like to talk to you," a woman said anxiously at the other end of the line.

"Sure, about what?"

"About Tobias Klingström."

"Can we meet right away?" Sara asked quickly. She didn't want to miss the opportunity.

"Yes, that's what I was hoping."

"Do you want to come to the station or do you want me to come to you?"

"It would be great if you could come to me."

Elin gave Sara her address, and she rushed off. It wasn't far to cycle.

The young woman opened the door and stared at Sara with a nervous look in her blue eyes.

They sat down on the sofa and Elin started talking about how she had come to suspect that Tobias was up to something strange.

"I'm not sure what it was, but I'm starting to realise he wasn't as perfect and amazing as everyone thought." She looked at Sara and clenched her jaws. "I think it had something to do with sex—masochistic sex."

Sara tried to help the young woman keep calm by sitting completely still with her hands resting on her lap. This was a trick that normally worked, although it didn't feel natural to her at all.

"How do you know this?" Sara asked.

"Someone told me," Elin said, and looked down. She obviously didn't want to tell Sara who had told her.

Sara moved on with the conversation.

"What do you mean when you say 'masochistic sex'?"

"No, actually. My mistake, I mean sadistic sex. More violent."

"And what did this sadistic sex entail?"

"What do you mean?"

"How do you know for sure it was sadistic sex?"

"Oh, I see what you mean . . . Well, as I understand it, it included putting someone in a cage and defecating on them. Something like that. I've never heard about anything like it before."

"No, that's understandable. It's not very common. When someone experiences sexual arousal and pleasure from faeces, it's called scat sex— or coprophilia," Sara explained to Elin.

The confident and determined look in the young woman's eyes was replaced by disgust.

"Gross," she exclaimed.

"Yes, a lot of people might agree with you there. But if everyone involved is into it, I guess it's their choice. However, the moment someone doesn't take part in this voluntarily, it's assault," Sara continued.

"I must say I have a hard time imagining any girls being into this voluntarily," the young woman said sharply.

For a second, Sara didn't know what to say.

"You're probably right," she said, finally, and decided to leave it for now. "How come you know about this?"

"Because I know people. And because Samira Khan is my best friend ever," she mumbled. "And I thought she'd met a great guy . . . But she hadn't. And now he's dead."

"Did you know Tobias?"

"Sure, our parents are close friends. But he's quite a lot . . . well . . . he *was* quite a lot older than me and my brother, so we didn't really spend a lot of time together as kids—or later in life. But he came to a party at my house once. That's where Samira met him."

"Did he pressure Samira into this kind of sex?"

"No way. She would never have agreed to it. He loved her. I know he did. She told me. But I've understood he was into these things when she wasn't around. And I've found out that he caused a girl to kill herself."

Sara flinched. *So it was true.*

"He and another guy, who I also know. My parents knew his parents too. But they're dead now. They died in a car crash ten years ago. I was there."

Sara flinched again.

"What's his name?" Sara said as if he were still alive.

"David Ljung," Elin said without hesitating.

"Who told you this? It would really help if you told me."

"I can't tell you."

Very defensive, Sara thought.

"Do you know a woman called Camilla? She's a bit older than you are."

Elin shook her head.

"Have you ever heard the name Candy?"

It was hard to miss Elin's reaction. Elin pressed her lips together as if she was scared of opening her mouth.

"No, I haven't," she said, and clenched her jaws.

Sara thought about it for a while and decided not to push Elin. She stood up.

"Well, thanks for calling me. It was great that you decided to tell me this."

Elin stayed on the sofa as Sara made her way towards the front door. Sara reflected on the contrast between the small flat and the gigantic house where David Ljung had lived. And she thought about Camilla—or was it Candy?

On her way home, Sara called Rita and told her about her meeting with Elin. They both wanted to know if Elin knew Camilla, or Candy, and how she would have known about Tobias's sexual preferences otherwise.

When Sara got home, she threw herself onto the bed. She didn't even brush her teeth. As soon as she had put her head on the pillow, she felt herself drift off to sleep. Dreamless sleep. The last thing she thought before she passed out was that she hoped for a good night's rest.

105

Samira paced back and forth. She made up her mind and picked up her phone. It had been given back to her after she promised not to call or text anyone—or use social media. She had sworn on an imaginary Quran.

Now here she was, dialling the number she knew so well. She knew her mother would be alone as it was her father's regular poker night.

Her mother picked up on the fifth ring.

"Hi, Mum," Samira said in Urdu.

She heard a gasp.

"Oh, hello my darling."

"I want to come home, but I've been told I can't as Dad will send me to Pakistan if I do. Mum, I don't want to marry some old Pakistani man. I want to become a doctor and I want to pick my future husband on my own."

Samira spoke quickly and her mother didn't interrupt.

"I'm trying to find a solution," she said when Samira had finished talking.

"They tell me there are no solutions," Samira said, and felt tears welling up in her eyes. She wanted to be an adult. She didn't want to cry and fought it as best she could. And she managed to push the tears away.

"I know. But Aidah is helping me. She's going to guide me. Guide us. I don't want to lose my only child."

"I don't want to lose you. Or Dad. Do you think someone could talk some sense into him?"

"I don't know. I don't think so. But Aidah is telling me she'll look into our options. She needs to do some sort of assessment first. That's what she said."

"I have to go. Promise you won't say anything to Dad. Promise."

"I promise," her mother said.

And Samira trusted her.

106

Jörgen called Sara to tell her he was about to go see Margareta Eriksson. "Her family owns one of the allotments close to where Tobias's body was found. She told me she and her husband have been friends with both Tobias's and David's parents for years."

"Eriksson . . . How come you decided to go see them?" Sara asked eagerly.

"I called every single person on the list with a surname ending in 'son' until I found a family with connections to both our victims."

"Do you want to go on your own, or . . . ?"

Sara wasn't sure if it was a great idea for Jörgen to conduct the interview.

"I normally don't question people, but as I'm the one who called her, I think it's a good idea if I do it this time."

Sara agreed. She called Ove Ovesson to check if he had Camilla's DNA test results.

"Yep, it's Camilla's DNA on the note from the rose. You'd better ask her about that."

"Woo-hoo," Sara said without much enthusiasm.

"Yep, that's the way the cookie crumbles," Ove said, and sounded as positive as always. There were no good or bad results if you asked him. The only thing that mattered was that there *were* results at all. In many ways, Sara could identify with his approach.

She called Baum, who sounded happy about the news.

"But who does the DNA on the cup belong to, then?"

Sara had to admit she didn't know yet. But they would bring James Elliot in to see if it was his.

Baum sighed but sounded pretty satisfied with the progress.

Sara walked into the conference room and waited for the rest of the team, except for Jörgen.

"It's pretty cool, actually," she said when Jonny, Torsten, and Rita entered the room.

"What is?" Rita wanted to know.

"Well, yesterday I talked to a girl called Elin Eriksson. She's Samira's best friend. Without giving away who told her about it, she told me Tobias Klingström and David Ljung had subjected a young girl to a perverted form of BDSM. The girl later killed herself. She must be talking about Jannice Karlsson. Today, I found out that Jörgen has found an allotment owner with ties to both Tobias and David. Elin's parents."

Sara took a break.

Jonny sat down on a chair. Torsten and Rita stood completely still without knowing what to say.

"Now, all we have to do is find out who the murderer is. Let's start with checking if it's James Elliot's DNA on that cup."

"Camilla must've known all along that Elliot drank from the cup," Jonny exclaimed. "He told us so himself."

"Yes, maybe she knows. Or maybe it slipped her mind. Either way, James Elliot has no prior record and no relevant connections according to Jörgen. But he did say something strange. He said he felt watched when he was in the house. Could someone else have been there?"

"Hmm," Jonny muttered.

"By the way," Sara said, turning abruptly towards Torsten. "What's James Elliot's phone number?"

"I don't remember, but I can look it up. Why?"

"I just realised we still have a phone number with no known sender. That text message Jonny received about David Ljung's holiday . . ."

They all gasped.

"Wow, I forgot about that," Torsten exclaimed with eyes as big as saucers.

"We have to look it up right away. And we need to bring in James Elliot. Now. What are we waiting for?" Sara stared at them.

Rita ran to her office to get her laptop and was back again in the blink of an eye. She started her computer and tried to log in to the database.

"What the hell?" she shouted. "The system is down."

Sara sat next to her and rebooted the computer. When it started up again, everything seemed to work as it should.

"Here," Rita said after calming down. "This is James Elliot's phone number. *This* is Candy's phone number, and here is the number Jonny received a message from. All numbers belong to different prepaid phone cards."

"Okay, but let's bring James in anyway. We need his DNA. And we need to bring Camilla in to explain the rose," Sara said, and stood up.

She gave orders to bring Camilla in for questioning right away as she was convinced Baum would support her decision. Then she called the prosecutor and, just as she thought, he gave her the go-ahead.

"Torsten, I need you to call Elliot and ask him to come to the station immediately."

Torsten left the room but returned a moment later.

"The number is not in use," he said, and shrugged his shoulders. "Shit, I can't believe I didn't think about this when I talked to him earlier and asked him if he'd had coffee at the house and all."

"Not in use?" Sara couldn't believe it. "It has to mean something. Who is this James Elliot? Does anybody know?"

"I called him just to check an alibi. Jörgen told me there wasn't anything more to it."

"Could someone else have been using this name without Camilla knowing about it?"

"I have no idea. I trusted Jörgen."

"Come on now, let's not blame each other. Look up James Elliot's address and go there immediately, Torsten. We have to at least find out if this guy is who he says he is."

Torsten left without a word to get the address.

Sara's phone rang. It was one of her colleagues who called to tell her that Camilla had been brought in.

"I'll talk to her," Rita said decisively, and went to question her.

107

Jörgen stepped into the conference room and brought some fresh autumn air in with him. Sara waited while he took off his coat and hat and threw them on a chair. Then he walked up to her.

"Margareta Eriksson told me she and her husband, Egon, are very close with the Klingströms. And that they were close with David Ljung's parents when they were alive."

Jörgen looked at the other two as if he was examining them. Studying them. As always, Sara was amused by his way of hunching his back, bending his neck and pushing his nose forward. There was something highly unusual about the way he carried himself.

"They own an allotment close to the cottage where Tobias was found. But they closed it down for the season weeks ago. They've owned it for a long time and told me they've lost interest in it."

Jörgen paused for a couple of breaths and Sara pushed him impatiently.

"Come on," she said.

"They have two children. A girl named Elin. She's in law school. And then a boy named Martin. He goes to med school together with Samira. Can you believe it? Where are Torsten and Rita, by the way?" he added when he realised they weren't there.

"Gone," Sara said without further explanation.

"Wow, great detective work," Jonny said sarcastically. "And what does this new information bring to the table?"

Jörgen frowned.

"At least now we know there are people connected to Tobias in the area. And to David."

"But David wasn't murdered there," Jonny said.

"No, but he *did* own an allotment there." Jörgen frowned again.

"Yes, these are all great observations," Sara interjected. "The connections you're mentioning are super relevant."

"Yep," Jörgen said, and sat down.

Sara took charge of the conversation again.

"So, Tobias knows Samira, Samira knows Elin, and Tobias knows David. Tobias, David, and Elin know each other and Elin's parents know both Tobias and David. And they are all connected to the allotment gardens somehow. But what's the motive behind these murders? And what does it have to do with Camilla—and Candy?"

Sara gave her colleagues a stern look.

"Think," she ordered them. "Think hard." She turned towards the whiteboard.

"Elin and Samira are best friends. Samira is Tobias's girlfriend. Tobias is friends with David and, together, they've subjected a young, self-harming girl to violent and sadistic sexual acts. David has a relationship with Camilla, who actually hates him. She's into BDSM but always respects the boundaries. David and Tobias are into BDSM too, but Tobias isn't having that kind of sex with Samira," Sara went on while drawing new lines between the names on the whiteboard.

"I don't believe for a second that Candy is the same person as Camilla," Jonny said.

"So, who is Candy?" Jörgen wanted to know.

"Who told Elin about Tobias's and David's sexual preferences?"

"Who would know—" Jonny interrupted himself and sneezed into the crook of his arm. "Sorry, dust . . . Who would know about the allotments and the fact that the Eriksson family's cottage had been closed for the winter?"

Jörgen turned to Sara.

"Could Camilla have told Elin?"

"Elin doesn't know Camilla. She didn't react at all when I mentioned her. However, I thought I saw a reaction when I mentioned the name Candy. But I could've imagined it."

Sara asked her team to take a break and go to their separate offices to think. She also asked them to come back and write their ideas on the whiteboard if they came up with anything.

She could feel they were close. But how close?

108

Camilla sat on a chair in the sterile interrogation room. Rita thought she looked proud and determined. *This is going to be a power struggle,* she thought.

"What now?"

"We need to clarify a couple of things," Rita said without giving away what she was thinking.

"Oh, what things?"

"We got the result from your DNA test. Your DNA matches the DNA found on a rose by a grave," Rita said, and waited for a reaction.

"What? What note?"

"A card attached to a flower. Does it ring a bell?"

"And what did the note say?"

"I thought you could tell me," Rita said with a neutral expression on her face.

"Well, I have no idea. Are you telling me I attached a card to a rose and placed it by a grave? I guess if I did, it would have been for David's grave. But I didn't."

"Did you ever write one of those little cards though?"

Camilla looked genuinely confused. She raised her eyebrows and opened her mouth slightly.

"Did you know a girl called Jannice?" Rita tried a different angle in an attempt to rattle the woman on the other side of the table.

Once again, Camilla raised her eyebrows. But this time she didn't look confused.

"No, I didn't know her. But I know who she was," she said.

Rita noticed that Camilla's face looked slightly tense, although her gaze stayed steady.

"How?"

"I knew people who knew her. James Elliot, for example."

"James Elliot knew her?" Rita couldn't hide how surprised she was.

"Yes, and now I remember something. When I met him for the first time, he asked me to help him write a note for a rose he was leaving by her grave. He said his handwriting was terrible. So I helped him." Camilla looked right at Rita.

"What did you write?"

"You're my one true love," she said hesitantly, "or something like that."

Bingo, Rita thought. *Here we go!*

"Thanks. I'm afraid I'll have to ask you to wait here for a moment. I'll be right back."

Rita stood up so suddenly that she almost tipped over her chair. She ran out of the interrogation room and up the stairs.

109

Rita rushed into Sara's office.

"James Elliot," she gasped.

Sara stood up as a reaction to Rita's rushed behaviour.

"What about him?"

Rita took a deep breath and waved her hands in front of her.

"James Elliot is the one who left the rose by Jannice's grave," she panted. "Camilla wrote the note for him. Come on, Sara, react. James Elliot, let's get him in here."

"His phone is off. We think he's using an assumed identity. Torsten is checking his address as we speak."

"What? Are you serious?"

"Yes, I am. But fantastic news that Camilla admitted to writing the note. Go back to her and try to get her to give us a description of this James," Sara ordered.

"Sure thing," said Rita, who looked a bit deflated, and left the room.

Sara's phone rang.

"This is Torsten," a deep familiar voice said. "James Elliot isn't our guy. According to his relatives, he's been in the USA for weeks. He's a teacher at Lund University Hospital. He's been teaching there for thirty-five years. So I think it's fair to assume someone has been using his identity. Maybe a med student?"

"Maybe," Sara said. "Get back here and I'll tell you what we've just found out."

When Torsten returned to the station, she gathered everyone except for Rita, who was still questioning Camilla.

She told Torsten what they had just found out and then she told him about the progress Rita had made.

"So, Camilla also thinks James Elliot is James Elliot?" Torsten concluded.

"Yes, that seems to be the case."

"But who the hell *is* James Elliot? Candy? Not the same phone number but he could have more than one phone. One thing is for certain if you ask me. We need to keep focusing on the connections here," Torsten continued.

"Yes, we could very well be looking for someone within the victims' closest circle here," Jonny said, confirming what Torsten had already suggested.

"There is one more thing we need to do," Sara said.

"What?" Torsten and Jörgen said in unison.

"We need to talk to Ann-Britt Karlsson again. I think it's starting to look like Jannice wasn't in love with David at all, but with someone else. Maybe she knows something more? Maybe there is a mobile phone or something else in that flat that can give us more information?"

Jörgen stood with his arms crossed in front of his chest.

"Yes, like a photo for example," he suggested.

"Exactly. Let's wait until Rita is done with her interview. Then I'll take her with me and go over there." Sara placed her hands on her hips and turned to Jörgen with a confident look on her face. She smiled at him.

Shortly thereafter, Rita returned. She beamed.

"Done," she said.

"Wow, you guys sure are confident today," Torsten said, and raised his bushy eyebrows.

"I've got a description of James Elliot—who I understand isn't really James Elliot?"

"Right," Sara confirmed, and looked at Rita.

"A young man, probably about twenty-five years old. Blond, quite tall, blue eyes, thick hair. No glasses. Fit but still quite gangly."

"How did Camilla meet him?"

"She was introduced to him by someone she didn't know too well. Someone who called herself—listen to this—Candy!" Rita laughed. "It was a contact from the BDSM world."

"What the hell? Couldn't she have told us this earlier?" Sara exclaimed.

"I asked her the same thing, of course. She told me there is an unspoken rule within her circle that you're never supposed to share information like that with anyone. Also, she has no idea who this Candy really is. So, she didn't mention it. I asked her why she didn't react when we mentioned Candy in connection with David Ljung's death. She said she didn't say anything because she didn't think it was connected in any way. She thought it was all a coincidence."

"Not her smartest moment," Jonny said, and grimaced.

"No, maybe not. But now we know."

"Maybe we should go have a look in Ann-Britt Karlsson's flat, then," Sara said to Rita. "Let's see if we can find something relevant. A photo, maybe?" She smiled at Jörgen again.

"Not today," Rita said firmly. "I've got a date."

"What?" Jonny said, looking baffled.

"Yeah, what about it?"

"Oh, come on, I'm only messing with you."

Torsten grabbed Sara's arm.

"I'll go with you."

"We have to search David Ljung's home again together with forensics," Sara said, and assigned the task to Jonny. She had already got used to the idea of ending her shift without Rita, who had disappeared into her office.

110

"Hi, babe," Rita said, and surprised herself with how quickly she had adapted to being in love with a woman. She giggled.

"Hi there," Linda said, and sounded a bit confused. "What's up?"

"Nothing," Rita said as she drew a little circle on the floor with the tip of her shoe. *Like a child*, she thought.

"Well, I'm looking forward to seeing you soon," Linda said.

"Well, that's the thing." Rita spoke quickly. "I think we've stumbled upon an important lead."

"Oh, so our date is off?" Linda said, and Rita could hear how disappointed she sounded.

"No, not at all. I'm just calling to tell you I might be a bit late. There is a key under the flowerpot next to the door."

"Oh, that makes me so happy to hear. I thought I wouldn't get to see you."

Rita's heart skipped a beat. *Wow, this makes me feel so alive*, she thought.

"Of course we'll see each other. There is nothing else I'd rather do. But take the key and do whatever you want. My home is your home."

Linda giggled at the other end of the line.

"Wow, that sounded so feeble," Rita said, and scoffed at herself.

"No, not at all. It was sweet," Linda said, and made a kissing sound.

"That was also pretty weak," Rita said, and made a kissing sound back.

Linda giggled again.

* * *

Rita headed over to Sara's office, but she wasn't there.

"Sara," she shouted, and received an answer from the conference room.

"What are you doing?" Rita said when she stepped into the room and looked at the whiteboard. The names and lines on it had all been blurred out.

"I'm trying to figure out who James Elliot is."

Rita studied the whiteboard again.

"Yes, your latest changes have made it all *much* clearer," Rita said sarcastically, and pulled a face.

"Oh, come on," Sara said. "I can easily put it back as it was again. But I felt the need to erase a few things to get a new perspective."

"Did it help?"

"Yes and no."

"Come on now. Let's go to Professorsgatan and see what the forensics team can find for us," Rita said, and pulled gently at Sara's hair.

"I thought you were going on a date?"

"I cancelled it," Rita said, a half lie. "And I still think we should go to Professorsgatan before we talk to Ann-Britt Karlsson."

Sara aimed a playful punch at Rita, happy about the cancelled date.

111

Ove Ovesson met them in the hallway. The house looked abandoned and it looked like Camilla hadn't been there for some time.

The forensics team walked around in white suits, plastic gloves, and protective covers over their shoes.

Ove showed Sara and Rita into the kitchen and headed into a storage closet.

"Someone has been here," Ove said. "Someone has been hiding here among all the stuff. Do you know how I know that?"

"No," Sara said.

Rita shook her head.

"There is a shoe print here," he said, and pointed at a patch of grey dust with a clear sole impression in it. "And I can tell someone has pulled down the blanket that has obviously been used to protect the fabric of this old armchair. It's clear that someone has been sitting here."

"So, someone has been here. This is so strange. James Elliot, who isn't really James Elliot, said he felt he was being watched. But if James Elliot is the murderer *and* the guy Camilla Brink had sex with, why would he be hiding in here?" Sara felt a jolt of adrenaline rush through her body and broke into a sweat.

"Who are you talking about?" Ove Ovesson said, staring at her.

"Well, a guy who visited Camilla in the house," Sara said, and felt a strange need to protect Camilla's integrity. She wasn't sure why she felt that need. Not long ago, she had suspected her of being the murderer.

"And?"

"He told us he felt as if someone else was in the house. And he isn't really who he says he is, but another person entirely—someone who probably murdered David Ljung," Rita explained.

"I'm not sure I'm following you here," Ove said. "Anyway, we've also found some hair in here and a green leaf—probably from a rose stem. It was most likely stuck under a shoe."

"Oh shit," Sara said. "Is there any way of finding out what rose the leaf came from?"

"Well, not really. But I don't think you'll need to know what rose it came from. The hair we found will probably be enough."

"Oh, of course."

Sara blushed.

"And," Ove continued, "we've found a SIM card. Pay as you go."

He paused and waited for Sara's and Rita's reactions.

"Oh my God, could it be one of the SIM cards we've been looking for?"

"Yes, it could. We'll let you know as soon as we can."

"This is incredible. Now we just have to find this guy," Sara said before giving both Ove and Rita a hug.

"We're off to see Ann-Britt Karlsson now," Sara told Ove, "but we'll talk again soon."

As they left the house, Sara was so excited that she couldn't help but skip along the street. Rita laughed at her.

112

Ann-Britt Karlsson welcomed Sara and Rita without asking any questions. Her window was wide open. The flat was cold but smelled better than it did the last time they were there.

She switched on the kettle and offered them a cup of tea.

"It's better to drink tea in the evening," she said, and sounded slightly apologetic.

"Thanks. And yes, much better," Sara said.

"I'd love a cup." Rita nodded.

They sat down with their tea and once Ann-Britt Karlsson had closed the window, they started asking their questions.

"If Jannice had a boyfriend, would she have told you about him?" Rita asked as she warmed her fingers on the teacup.

"I don't know. She didn't say much to me. She spent most of her time in her room or in bed. She locked her door quite often."

"Did she ever mention someone who might have been close to her somehow?"

"When I think about it, she went for a lot of walks. Maybe she met with someone then. But didn't you guys take her computer?"

"It was empty. There was nothing on there. Maybe she didn't have any contacts?" Sara didn't sound convinced by her own suggestion.

"Yes, that's probably it. But I know she spoke to someone over the phone now and again," Ann-Britt Karlsson said hesitantly. "I don't have it though."

"In what way would you say Tobias Klingström approached Jannice?" Rita asked, and changed the subject.

"She didn't tell me much, but she called him gross and told me he wanted to sleep with her. I wasn't sure if she was telling the truth as she was always feeling so bad. But something must have happened to her, I'm sure. Because she started cutting herself more and more after seeing him. And she went missing now and again. I had no idea where she was. Sometimes when she returned, she was super happy . . ." Ann-Britt stopped talking and ran her hand across her face. "Maybe she was in love?" she continued, and hesitated for a second.

"Yes, maybe she was. Were there times when she came home and wasn't super happy?" Sara asked.

"Yes, sometimes she came home and seemed absolutely miserable. Angry at the same time as she felt . . . It's hard to explain. She felt small somehow. I wasn't allowed to touch her or be near her. She didn't want me to comfort her. She called me disgusting. I thought it was strange. And sometimes, she reeked. I know . . . This place isn't the cleanest and I've been a horrible mother, but still."

The woman in front of them looked small. *What she felt was probably the worst thing one could feel as a mother*, Sara thought. Ann-Britt's hand rested on the table and Sara placed her hand gently on top of it.

"I'm sure she was being used by that Tobias Klingström," Ann-Britt said, and it sounded as if she had just realised she might have been right all along.

"Wasn't that why you wrote to the social services director?" Sara asked.

The tension in the room was so thick one could almost cut it with a knife "Yes, but I wasn't sure."

"I understand. Do you know if your daughter had pictures anywhere?"

Ann-Britt stood up and walked over to a chest of drawers in the hallway, next to the kitchen. She pulled out one of the drawers and handed them an envelope. In the envelope, there was a mobile phone.

"This was Jannice's."

"Why did you tell us you didn't have it?" Rita said, and sounded slightly annoyed.

"I wanted something from her life to belong only to her. I'm sorry."

113

They all gathered around the mobile phone in Sara's crowded office. Jonny tried to lean over the others to get a better view and let out an irritated grunt.

"Let's connect the phone to a computer instead," Jörgen suggested. "Then I can use the projector to show you the pictures."

Sara nodded. He took the phone and left. Within half an hour, he returned and asked them all to join him in the conference room.

He started the projector, and soon they were watching a slideshow on the wall.

They carefully went through photo after photo. There were a lot of photos of Jannice. She had snapped selfie after selfie in different poses, just like most young people did nowadays. Then there were a bunch of photos of the cuts and scars that were covering her arms. And a photo of a cut on her face followed by a scar in the same place.

Suddenly, there was a photo of Jannice and a young man, who was kissing the scar on her face with a smile on his lips. Jannice had a different look in her eyes. She looked happy. Then there was a picture of only him. His hair was long and blonde and tied back in a ponytail. His smile showed a row of perfect white teeth. His eyes were full of joy. Confident eyes. Judging by his clothes and general appearance, it looked like he was quite wealthy. The photo was old. Taken two years ago. The man in the photo was probably nineteen or twenty, but it was hard to say.

A gasp spread through the conference room.

"James Elliot," the team said in unison, and everyone started squirming in their seats.

"Should we talk to Camilla Brink?" Jörgen asked, and broke the silence.

"Absolutely." Sara raised her palm to her forehead and tapped it. There was a thought in there that refused to come to the surface. But then she remembered her conversation with Elin.

"Maybe I have another solution," Sara said.

"What solution?" Jörgen asked, and gave Sara a curious look.

"I'm thinking about Samira's friend, Elin Eriksson. Her parents own an allotment close to David Ljung's allotment. She grew up in Lund and, as we all know by now, people who grew up in Lund are often known to each other. I want to show her this photo. We don't know how old this man is here, but I'm guessing he's in his twenties. Maybe she'll recognise him. She's a student. We can't know for sure, but doesn't this guy look like a university student?" She turned to her team. "Am I being judgemental now?"

"Yes, very." Rita laughed in the middle of the serious situation.

"Maybe I am, but it's worth a try. If he was nineteen in this photo, he should be twenty-one by now. Elin is twenty-three, which means she could have gone to the same school as him. If he's also from Lund, that is. It's fair to assume he might be."

"Sounds like a good plan. At least better than no plan at all," Torsten said. "If you don't mind, I would like to leave as soon as possible though. Veronica is waiting for me."

"I understand, but I'm sure she's used to it," Sara said, and put a hand on Torsten's shoulder.

"Yes, of course. She's used to a father who's never there but always busy solving murders. But things are different now and have been ever since she moved to London. I don't want her to sit around and wait for me now that she's finally here."

"You can go home," Sara said, feeling generous. "I'll call you if I need you. Okay?"

"Thanks, that's nice of you," Torsten said. Then he took her hand from his shoulder and kissed it. He smiled professionally and stood up.

Before he left the room, he turned around and blew a kiss at his colleagues. Sara smiled when she heard him whistling as he walked through the corridor.

Not long after, Ove joined them in the conference room.

Sara and Rita circled him like vultures while Jonny and Jörgen stayed seated.

"The SIM card belongs to Candy," he said after a while.

"No way!" Sara exclaimed, and jumped up and down.

"Yes, it's true."

"Hurrah! Another step in the right direction. So this is the person who lured David into the basement. And it's starting to look like it's the same person who claims to be James Elliot, and the one who murdered Tobias Klingström."

Jonny gave a hollow laugh.

"I'll have a look at all the data," Jörgen said, and left the room.

Sara called Camilla Brink, who didn't pick up. *Shit. Has she skipped town?* Sara thought. She had a headache but forced herself to keep moving. She called Elin Eriksson. Success. Elin promised to come to the station right away.

"I'll ask my dad to drive me."

"That would be great," Sara said, and let out a relieved sigh.

It would have been a disaster if she hadn't been able to get a hold of her either.

114

Elin sat in one of the interrogation rooms. It was late and Sara had asked Elin's father to remain in the waiting room. He had looked very worried. Sara had done her best to keep him calm by telling him that she only wanted to show Elin a couple of photos, and that his daughter hadn't done anything wrong.

"I want to show you a photo," Sara said. "As you're raised here in Lund, I assume you know a lot of people here."

"I'm not sure I know that many people, but I suppose I'd recognise quite a few."

Sara put a photo down on the table.

Elin stood up. She opened her eyes wide and started to tremble. She pointed at the photo and gasped.

"Why are you showing me this photo?" she panted.

"We need to find this man," Sara explained with a surprised expression on her face. So Elin did recognise him. But why the violent reaction?

"Yes, but why?"

"I can't tell you any details, but we believe he has some important information to share with us."

Sara studied the girl closely. She was obviously upset by the photo.

"That's . . ."

Sara gave her an encouraging nod.

"That's my brother. His name is Martin."

Elin sat down again.

"Your brother?"

"Yes, my brother."

How the hell could we have missed this? Sara thought. She knew she had to gather herself and focus, so she took a deep breath to regain control of her heart rate, which was going through the roof.

"Thank you. You can go home now," she said, and tried to sound as friendly as possible.

Elin stood up again, and Sara walked her out to her father to let them both out of the station. The father shot Sara a murderous look when he saw the expression on his daughter's face.

Sara called Åke Baum, who was expecting her call.

"We need to bring in Martin Eriksson right away. Like, right now. It's been confirmed that he was Jannice Karlsson's boyfriend, and as Camilla Brink's description matches the appearance of this young man, we can also confirm he's the one who calls himself James Elliot."

"In that case, I'm issuing a warrant for Martin Eriksson's arrest. You have my go-ahead to proceed."

115

His phone vibrated in his pocket. He ignored it. He needed to go to the bathroom. The house was silent and he made his way to the main hallway and into the enormous bathroom to the right.

On his way out again, he picked up his phone to read the message. He felt cold.

What have you done? Why are the police looking for you?

He deleted the message and took a deep breath to calm down. He walked into the big bedroom. It was cool and dark in there. He lay down on the bed and fell asleep.

She came to him in his dream. She came to him with a sunny smile on her lips and beautiful eyes full of joy.

"I love you," she said. "Come to me. It'll be amazing, James."

He woke up, drenched in sweat. *James*, he thought. *I'm not James. I'm me. Come back.*

116

Sara, Rita, and Jonny stood outside the door to Martin Eriksson's student residence. Two uniformed officers had joined them as well. Sara rang the doorbell.

A skinny young man opened the door and asked them what they wanted.

"We need to talk to Martin Eriksson; we've been told he lives here," Sara said, keeping her tone as friendly as possible.

"Why?"

"We just need to talk to him," Sara replied, doing her best not to sound frustrated.

"Okay, but it's been two days since the last time I saw him. So I can't help you," the young man said, and stared at them.

"Well, we still want to come in for a while to take a look at his room," Sara said.

The others stayed silent.

"Why?"

"Enough with the questions," Jonny said. "Let us in."

"What did he do?"

"Enough with the questions," Jonny repeated.

The young man reluctantly opened the door wider to let them in. The door to Martin's room was locked, but Sara ordered one of the uniformed officers to break it open.

The room looked like a typical dorm room. Sparse. There was a computer on a desk. Sara nodded to the uniformed officers, and one of them picked it up as the other asked the guy who had let them in to leave.

"Well, he's not in here," Sara said, stating the obvious. "But . . . where is he?"

Jonny shook his head.

Sara looked at Rita and saw that she had just had a lightbulb moment.

"In the house on Professorsgatan," Rita said. "That's where he is."

"Shit," Jonny said, "of course he is."

They left the uniformed officers to search the room and rushed out.

They jumped into the car and Rita took off with a flying start.

They parked the car on a parallel street to Professorsgatan to avoid being seen. Then they made their way as discreetly as possible along the hedges until they reached David Ljung's home. It was dark inside the house.

Sara waved to the others to follow her as she walked through the gate. Rita closed it behind her, careful not to make a noise.

"We have to check for exit routes," Sara said to her colleagues. "Jonny, check the back."

"Shouldn't we call for backup?" Rita whispered.

"There's no time," Sara answered.

Jonny returned.

"There's a deck on the back."

"I need you to keep an eye on it," Sara said, and pointed to the back of the house.

Jonny made his way back to the deck while Sara and Rita sneaked up the stairs.

Rita pulled out the crowbar she had brought with her from the car. Now they needed to move quickly. They didn't want to give him a chance to react. Sara nodded to Rita, who wrenched the door open even quicker than Sara thought possible. In the dark, Sara saw a smile on Rita's lips.

Sara could hear her own heartbeat. She wondered if her colleagues could hear it too. Once the door flew open, they rushed into the house.

Rita switched on the lights in the hallway and the light blinded Sara. Suddenly, she heard a noise from one of the rooms. The next thing she knew, a man rushed out towards her. Sara just had time to think *That must be Martin Eriksson*, before he punched her right in the face. She fell backwards and landed on the floor. Rita shouted at Jonny, who ran after the swift youth.

Sara sat up.

She felt dizzy but managed to stand up and make her way to the hallway.

On the path leading up to the front door, Jonny straddled the man who they all assumed was Martin Eriksson.

Sara grabbed her phone and called the operations centre.

"We need a car at Professorsgatan," she said. "We've made an arrest."

Sara's nose hurt like hell on the way back to the police station. She was sitting in the back next to Martin Eriksson.

"I'm a pragmatic person," he said suddenly.

"Yes," she answered.

He didn't say anything else.

117

Torsten sat across the table from Martin Eriksson. He studied the man carefully and thought about what a shame it was for someone as young as him to ruin his own life the way he had. A brilliant future washed down the drain.

Torsten started the video camera and began the interrogation by stating the name of the interviewee, as well as the date and time for the interview. Then he stated his own name and title.

"Could you tell me how you got to know Jannice Karlsson?"

Martin seemed to realise that it was an order rather than a question.

"I was at the Lund University Hospital for a visit with school when I met her. I bumped into her in the waiting room. I saw her and thought she looked cute. And lonely. We were there to interview people about why they had come to the emergency room. She agreed to be interviewed. She liked me too. And we started seeing each other. She told me a lot about herself. It was horrible, hearing what she was going through."

"I understand," Torsten said. He felt for the young man. There was something very likeable about him and he seemed empathetic.

"And how did your relationship develop?"

"We fell in love. I think I can say I loved her."

Torsten gave him an encouraging nod.

"I found out she was receiving help from social services and that she had been assigned a case handler there—someone who was responsible for children's and youths' health plans. And she told me the fucking guy was using her. She was hurting herself and was very fragile. She was a young girl who couldn't put up a fair fight. It devastated me."

"And what did this social worker do?"

"I know her mother reported him and after that, he relocated to Hörby. But I know he kept putting her through . . . kept using her."

"In what way did he use her?"

"He put her through loads of disgusting shit. He put her in a cage and pissed on her. He made her lick up his urine. He tied her up and forced her to wear a mask. He dressed himself in leather and wore a mask. Then he raped her, over and over. I don't have it in me to say much more about this, but she told me a lot more. And still, he was allowed to keep his job at the social services office and he got to be the guy responsible for the well-being of children and young people every day. It's fucked up."

"Unfortunately, I need to ask you to give me more details," Torsten said, although the last thing he wanted was to force the man in front of him to tell him more about how Jannice had been abused. But he had to. There was so much pain in the young man's voice and the look in his eyes pierced Torsten's soul. *Poor child*, he thought.

"Well, he brought a friend too. A real scum. Just the same as Klingström. David Ljung. And then they tortured Jannice, both of them at the same time."

In a flash, Martin scrunched up his face in pain and started crying.

Torsten, who knew he had to stay professional, wanted to hug the young man and comfort him. But he didn't. Instead, he listened and took notes.

"Can you imagine how much I hated them? How could they do something like that? What the hell is wrong with people? Fucking scum."

"I understand," Torsten said as calmly as he could without showing how much he shared the young man's pain.

Martin kept talking and Torsten let him. As he talked about the horrific things people were apparently capable of doing to each other, the whole room filled with an intense feeling of shame and disgust. Everything felt filthy.

"What happened to Jannice?"

"She couldn't live with it. So she killed herself."

Martin's crying intensified. He sobbed and hunched over from the pain.

"Yes, she did. And what happened to you then?"

"Something inside of me died. I went to uni. I attended the lectures and studied hard. But everything felt empty and meaningless."

"How did you manage to keep up with your studies?"

"I was driven by anger. At first, I felt empty. Then, I felt rage. And hate. I hated those assholes. Once I had made my mind up, I felt better. I started seeing the people around me again and found a purpose to keep on living—to make something of myself."

"What decision did you make?"

Martin made a failed attempt to look superior, but his chin trembled and it looked like he had to struggle to keep a straight face.

"What do you think?" he said.

"I never think anything. I ask to know."

"But you know already," Martin answered.

"I would like you to tell me, so I don't have to guess."

"I decided to erase them—not only from my brain but from the world. They didn't deserve to live. They turned Jannice's life into a living hell. And my life too. They were scum."

"And how did you plan to do this?"

"I thought about doing it as quickly as possible, but once I got my hands on Tobias, things turned out differently. I was overcome by hate—a hatred I thought I would be able to control, but couldn't. Once he sat there in front of me, I wanted to torture him. And I did. I discovered a new side of myself. I was stone cold. I tricked him into that chilly, empty allotment cottage. If you're wondering—that's where I killed him. I didn't force him to go there. He thought he was meeting 'Samantha.' I made her up. And I became part of that circle, but I never hurt anyone. And do you know something? While I was torturing him, I felt nothing. He had tortured Jannice. He deserved it all."

The young man was well-spoken; it surprised Torsten that someone so young could handle himself so well, especially in the situation Martin found himself.

"Do you know a person named Candy?" Torsten asked. He tried to keep as much distance between himself and the young man's story as possible.

Martin Eriksson laughed.

"That idiot, David Ljung . . . He was so gullible. I sent him a text. I'd found out how things work among these people, you see. It was so simple to gain their trust. You have no idea how much I've learnt about them."

Although Martin's eyes were red from crying, he looked triumphant. As if he was proud of what he'd done. As if he still hadn't grasped the serious nature of his actions.

"Candy," Torsten repeated.

"I called myself Candy and asked David to meet me in the basement on Krafts Torg. The Swedish Wine Association. I knew the number of people who had tried to break into that place before me would make it harder for you to trace me. Either way, I expected you to come. I knew you would find me eventually. That's why I decided to become James Elliot. To humiliate David even more. I called myself Candy and put Camilla in contact with James."

"Let's talk about James later. What happened when David came to the basement?"

Torsten felt physically ill but ignored it and stayed focused on the conversation and his own thoughts.

"He arrived and knocked on the door. I opened it. He was expecting a girl, and I could tell he felt unsure when he saw me. It was obvious. So, I grabbed him and pulled him inside. He tripped and I overpowered him. Then I tied him up. And when he had suffered enough . . . he whimpered and tried to break free. I could tell he was terrified. Then I walked up to him holding my flashlight and my knife in one hand like they do in American thrillers. Well, I guess they usually have a gun instead of a knife in those movies, but still. The flashlight blinded him. I slit his throat. And while he was dying—I'm a med student so I know exactly what I'm doing, you know—I stabbed him in the cock. I made sure he got what he deserved."

Torsten felt like throwing up but stayed strong.

"And then what?"

"I watched him die. Slowly."

Martin Eriksson no longer looked proud. Or sad. He had a blank expression on his face. As if he had accepted his fate. As far as Torsten was concerned, it wasn't that strange that people like the young medical student existed. As long as there were bad actions, there would always be people willing to cross every line to get revenge.

"How did you handle Tobias Klingström? He was a big and strong fella."

Torsten heard how silly the question sounded, but it was too late to take it back.

118

Sara knocked on the door to the interrogation room and stepped inside. She walked over to Martin and held out her hand. He shook it with confidence. *Vindication*, she thought. *He isn't scared at all.*

It wasn't until much later she realised that in a way, he represented her own longing for vindication.

Martin looked at her nose. Broken, twice in one year. But she didn't care.

"Sorry about that," he said.

"It's okay," she said, and brought her hand up to her sore nose.

She had listened in on the interview and realised it was too heavy to handle alone. Torsten needed backup. She knew very well that the mix of disgust and empathy he must be feeling could be overwhelming. Torsten was a sensitive person, but she had never seen him act unprofessionally. No matter what he was forced to hear.

"How did you get Tobias Klingström to come to the allotment? And how did you know the owners wouldn't be there?"

Martin looked at her as if she was an idiot.

"Of course I knew which cottages were in use and which cottages weren't," he said as he kept studying her.

"How?" Sara wanted to know. She was also nauseous, but not necessarily for the same reason as her colleague.

"I grew up there. My family owns an allotment there, but I'm sure you already know that. A piece of shit like Tobias Klingström only cares about one thing," he said as if it was obvious.

"And that is?"

"He's perverted, the fucker. All he cares about is violent, sadistic sex. All I had to do was say the right thing."

As cold as a fish, Sara thought. She looked at her colleague, who looked pale.

"And what was the right thing to say?"

"Well, I wrote him a message and gave him the idea that I offered the type of sex he liked, just as I did with David. But I used the name 'Samantha.' I think I told you that already. I have his phone if you want it."

"And what exactly did you write in the message?"

Sara had mixed feelings. A small part of her could taste the sweet taste of revenge. But the rest of her felt disgusted.

"I told him he should come to the allotment gardens and that he would know exactly where to go if he just followed the lights I had put out for him. I knew he would be tempted by it."

"And what happened next?"

"Well . . ." Martin hesitated for a second. He picked at the table as if there was something in front of him, something nobody else could see.

This young man's conviction that he has the right to end another man's life contradicts the pureness of youth, Sara thought.

Torsten sat next to her and repeatedly ran his hands through his hair.

"He knocked on the door and I opened it. The moment he saw me, he took a step back. I knew he would be hesitant, so I had a plan. I told him we would share a girl. He came in and I told him the girl was getting ready in the shed next to the cottage. He sat down. And I pulled out a gun."

"A gun?" Torsten said. He sounded surprised.

"An air gun, but still. *He* didn't know that. I forced him to lay down on his belly on the floor. Then I tied him up. When he sat there on the chair, I was overcome by rage."

"Did you know Samira and Tobias were a couple?" Sara asked calmly.

"No, not then. But I do now, and I must say I feel horrible about it. Both about her not knowing who he really was, and about her family's honour-shame approach."

Fleetingly, Sara saw something in Martin Eriksson's eyes. Empathy.

"I tried to make Elin realise it wasn't Samira's parents who killed Tobias, but she didn't get it."

"Not so strange, perhaps?" Sara said, and glanced at Torsten, who nodded. They had both heard enough. They were both exhausted and needed a break.

119

It was late when Sara came home. She was tired, but happy to finally have a resolution to the mystery and a perpetrator in custody. She still had something she had to take care of though. And she had to take care of it straight away, before it was too late. She walked into the bathroom and ran her fingers through her messy hair. Then she washed her face and put on some lip gloss. She drank water straight from the tap and accidentally got her hair wet. She dried it off as best she could and walked out into the living room, where she sat down cross-legged on the sofa. She had her laptop with her.

She started Skype, took a deep breath, and clicked on Anders's picture. It rang for a while and she was just about to hang up when he took the call.

"Hi," she said, "please don't hang up."

"Hi there. I'm not hanging up, don't worry."

"I've missed you terribly. I'm sorry. Sorry for being so mean and sorry for hurting you."

She didn't even realise tears were streaming down her face until she felt them trickle down her throat.

"Don't cry," he said. "I've missed you too. I thought I would die without you. Sorry for being so egotistic and not understanding you better— not understanding what you've been through."

"I really hope you're willing to give this another try. I promise to tell you when I'm not feeling well."

"And I promise I'll be able to deal with it," he said. "I love you."

Sara realised she had been right from the beginning, even if she had lost her way in all the misery. He was the one for her.

Suddenly, she started laughing. She felt incredibly relieved.

When they ended the call, they did so with kind and loving words to each other. She knew it would be okay. Everything would be okay.

120

That was both the easiest and most difficult interrogation of my career. Normally, the perps are difficult to talk to and refuse to admit to what they've done. This was different. Anticlimactic, in a way," Torsten said to his colleagues.

Once they had watched the video recording of the interview, they all understood what he meant.

The intelligent and well-spoken Martin Eriksson didn't match the story he told them about a world none of them knew or understood.

"It's easy to see where his hatred comes from," Rita said gloomily.

The others nodded.

"Unfortunately, it doesn't matter," Torsten said after a moment of silence.

Rita sighed.

"No, but I'm just saying I can understand why he did what he did. He loved her and what they did to her was disgusting. And nothing happened to them. He witnessed her feeling worse and worse. And then she killed herself. How are you supposed to deal with and handle an experience like that? Especially if you don't have anyone to turn to?"

Sara didn't say anything. She was overwhelmingly tired.

"All that's left to do now is to match Martin's DNA with the hair found in the closet. But it shouldn't change anything. And we have to arrange the murder reconstructions. His whole story matches our theory.

We have Tobias's phone, as well as Martin's phone and his three SIM cards," she said, finally.

"He admitted to the circumstances rather than confessing to the murders," Torsten said. "But yeah, I guess you can call it a confession."

"I think we should be happy with the progress. As always, this is not the same as being completely satisfied. Perhaps we could have stopped this guy from murdering David if we had acted even quicker. But it's never that easy," Sara said, and ended the meeting.

They drank coffee and took a moment to talk to each other. It was important to Sara that everyone onthe team felt good after a case was closed; she always made sure nobody felt like there were any loose ends to tie up.

The two murders were solved. It was a relief. The sad thing about it all was that a young person's life—that could've been great—would never be the same again. Martin Eriksson and his family had a long road ahead of them. In more ways than one, Elin Eriksson had also lost. Camilla Brink had also been lured into a web of lies and games, but she was the only one who had a chance to walk out of the situation unharmed. Nobody else was as lucky.

"There are no winners in a situation like this," Sara said as she hugged the members of her team. "But I'm so glad you're here with me, doing such an amazing job."

She grabbed her jacket and left without looking back. As she exited the police station, the crisp air felt great against her face. She stepped into the cool autumn night, stopped on the stairs for a second, and looked up at the sky, where stars were glistening.

She took a deep breath, got into her car, and drove to Anders.

EPILOGUE

Samira hurried into the classroom. She sat down next to her best friend, Anja.

"Late as always, Barbara," Anja whispered, and pinched her arm. Samira giggled. She still wasn't used to her new name.

"Today, we're visiting Saint George's Hospital, which is one of the best hospitals in England," the professor said with a French accent.

"He's gorgeous," Anja whispered, and showed off the goose bumps on her arms.

"That's all you ever think about," Samira whispered to her friend, and loosened her headscarf. Her hair was shorter and healthier and she no longer wore it in a braid.

She felt happy again. She could breathe. And the memory of Tobias was slowly fading.

Although she wasn't really supposed to, she called Elin from time to time. She had moved to Australia—far away from anything that reminded her of Martin. Samira found it sad. But they had decided that Samira would join Elin in Australia in the future. They were both excited about it. Aidah Iskander-Svensson and the police had helped both Samira and her mother to leave the country and move to London. Now they lived in a nice little flat just outside the city. They liked it there. They really did. Samira thought about her father now and again, although she did her best to push those thoughts away. She hoped that they would see each other again one day. One day.

After the lecture, Samira and Anja stepped out into the fresh air.

Samira picked up her phone.

"Hi, Mum," she said. "I'm going to be late today. We're going to Saint George's Hospital. I'll be home around eight. Is that all right?"

"Sounds exciting, honey. Have fun."

THANK YOU

I'm grateful to a lot of people and I want to take this opportunity to mention some of those who made *Vigilante* possible.

My dear husband, Torgny, who puts up with me during periods when I barely answer when spoken to, supports me in every possible way, and loves me despite it all.

My beloved children, who are always there by my side.

My mother, who listened to the first half of *Vigilante* and who always believes in me.

Bahare Mohammadi-Andersson, my dear friend and colleague, who has been an amazing advisor regarding honour-related issues. She has been the model for Aidah Iskander-Svensson and she has also helped me in the creation of the Khan family.

My dear friend Ami Messa, who has joined me for many long conversations, read the novel and consulted me when it comes to honour-shame culture.

Lena Körner, prosecutor and amazing friend, who has patiently answered all my questions related to court proceedings and criminal classifications.

Beautiful and fantastic Jenny Bäfving, who has guided me when I've taken the wrong path, listened to my thoughts about the development of the script, had dinners with me, joined me for long walks on Österlen, and been my biggest cheerleader!

All those close to me who have listened to me and put up with me.

Hörby municipality and its residents for letting me borrow Hörby for my novel.

And I want to apologise to Hanna Wollinger for once again using one of her favourite places as a backdrop for horrible events.

If anyone at the social services office in Lund would feel offended by my description of your workplace, I want to assure you that none of this is based on real people or events.

Any similarities between this novel and real events or people are coincidental. *Vigilante* is a fictional story. Only Aidah is real.

Cecilia Sahlström
Lund, 2007

ABOUT THE AUTHOR

Cecilia Sahlström is a popular Swedish crime writer based in Lund, in southern Sweden. Sahlström worked in the police force for twenty years before becoming a writer. Her first novel, *White Lilac*, has been praised for its gritty realism and authentic portrayal of police investigations.

Podium
DISCOVER
STORIES UNBOUND
PodiumAudio.com